Additional Books by this Author

Bitter Lakes

The Little Green Woman Who Fell to Earth and Other Tales of
Roswell... and some other places

Second Edition

Interrupted
Weekend

A Subic Story

To Dave Barry

R. L. Scifres

R. L. Scifres

This book is dedicated to my lovely young bride, Joanie Cole Scifres, who has tolerated my storytelling for over 25 years of marriage.

Olongapo, Republic of the Philippines
Located on Subic Bay

Photo by R.L. Scifres

Interrupted Weekend

A Subic Story

Friday

Chapter 1

Damn, things were hot. The air temperature was probably in the high 80's, but the humidity hung heavily, almost oppressively. Roy swore he could see the air swirling slowly around him in lazy waves. The Naugahyde upholstery of his chair was soft and tacky, and the slight shade offered by the barracks' awning did little to cool him. He thought he might even be able to smell the heat. Recent rains had left little puddles here and there and some small thrushes were bathing in them. The only respite from the heat for Roy was contained in the cold, brown bottle currently forming a circular pool of sweat on the wooden arm of his chair. He sniffed the rich, cool beer and took a drink.

He had sat on the front porch less than a minute ago and already his back was slick with sweat, causing his thin polo shirt to stick to it and to the green skin of his chair. At 36 years old, he noticed his eye sight was starting to deteriorate slightly, but he took little consolation in the fact that his sweat glands seemed to still be working just fine. He leaned forward slightly and squinted out into the bright sunshine looking for the cab he had called about ten minutes earlier. His short cropped brown hair, sporting a growing collection of gray ones, was also starting to feel tacky. It was long enough to trap the small beads of sweat emerging from his scalp.

The chief's barracks, his new home, was situated about halfway up a hill overlooking much of Cubi Point Naval Air Station and the dark blue waters of Subic Bay beyond. Although several other buildings of various design dotted this hillside, his view was obstructed by only a few coconut palms, un-stirred by any breeze and three cars parked in front of the barracks. To Roy's right, farther along the coast of the bay, were the ships and warehouses of Subic Bay Naval Station. Beyond that, spreading out through the valleys and hills of Zambales province, was the city of Olongapo. From this vantage he could see emerald forests and jungles, glimmering water and bustling humanity; however, there was not one taxi to be seen.

Additional beads of sweat grew slowly on his pale forehead until,

3

gradually, succumbing to gravity, they trickled into his squinting, hazel eyes. He mused silently that it was not the heat he smelled. Rather, it was the decay of his own sweat, dying in its attempt to cool a body not yet reacclimated to the tropical conditions.

"Jesus shit," he said under his breath and wiped perspiration from his brow and onto the leg of his jeans. He lifted the cold San Miguel beer to his lips and took two deep swallows before rubbing the bottle across his forehead. He used his shirt sleeve to wipe his eyes again and set the sweating bottle back precisely onto one of the many circular stains which mottled the dark wood of his chair.

"Is it always this fucking hot?" He had asked the question more or less to himself, but a house boy who had just emerged from the air-conditioned barracks answered back.

"Not always," he said in a clipped Filipino accent. "Sometimes, it's to be more hot and sometimes, not so hot."

Roy looked over at the short, thin man who was now squatting on his haunches, sucking on a cigarette. Roy recognized him as the house boy who had been assigned to his room and remembered he was named, or at least called, "Daddy."

He assumed Daddy was going home for the weekend because the tee shirt and rubber sandals he had been wearing earlier had been replaced by a casual, button-down shirt and brown leather, slip-on loafers. In place of tattered khaki shorts were some type of polyester, yellow trousers. He still had no socks on his feet. He was obviously comfortable in this squatting position and he let cigarette smoke slowly escape his thin lips as he rocked back on his heels. Adding to the evidence of his departure was a brown paper bag, its top rolled into a handle, sitting on the cement floor beside him.

"Is it any cooler where you come from?" Roy asked.

"No. Mariveles is close from here, across the ano... the bay from Manila." Daddy's dark face was deeply lined, and its expression changed little as he spoke. He gestured in the general southerly direction as he mentioned it and then ran his calloused fingers through a tangle of curly, salt-and-pepper hair.

Roy knew that Manila was a few hours trip over the winding, perpetually-under-construction roads, but he had no idea what lay across its bay. He now knew that, at least, Mariveles was there.

"How often do you go home?" Roy asked casually.

"On the weekends I go there sometimes. I stay to my cousin's house till then. He is there in East Bajac-Bajac." Daddy gestured again, this time toward Olongapo and smiled easily. "Tonight, I go home." His grin revealed a substantial investment in dental work and the potential for more, but the effort seemed to take ten years from his fifty-something face. "Will you have clothes next week?" His smile dimmed only slightly as he asked about Roy's laundry.

"Yeah," Roy replied. "I only carried a couple of things with me, but I mailed some stuff last week before I left the states and then I have a household goods shipment that should be here in a week or so. I'll get my money's worth from you then."

Roy smiled at the facetious comment, because he knew that the house boys' services were really a huge bargain. For twenty dollars a month, a house boy would shine shoes, do laundry, make bunks and generally square-away a barracks room every day, as well as sweep, mop and polish the floor once a week. They would do other chores, for an additional fee, which just about eliminated any of the hassles generally associated with living in a barracks. On top of all that, they provided most of their own supplies.

Roy almost didn't believe the deal when he had first been told about it that morning by the barracks manager. Although he had heard stories about the Philippines since his first day in boot camp, few had involved barracks life. He remembered thinking, after paying the barracks manager for his first month of services, that if he could get all this for so little, perhaps at least some of the other stories he had heard about Olongapo were true.

"Okay," Daddy said, oblivious to the joke. He rose to his feet after smashing his cigarette out on the cement. He tossed the butt into a shit-can and clanged its dull metal lid back into place just as a red jeepney, packed with passengers, pulled in front of the building. He opened the door to the barracks, yelled something in Tagalog and then turned back to pick up his makeshift satchel.

"You are Senior Chief Thompson, yeah?" Daddy asked.

"That's right." Roy replied.

"Well," he said as he walked toward the jeepney, "have a good weekend. But be careful, hah?" He flashed his gold trimmed smile again and waved just before climbing into the back of the vehicle.

Before the jeepney left, two more house boys hurried out of the barracks and piled into its back. Finally, its rusty springs moaning from the strain of a dozen passengers, the jeepney chugged away from the curb, belching and farting. Its wasted brake shoes squealed angrily as it slowed slightly for a stop sign and then fell silent as the jeep gathered speed going down the hill.

Interrupted Weekend

I hope my taxi isn't one of those, he thought. He was anxious to begin his investigation of Olongapo, but not in a carnival ride contraption like that.

Roy watched the jeepney turn a corner and a familiar aching pain seized his gut as he remembered how he and Lisa used to take her jeep into the country surrounding Norfolk in Virginia. Driving with the top down, her long red hair would whip around her head in an ecstatic electric dance, leaping around her beautiful face, competing with her smile for attention.

She had talked often about how she was going to trade her old CJ5 in for a brand-new model, but he knew that before she would part with that particular jeep, it would be way too old and beat up for any trade-in value. Once she found something she liked, she hung onto it. Details of that beautiful face were already starting to fade. Would he forget the way her smooth cheeks wrinkled when she smiled? Would he forget her miraculous green eyes that seemed to change tint when she got angry or horny? Regardless, he didn't think he would ever forget her dancing red hair.

A quick glint of reflected sunlight poked his eyes, and he was happy for the interruption to his thoughts. Roy squinted to see a small, white Datsun sedan coming toward the barracks. The Japanese company had changed its name to "Nissan" a few years back, but Roy knew there were several more years of service left in the car. It pulled next to the curb and lime green lettering on its side told him it belonged to the "Guerrero's Taxi Fleet." Its driver wrote something on a clipboard and then looked expectantly at Roy.

Roy waved to acknowledge the driver and pulled his 6'1" frame easily from the chair. He downed the last of the beer and set the empty bottle in a green, plastic case next to the barracks door. Walking toward the cab, Roy shifted his wallet from his hip pocket to a front pocket and rubbed the bare spot on his wrist where his watch had been until just before showering. This was a pre-liberty ritual that Roy had unconsciously developed over many years of being an American sailor exploring foreign ports and was one which had served him well.

Settling into the cramped back seat of the taxi, Roy said, "Main Gate, please."

Buildings, cars and people whizzed by the car window. Roy watched them blur together and yawned. His brain registered the several hangers and offices of Cubi Point, as well as the Navy Exchange, Bank of America and a go-cart track. Although they all registered, none was very high on his interest meter. Endless Tagalog chatter came from the dispatch radio and the meter seemed to click another dime with every bump in the road, but after ten minutes of the driver's Mario Andretti-like maneuvers, the cab arrived at the main gate.

His total time in the Philippines was just slightly less than twelve hours. The nap he had gotten on the way over the Pacific wasn't necessarily quality sleep, but it had charged his batteries enough to get him through the day. Perhaps the cat nap he'd grabbed at the barracks would get him through a little liberty. At any rate, he thought he deserved to get a glimpse of the town after the trip he'd just had and hoped that a little time out there might help reset his internal clock.

Stories about the Philippines were circulated by shipmates at every duty station he'd had over his seventeen-year career. It was now 1989 and he didn't really expect the situation to have changed much. He was just a little concerned about the temptations which awaited him outside the main gate.

His critical thinking skills might be compromised by lack of sleep, but he thought he could handle a few beers without getting too stupid. His days of getting excessively stupid were over, and he knew also that fatigue would help curb any such inclinations to get laid.

The faint possibility of sex triggered yet another painful memory of Lisa. She'd killed herself just days before Roy was set to propose marriage. That had been nearly a year before, but he still thought about her every day, and honestly didn't know if that was a bad thing or a good thing. Additionally, he still felt unjustified guilt about how she died. He knew it was illogical and misplaced and had been told so by friends and family since it had occurred, but still it lingered. Hoping for a distraction from fixating on Lisa, he recalled the events leading to this taxi ride to his next adventure.

The military-chartered Boeing 747 which brought him to the islands had touched down at Clark Air Force Base a little after 5:00 AM that morning. After a sometimes-bumpy flight, his last overseas assignment – perhaps last ever assignment – began with an even bumpier bus ride.

At just over two hours, the bus ride down to Subic and Cubi hadn't been near as long as the marathon flight from Los Angeles but was filled with considerably more scenery. The flight had short layovers in Honolulu and Guam and there hadn't been much time off the plane. But between Clark and Subic he witnessed jungle covered mountains on the horizon; flat plains filled with rice paddies, sugar cane and coconut palms on either side of the highway; carabaos pulling plows and carts and being ridden by children; roads filled with colorful jeepneys and commercial motorcycles with sidecars; small nipa huts built with bamboo poles and thatched roofs and walls. He had expected it all, had heard about it for years. He was well read and prided himself on his overall knowledge of the world, but still Roy was overwhelmed by both the beauty and the simplicity of the place.

He had yet to witness much of the poverty he knew existed here. The neighborhoods he'd passed through on the bus ride didn't seem that bad. He had been to many third world countries and what he'd seen here so far seemed to be about on par with most Caribbean nations. He had seen lots of poor people, working like hell to get through the day, but no fly covered babies, bloated by malnutrition. He had seen nothing yet that would make Sally Struthers want to do a television spot.

The bus had dropped him off at the chief's barracks in Cubi Point, where he was met by his sponsor, a Torpedoman Chief named Bill Eikleberger who took Roy around to check into a few places like the Personnel Support Division, Disbursing and the barracks.

As a person trained to remain objective, Roy tried never to jump to conclusions; however, Chief Eikleberger presented a very poor first impression. Eikleberger's khaki shirt threatened to jettison buttons every time he moved and at 5'9", his 190 pounds seemed to be located mainly above his invisible belt and in his fleshy arms. He reminded Roy of the worst possible example of a Navy CPO. It didn't help that Eikleberger fumbled his sponsor responsibilities and leaned on the excuse that things were tough at work and how busy he was there and at home. Regardless, Roy was grateful for transportation at Cubi Point.

The site of the Naval Magazine itself, reachable only by one long and winding road, by helicopter, or by sea, was located a few miles from the Naval Station and the Naval Air Station at Cubi Point, which handled all its administrative and support matters. The XO felt Roy would need to recover from jet lag and "get situated" over the weekend, so he told Eikleberger not to bother bringing Roy to work until Monday morning. Roy thought that idea was just fine, and he was looking forward to a nice, uninterrupted weekend. He also felt he might get along great with his new XO, a Lieutenant Commander named Franklin W. Pillsbury, III.

Roy was grateful that he would have the weekend to relax, but at the same time he was quite anxious to get to work and see what was going on there. His communications with the base, from the time he had received his orders until now, had been sketchy at best. Roy still wasn't sure what the scope of his duties would be. The person who had held the job previously left the command quickly and was already gone by the time Roy received his orders there. He was certain he would be involved in the physical security of the base but having never been assigned to a Naval Magazine before, Roy felt a bit apprehensive about what kind of responsibilities he would have. He knew security at a NAVMAG was second only to safety and a very close second at that.

Beginning the check-in process and the quick tour of the base had eaten up a good chunk of the morning, so Roy spent the remainder of the afternoon getting settled into his one-man room and getting ready to explore Olongapo. A short nap, another quick shower, a phone call for the taxi and a cold beer were all squeezed in between when Bill had dropped him at the barracks and when the taxi had arrived.

Chapter 2

The intruder closed the kitchen door silently behind him and stood still for a full three minutes, listening to the sounds of the house. He heard mostly refrigerator noises and the sound of children and dogs in the distance. Other sounds, the sounds of nature, he sensed at a deeper level. He could smell the artificial lemon scent of an American cleaning solution and thought how it offended his nose.

The key worked perfectly, fitting both the doorknob and dead bolt, as if it were the original. He only hoped that the rubber gloves on his hands worked as well and wouldn't interfere with his work. He had been given explicit instructions along with the key and the gloves; he was to touch nothing, he was to wear the gloves at all times to protect against accidentally leaving fingerprints, he was to disturb nothing and he was to take nothing. Nothing, that is, except the life of the house's occupant.

In return for that life, he was to leave an envelope where it would be easily found. He did not know what was in the envelope; only that it was to be handled with gloved hands and left in a conspicuous place. He didn't care what was in the envelope.

He was to kill a large, black American man. The American should be wearing a brown uniform and arrive at this house shortly after 5:00 PM, alone and driving an old blue jeep. The only other thing the intruder knew about the American was that he worked on the naval base and lived alone in this house in Barrio Barretto.

The intruder was given no instructions on how to take the American's life and needed none. That was a sacred matter between him, his god and his prey.

Standing motionless inside the door, he could see everything in the small kitchen and most of the living room. The eastern wall of the space was dominated by jalousie windows draped with green curtains, hung more to hide the house's contents than to block the sun. However, they effectively dampened the sunlight, giving the space a soft and somber glow. A wide, wooden counter separated kitchen from living space and over its top could be seen the circular, rattan frame of a papa-san chair and other rattan furniture covered with green and brown patterned cushions. The dark wood paneled walls of the living room were studded with prints of Japanese peasants, temple rubbings from Thailand and cheap Malaysian tapestries. The only things on the wall the intruder recognized were a huge spoon and fork, hand-carved from Philippine mahogany. An oscillating fan stood tall and motionless, ready for service, between one end of the rattan couch and the front door.

He had been hiding outside the house for over an hour before coming through the kitchen door. He had watched the frosted windows, covered by iron bars, and listened intently for any signs of life stirring within. He felt confident there was no one else in the house. Still, he remained silent, moving only his eyes and listening. Over an hour remained before the American was to arrive and he wanted to determine the best vantage for his purpose.

Eventually he moved around the small kitchen table and towards the front door. The wall to his right, which held most of the items the intruder could not recognize, was broken about midway by a wide archway. He walked to it quickly on soft soled shoes and stopped to lean his head around the corner. Three open doors greeted him; two bedrooms, separated by a bathroom, all empty.

He heard a car coming up the drive. It was invisible because of the drawn curtains, but this house was its only possible destination.

The early arrival of his target didn't distress the intruder – he wasn't needed elsewhere until later in the evening – but his pulse quickened, and his stomach muscles tightened ever so slightly. A smile flashed across his face and disappeared again as the intruder recognized the familiar feelings as a precursor to what lay ahead for him. A flush spread slowly up his face and the hairs on his ears began to tingle. He likened these feelings to the growling stomach of a starving man and his gush of salivation when finally presented with a meal.

He looked quickly into one bedroom on his left and, deciding it was the master suite, ducked quickly into the smaller bedroom on his right, backing against the wall behind the door. There was about two feet between the edge of the open door and the side of a closet which protruded from the wall. He didn't get all the way behind the door because he wanted to be able to move through the portal quickly and take the American from behind. Instead, he closed the door just enough to hide himself from a casual glance and stood with his back to the wall.

He reached into his back pocket, closing his right hand on the butterfly knife that resided there. Normally, he would withdraw the knife, flick it open and lock its blade into place with one fluid motion. This time, the gloves he wore forced him to use both hands to unfold the knife and get it ready for business. Then, with his blade securely in hand and with the exaggerated wiggle of a pitcher getting ready to deliver a fast ball, he returned his arm loosely to his side and tapped the cold blade rhythmically against his pant leg.

The car pulled under the car port, directly outside the front door and cut its engine. A familiar rhyme, learned while hunting in the jungles with his father, rose from his memory and began dancing in his head like a frolicking child:

"Monkey, oxen, pig and hen,
All become the food of men..."

The intruder faintly heard an unfamiliar tune being whistled by the American but couldn't tell if it was being muffled by the walls which separated them or the blood now rushing through his own head. He waited.

The key clicked in the lock and the whistled tune became clearer as the front door swung in.

"All the creatures of the land,
served to man from God's own hand..."

The intruder's vision was limited from his hiding place, but through the crack between the bedroom door and door jam, he could see the front door opening and closing. The tune continued and was accompanied by a soft whirring as the American clicked on the fan next to the entrance.

"All the creatures of the sea,
food for man through God's decree..."

Instead of brown clothing, the intruder caught glimpses of red through the gap of the door as the American approached the bathroom, but he could make out the tightly curled, black hair of his prey.

"Thanks to Him on high for food,
man must prove that he is good..."

The American was not as big as anticipated, although definitely taller than the intruder's five and a half feet. As the American turned his back slightly to drop a gym bag inside the door of the other bedroom, the intruder slipped from behind his shield and with one silent step was at the American's back.

"If he fails to heed the call,
Man becomes the food of all."

As the American straitened, the intruder cupped his left hand around his prey's mouth and, with one violent move, thrust his knife into the base of the smallish skull, snapping back the head as hard as he could. With rapid, circular motions, the intruder jerked the knife handle around, slicing through the brain, as if scrambling an egg still in the shell.

An initial muffled grunt was the only sound the American made, but his bare left leg kicked spasmodically several times as he collapsed back onto his killer. The body seemed almost weightless in the adrenaline-soaked arms of the intruder and offered only a small burden as it was lowered to the floor. The murderer could feel the muscles of the American flexing and relaxing spasmodically and noted their leanness. He clung tightly to the head and pulled the knife quickly from the skull, wrapping his right arm around the chest of his victim and dragged him back into the smaller bedroom.

It was only then, with heart rate slowing and adrenaline levels subsiding, that the intruder noticed that his prize was a woman. He dragged her corpse further into the room and gently lowered it in front of a small closet. He knelt on his knees next to the body of Winifred Jackson and felt for a pulse in her limp wrist. As expected, nothing stirred beneath the smooth, cocoa skin, still warm and tacky with tropical sweat. The murderer smiled reflexively, and placed Winifred's lifeless hands over her still breast. He methodically wiped his blade across the leg of her cut-off blue jeans, stopping only to admire the symmetry of the narrow stains of blood as they fanned out across her thigh. He was acutely aware that the blade moved smoothly across the denim. It was honed to near perfection, with not the slightest barb to catch in the fabric. Again, a reflexive smile creased his face and then disappeared.

After one more quick glance toward the living room, the murderer lowered his head and, still holding the knife, clasped his hands in his lap. He whispered his thanks to his god for the life he had just received and for allowing him to be a part of the great plan. It was a prayer he knew well and had recited too often.

With that chore done, he now had time to survey the bedroom from his kneeling position. Its walls were covered with the same dark, wood paneling which lined the living room and was minimally furnished, containing only a plain bed with no headboard and a small, wooden nightstand which held a small electric fan. A red, rattan swag lamp hung lifeless from one corner of the ceiling, opposite the small closet. These windows too were covered with ugly, green curtains.

The murderer glanced quickly through the door into the living room, then scooted back around to the top of Winifred's body and grasped her under each arm. He pulled her across the smooth, tiled floor toward the corner of the room and noted with satisfaction that only a small amount of blood had escaped the wound. She had died quickly and with little pain. Another grin flashed involuntarily across his face.

He considered briefly dumping the body into the closet, but it was stacked with several packing containers filled with books, as well as shoe boxes and two suitcases. The murderer closed the door quietly and continued to pull Winifred's body with him as he walked backwards into the corner where the closet joined the bedroom wall. He stood and pulled her up with him as far as he could and then sat her in the corner, facing the bedroom door.

After folding her hands neatly in her lap and then leaning her head back into the cradle of the corner, the murderer studied her more closely. In addition to the denim shorts, she wore a red tee shirt with a white Nike swoosh on the front. Her hair had been cropped short and her body was lithe and muscular. She was a beautiful woman and had been aging gracefully until a few moments ago. Her skin was unmarked and stretched evenly over the now flaccid and expressionless muscles, betraying only the finest of wrinkles. He guessed she might have been in her late twenties or early thirties. She smelled of fresh soap and powder, with just the faintest trace of a flower the murderer could not identify. She reminded him of a tired laborer, or perhaps a harried mother, taking a midday nap after the noon meal.

He had no idea who the woman was and at this point, didn't much care. She was here and she was dead, and she had been his gift. The murderer's only concern now was to ensure he completed his purpose for being here. His original plan remained unfulfilled, and he would have to stay until the job was completed. He had other things to do, but he still had plenty of time. He had been in the house less than ten minutes.

There hadn't been much blood, but he did not want to leave even the tiniest hint for the next victim of what was to come. As he looked for signs of blood, he spotted the gym bag next to the other bedroom door and retrieved it, tucking it between the lifeless body and messy closet. He went into the bathroom and meticulously rinsed the small amount of blood from his gloved hands and dried them on his next victim's towel. He repeated the process with his knife, but with more reverence.

Gathering two large wads of toilet paper, he returned to the sink and wet one of the wads. He glanced at his reflection in the medicine cabinet mirror. The dark eyes reflected in the mirror spent no time lingering over the dark, smooth face in which they sat. He had no need to admire his own image. The thin face was otherwise nondescript and the few, thin whiskers which had dared to surface that morning had been carefully scraped away, just as they were every morning.

He retraced his path into the bedroom, stooping to clean tiny puddles of blood from the floor, first wiping with the wetted paper, then drying with the other wad. He stashed both wads of paper behind the body in the corner after the cleaning job was complete.

The murderer took up his original position behind the door and again began to wait. He had just begun to slide down the wall to settle on his haunches when he heard a sound from outside. He stopped and listened intently. It sounded like another car coming up the drive, perhaps a jeep and he grinned, quick and fleeting. He stood erect and once again reached into his pocket for the butterfly knife. The tune the woman had been whistling played in his head. This time, though, it had accompanying words.

"Monkey, oxen, pig and hen,
All become the food of men..."

Chapter 3

The cab took a right turn into a large parking lot, which accommodated several buses and personal vehicles, in addition to the taxis. Around the asphalt parking spaces were several single-storied buildings which housed Pass and I.D. offices, vehicle registration offices and similar places associated with controlling the flow of people and property through the main gate. A long, covered driveway was filled with other taxis awaiting dispatch.

Roy got out of the taxi, paid the driver and started for the gate without waiting for his change. To his right, as he walked toward the gate, were several money exchange windows set into a small white building. Ahead of him, across the two-lane street leading out the gate, was the Office of the Provost Marshall, flying both U.S. and Republic of the Philippine flags.

The image of those flags triggered Roy to recall a report he had read recently concerning the NPA. The New People's Army was the military component on the Communist Party in the Philippines and it, along with some other separatist groups, had initiated random attacks on Americans and others over the last several years. He didn't really fear that he might become the target of a "sparrow" attack, but it was just one more thing about the P.I. he felt needed to be kept in mind. His duties at the Naval Magazine would probably require him to be more concerned about the organization in the future but for now, he was going on liberty. Of all the stories he had heard about this island nation, its history of various rebellious groups was the least mentioned and for tonight, the least troubling.

Roy stopped at the money changers and cashed in forty dollars at about twenty-four pesos to one and continued toward the gate. He didn't know what the price of beer in Olongapo currently was, but he was satisfied he had enough for this first night on the town. He stuffed the bills of varying colors into his billfold and as he replaced the wallet into his front pocket, the long-forgotten words of his boot camp company commander rose from his memory like swamp gas from rotting vegetation. "I love the P.I." he had said, "It's the only place left in the world where a guy can get fucked, fucked up and fucked over for less than ten bucks."

Roy slowed his pace. If a fraction of the stories he had heard about the P.I. were true, how would he fare in the middle of it? He was older and more mature than most of the service people now winding their way out into evening, but he wasn't sure he could remain any more virtuous than they over the long haul. However, he was confident that he could for at least one night.

Fleeting memories of past liberty calls in Panama and Puerto Rico and the Virgin Islands played in his mind like an old video. In those, he saw himself as young, carefree and careless. Back then, his only goals were to have a good time and to do a good job for the Navy. He had worked hard and he had played hard and his goals had been met. Many goals had changed since then.

Lisa still lingered in his memory as the complex and perplexing image experienced by anyone who has lost a loved one. Her image was both a painful reminder of personal loss and vigilant sentinel of warning against getting too close to others emotionally or physically. The mixture of emotions associated with her, as well as the circumstances surrounding her death, still pulled at his core. But, of course, those were not the only recollections competing for his attention.

And now, here he was at a crossroads. Short-term goals? Have a couple of beers and see if there was any truth in what he had heard about the P.I. Long-term goals? Don't think about them for now. Plenty of time to worry about that, he thought. He walked on.

Splitting the two lanes of vehicle traffic at the gate was a guard shack manned with both U.S. Marines and Philippine soldiers. They shared the duties of operating the counter-weighted levers – one on either side of the guard shack – which controlled entrance to and exit from the base. Running parallel to the street was a wide, covered sidewalk which had been partitioned into two paths, one going out and one coming in. This sidewalk led past another sentry post where Marines and Navy shore patrol checked identification cards and were always on the lookout for someone either trying to take a controlled item off base or trying to bring unauthorized people on. It was a job Roy did not covet.

His first sight after coming out the gate was the infamous Shit River and the narrow bridge which spanned it. It was just a drainage channel, but virtually everyone, including the base commander and the mayor of Olongapo, called it Shit River. It was about forty yards wide and derived its nickname both from its fragrant bouquet as well as from its contents. It was connected to other water ways around Olongapo but separated it from the base and served as a receptacle for much of the sewage discharged from the city. In addition to the sewage, it had also received heavy doses of run-off consisting of who-knew-what kind of chemicals from both the base and the city. Environmental protection regulations were late in coming to the Philippines and largely ignored once they got there.

A sidewalk stretched along one side of the bridge and was separated from both the car traffic and the river by waist-high, iron, handrails. Roy saw several people leaning against the rail overlooking the river and confirmed another rumor about the place he had heard for years. Some of the young sailors and marines were tossing coins, but most were just hooting and hollering at people in the water.

Roy stepped to the edge of the bridge and looked down to the river's surface, perhaps ten feet below. The first thing that caught his eye were young girls, maybe eleven to thirteen years old, standing in the middle of crude canoes, called bangkas. Each stood on a platform built in the middle of the bangka and were dressed in long, flowing dresses which covered their feet and most of the platform. Purposefully or not, they were decorated like little prostitutes. Dark mascara and bright red lip gloss glowed in contrast to the murky sewage in which their boats floated. They all held long poles fixed with a basket at their ends, designed to catch the coins tossed from above.

"Hey Joe!" the girl closest to him called. "Throw pesos!" she implored him.

"My name's not Joe," he said and smiled.

"Come on, Joe, throw pesos!" the call could be heard from more than one girl now. Roy just waved and started to resume his walk across the bridge.

"Oy! Throw me pesos!" This time the voice was that of a male, probably in his early teen years. Roy stopped and looked down again. To his amazement and disgust, he saw three boys swimming in the water in front of the girl's boats. He had missed them earlier because they were close to being beneath the bridge. Each was treading water and holding out a hand to catch whatever he might toss them.

Up ahead, a young man wearing a marine's high and tight hair style, said, "Hey boy! Catch this!" With that, he threw a coin straight down with enough force so that neither the girls nor boys could get to it before it hit the water. To Roy's further horror, the boys immediately dove down into the fetid brew to retrieve their treasure. The marine didn't wait to see if his gift had been retrieved; he just continued laughing and talking to his friends as they moved toward the city.

Roy didn't wait either. He was anxious to see what lay on the other side of this river of shit.

Chapter 4

There was something shiny down there. She didn't know what it was, but it was shiny and by the virgin, she was going to get it.

She no longer wasted energy swatting at the flies buzzing around her head. They lit where they pleased and danced back and forth across her dirty face, licking up invisible morsels. As soon as the glint from the hidden treasure had stabbed at her right eye – her only good one – Luz's concentration was re-focused on digging in the pile of rubbish.

She glanced around quickly to see if any competitors were nearby. The closest people were Jun and Yollie. They were only about thirty feet away but concentrating on their own search and paying her no mind. Several others were down along the wall, but also paid little attention to the ten-year-old girl. She didn't recognize any of them and dismissed them as idiots if they expected to find anything good where they were looking.

She reached for the sky, stretching nonchalantly and continued looking around until Jun and Yollie got a little farther away. Luz stuck her fingers in her short, black hair and gingerly tugged at the matted knots in a half-hearted attempt at untangling them. Her smooth, dark face, smudged with dirt from days of foraging, tightened into a frown as her tresses fought the freedom offered them. Although blind in her left eye, the tear duct still worked well and was in full production when Luz gave up on her hair. From her two-dimensional vantage point toward the top of the heap, she could just see over the wall at the tops of colorful jeepneys jockeying for position along the boulevard. The early morning sun was rapidly warming the piles of garbage and coaxing even more odors from their depths.

The rancid smell of the dump had never bothered her, as far as she could remember. She could still discern the different odors that lingered over and around the mountains of garbage and the nearby shanty she shared with her sister and their grandmother. And when the wind blew from different directions, she could detect the odors of the city. The exhaust of thousands of vehicles mixed with the scent of the fish market two blocks away. Occasionally, a tantalizing blend of aromas from the various food vendors

21

along the boulevard would sneak in. High, white-washed walls hid most of the sights of the outside life from Luz, but it could not hide the sounds and fragrances.

When the walls first went up, Luz had asked her grandmother why they were built. "Mrs. Marcos is concerned for the safety of the children. She is personally building the wall so you won't get run over by those *loko* jeepney drivers! The woman is a saint." *Impó* always stopped whatever she was doing when she talked about Imelda Marcos, as if it were a sin to divide her attention between Marcos and anything else. "The woman is a saint," were her grandmother's final words in any discussion of Imelda Marcos.

The fact was that the walls had been built to hide the dumps and their symbiotic shanty towns, from foreign visitors. In various attempts to lure international attention and investments, Imelda Marcos embarked on a program of beautification for the capitol. These walls were cheap and seemingly effective.

When the wind blew from the north, the smell of sewage grew stronger, and Luz knew it was because there where even more shanty towns up that way. Any breeze from the west or south brought the fetid essence of Manila Bay and the familiar sounds of a busy port conducting international trade.

Of all the things that assaulted Luz's senses, she definitely preferred those emanating from the street. She also enjoyed watching the busy activities on the street, when she could. She liked the jumble of colors as people and machines competed for the limited space of the city; people going to important places and talking about important things. The cacophony of un-muffled engines, blaring horns and human voices added an ambiguous richness to the sensual assault that Luz found exhilarating. She dreamed of the day when she would be out there among those people, wearing nice clothes, eating good food and doing anything she wanted.

She enjoyed those dreams when she had the time. Most of her time, like this morning, was spent trying to sift a living from the mountains of refuse that was her neighborhood.

Jun and Yollie eventually moved out of sight, allowing Luz to quickly shrug off the denim bag, which had been dangling from her shoulder and loosen its draw strings. Squatting before the enticing shimmer of light, Luz began to work.

Sea gulls took to the air as Luz flung chunks of cement and scraps of gypsum board in all directions. Her fellow scavengers squawked noisily and returned to their perch, in hopes of finding another elusive scrap.

At last, Luz pushed aside a larger piece of gypsum board and uncovered her treasure, a chrome plated bathroom faucet. She wasn't sure just what she had found. It looked kind of like the spigot from which she and her sister got their drinking water, but it was different. Why would anyone want to run water through something so shiny and pretty? Except for a few nicks and scratches, its surface was smooth, and the handles were two rounded cylinders with indentations scooped out for gripping. That was another thing; why were there two handles? And why were there no threads with which to attach a hose?

These were fleeting questions, unimpeded be answers, as Luz stared silently at the fixture for a few moments before reaching reverently for it. It was heavier than she at first thought and was anchored in its grave of garbage by some unseen shroud. As she worked at dislodging her prize, the wind whipped Luz's yellow cotton frock over her head, revealing her tattered panties and filthy legs, scarred by many battles with the vast fields of garbage. The healed wounds were testaments to the ability of the human body to fight off infection. Luz's lack of concern for the lay of her dress hem was testament to the fact that modesty was not a high priority here.

As was normally the case, the heap released its bounty reluctantly. Luz gave one last tug and stumbled backward slightly as the faucet came free. She pushed her dress down and smiled broadly as the reason for the snag became apparent. Attached to the back of the mysterious treasure was a foot-long length of thin copper tubing which had been caught up in the surrounding masonry. Luz smiled because she knew the tubing would fetch a good price from the traders, regardless of what the shiny thing was worth.

Reaching for her bag, she allowed herself another mindless swat at the flies as she made ready to end her morning search. The tubing had been kinked about halfway down from the faucet fixture, making it hard to pull from the dump but it had straightened a bit when Luz retrieved it. Using that same kink to bend the copper tubing to fit in the bag, the girl shouldered her burden and started toward home, fantasizing about what she would like to do with the extra centavos she was sure to collect for this find. The reality was that whatever money the faucet brought would be used to feed her small, struggling family for a short while longer.

Luz slowed as she approached the shanty. From inside could be heard the angry, staccato words of her grandmother. She wasn't sure at first who was the focus of her grandmother's tirade but was glad it wasn't her. As she got closer though, she realized the only other person who could possibly have gotten such a reaction from *Impó* was her sister.

The glow of finding the faucet faded to black as Luz began to understand what was being shouted inside the shack. She reached up and timidly pulled aside the scrap of burlap which served as a door, peering quietly inside.

The room was about eight feet by ten feet and was all the home that Luz had ever known. The walls were a patchwork of cardboard, plywood and tin which bore the logos of the Baguio Cooking Oil Company, the San Miguel Brewery and just about every other manufacturer in between. Except for the door into which Luz now stared, there were no other large openings. Ventilation wasn't a problem because of the gaping cracks between the multifarious building materials. Its roof, coveted by several neighbors, was mainly corrugated tin, reinforced here and there by plastic to stem the rain.

Morning sunlight squeezed through the porous walls and spot-lighted a woven bamboo mat, spread on the far corner of the dirt floor, which was bed and dining area for all three of the shack's inhabitants. Emmy was kneeling on the mat, rapidly stuffing what few pieces of clothing she owned into a plastic bag. Luz stared uncomprehendingly at the logo emblazoned on the side of the bag as she listened to her grandmother. She seemed unable to move her eyes away from the bag as it stretched more and more with each added belonging.

Emmy's pretty, fifteen-year-old face, unblemished and freshly washed, was a study in adult determination. Her large brown eyes, normally soft and just a little too far apart, now seemed hard and flinty. Her full lips were turned down ever so slightly at the edges and her shoulder length black hair, also freshly washed, dangled erratically as she reached for this and that, stuffing her bag.

"Where will you stay? You know there is nothing but whores there! What about me and your sister?" *Impó's* voice quivered and subsided as she saw Luz at the door. Fueled by agony and rage, *Impó* paced in the small space behind Emmy, wringing her hands, emitting short groans and sighs.

Emmy glanced up at her grandmother and then over to Luz. "Don't worry," she said, more to Luz than the old woman. "*Ateh* Mari says that I can stay with the other waitresses who work in the restaurant. I will be able to send lots of money back for you two."

Emmy took a last look at the small pile of clothing left on the mat – two tee shirts and a pair of panties – as she got to her feet. "You can have these," she said to Luz. "I am going to have all new clothes and new shoes and I will go to the movies every day if I want."

She looked over at her grandmother, now silent and staring at the dirt floor. "After I pay back *Ateh* Mari and save a little money, I can send for you two," Emmy said, her voice filling with hope. "We can have our own apartment, maybe even a separate kitchen! That will be great, okay?" she said, smiling at Luz.

24

"Mari is already a whore," Impó said softly, all of the earlier rage having drained her. "She is a whore, and she is going to turn you into a whore." Her thick, grey hair, cut short, barely moved as she shook her head slightly from side to side. The faded purple flowers printed on her dirty, long frock seemed to grow even paler as *Impó* twisted her hands into the fabric.

Luz stared silently at the two through one misty eye, her prize forgotten.

*　　　*　　　*

"Luuuuzy, I'm home!" The fake Ricky Ricardo voice brought Luz back from her reverie, but she came reluctantly.

"Hi Scott, where's your friend, tissue?" Luz said. She thought she had heard the Cuban accented voice before somewhere but couldn't recall where. At any rate, coming from Scott Chalmers, she knew it was supposed to be some sort of lame joke, so she made one of her own.

'Yuk, yuk, very funny," he said, coming the rest of the way into Ace's Place and allowing the hydraulic cylinder to close the door. He looked around the square room, lit mostly by the afternoon sun sifting through dusty old curtains in the front windows. A tired, capiz shell lamp above the scarred countertop tried valiantly to scare away some shadows, and strobes throbbed and flickered on the silent jukebox. An oscillating fan on a meter-tall stand swept the room, pushing warm air and the lingering odor of fish paste over the empty tables and chairs. "Where's all the customers? You scare 'em away?"

"No ships come here. You station guys are so late, too. I don't have very many customers today." Luz ignored the barb and resumed putting beer into the cooler behind the bar, which she had been doing automatically while caught up in the memory of the last day she had seen her sister. "You want beer?"

"*Oo, talaga*," he said, covering the short distance between the door and the bar. He spoke this Tagalog phrase in a thick, fake, southern drawl.

"Hey, listen, there's going to be a new guy stationed here," he said in a much less pronounced drawl, which passed as his normal voice. "He's a cherry boy in the P.I., but he's a Senior Chief so I doubt he's a cherry boy in life."

Scott stretched on his tip toes to slide his butt onto the stool and put a ten-peso bill on the bar. Although only 5 feet, 8 inches tall and 145 pounds, the bar stool creaked as loudly for him as it would any man. In one well-practiced move, Scott slid his right hand across his forehead, moving a shock of blonde hair out of his eyes and simultaneously wiping sweat from his brow. He then wiped them on the leg of his jeans and leaned against the bar in anticipation of his beer.

"He is a good friend to you?" Luz asked, quietly placing the San Miguel on a cardboard coaster.

"Naw, haven't even met him yet. He just got here this morning and his sponsor was taking him around the base today. But I hear he is single, and I know he'll get out here eventually. Everyone comes to "Ace's" for the coldest beer and the hottest women." Scott said that last sentence with a cheesy grin. He twisted his finger in the mouth of the beer bottle and then wiped the rim where the cap had been. And, after tipping the bottle in Luz's direction, took a long pull of the beer.

Luz looked around at the silent jukebox and the five empty tables. "The girls are at the movie," she said. "If he comes now, I hope all he wants is beer."

"I doubt he'll be coming out anytime soon. Hell, I'd be taking a nap if I was him. He's probably taking the big *tulog*, even as we speak." Scott reached in his front pocket, fishing for more money. "Anyway," he said, finding only lint, "his name is Roy Thompson and I want him to be in a good mood for the rest of the time I have left here, so we need to make sure he has a good first weekend to get him off on the right foot." Scott took another swallow of beer and said, "So don't let him take any girls from here, okay?"

"Like you?" she said, ignoring his attempt at wit. "Is Judy back from the province yet?"

"Naw," he replied. "Couple of days."

"Are you to be working with him?" Luz's banter was only slightly more contrived.

"Well, not directly," he said. "He's gonna be in charge of security and he'll work straight for the XO. But, since I work for the CO, I figure we'll be doing lots of stuff together. The easier life he has here in the P.I., the easier life I'll have. Know what I mean, jellybean?"

Luz didn't answer. She tried never to answer a question which rhymed with itself, hoping in vain that Scott would stop the annoying habit if she ignored him. She was learning human nature, but still naïve about cocky, young Americans.

"Maybe I'll be the one," Luz said.

"What, you?" Scott looked incredulous. "Everyone knows you're the oldest virgin on Gordon Avenue. And I'm sure no self-respecting Senior Chief wants a thirty-year-old cherry girl." Scott chuckled quietly. He didn't know if she was a virgin or not, but he had never seen her take a short-time or over-night.

She didn't really look like a thirty-year-old virgin either. She was only twenty-three and actually looked younger. With dark, long eye lashes and lips that were full and wide, she seldom wore makeup. Her coffee-with-cream colored face was free of wrinkles or blemishes and perfectly complimented the sparkling smile which visited there often.

"How do you think I am like that?" Luz asked in mock anger. "I am being the number one girl here, but I go to rich guys *lamang*. You are not the one to see that!"

Scott laughed out loud and finished his beer. "Well," he said, settling the bottle on the bar and scooting out of the stool, "I guess a Senior Chief should be able to afford the "number one girl" at Ace's Place." He picked his two pesos of change off the bar and checked his wallet for more cash as he walked to the door.

"I gotta go change some money and meet some guys. We'll be back *mamaya*. Okay?"

"Okay, bye," she said plainly, as he reached the door.

"Oh, and if Ben comes in, will you let him know I'm still waiting for that new wallet? He was supposed to have that for me last week." Scott opened the door, allowing the sunlight to stream across the worn tile floor and wash away the shadows for a few seconds.

"*Oo, mamaya*," she said, flapping her hand at him in a half waving, half shooing motion, as if to hurry him along. "I talk to Ben," she said to no one, as the door clicked shut. "I always talk to Ben."

Chapter 5

Olongapo did not usually disappoint those who sought what it offered. It was a bustling city of around 200,000 people and had for decades provided almost anything an American marine or sailor could possibly ask for in the way of exotic liberty and cheap goods. It had done the same for all types of seagoing adventurers since the end of the 18th century.

The mythology of the city's name involved the missing head of an assassinated village elder. Weeks after the elder's corpse had been located, a boy supposedly found its head perched atop a bamboo pole, prompting him to run around yelling "*Ulo ng apo! Ulo ng apo!*" The remaining elder's must have thought it a good idea to name the place "head of the elder." Olongapo grew continuously under British, Spanish and American rule as operations at the port increased. Even after the Philippines was granted independence following the end of the second World War, the city remained under the administration of U.S. Naval forces until the middle of the 20th century.

Now, of course, Olongapo was packed to the gills with bars and clubs. They ranged from one room beer bars, lucky to have a jukebox to multi-floored nightclubs, rotating several bands and serving the finest food and liquor available anywhere in the Pacific. A person could get a beer almost anywhere, but Olongapo offered so much more.

For every bar, massage parlor, or nightclub, there was a restaurant, a sari-sari store or a marketplace. And though severely outnumbered, there were chapels, reading rooms and service centers representing many faiths, to lend a counterbalance to the effects of each den of iniquity.

In addition to the entertainment, food and redemption, there were thousands of small shops where one could purchase hand-sewn, tailored clothing or made-to-order shoes and boots for just a few dollars. Hand-carved furniture, crafts and musical instruments could be acquired so cheaply that many Navy warships sailed to the U.S. with not a single void left empty. There were whole buildings located on the Naval base filled with people whose sole purpose was to pack and mail parcels out of the country.

Whether one were young or old, black or white, country or rock, male or female, straight or gay, or anything in between or outside all those things; one could be accommodated in Olongapo. Forget Las Vegas; for the deck-plate seaman returning from three months at sea, this was the entertainment capital of the world. Forget U.S. network television's idea of fantasy; for the eighteen-year-old marine fresh off the farm in Iowa, this was the real "Fantasy Island."

However, it was by no means everyone's idea of fun. It was not unheard of for a person to spend a full tour there and never leave the base. Many military members or their spouses were so sickened by the lasciviousness of the place that they refused even to venture out for a meal or to view the scenery. If they did, they would find that the streets and sidewalks seemed in constant need of repair and that little effort was made to "beautify" the city. The base offered everything they needed and provided a prophylaxis from what they considered unclean.

To be sure, the place was far from clean, morality notwithstanding. Olongapo's idea of a street sweeper was some underpaid laborer clearing trash from in front of a business and there was no such thing as an Environmental Protection Agency in the Philippines. The exhaust from the jeepneys alone was enough to foul the air of the city but add to that the exhaust from Victory Liner and Rabbit buses, several thousand motorcycles, as well as private cars and taxis, and the air became a haze which seemed to drain energy from the sun even on the clearest of days.

The air was no clearer over the base, despite the fact that the cars there were well tuned, shipped from the states and maintained for bargain prices at the large Navy Exchange Garage. Most of the cars from the city were not allowed on the base, whereas most of the American owned vehicles were allowed out. When on the base, they rode over roads that were patched as needed and resurfaced regularly.

Between those roads and the many buildings on the base were lawns and gardens and parks and athletic fields and golf courses, maintained by armies of local Filipinos, happy to work on the base in any capacity. They could be seen daily, grooming the vegetation and clearing the streets of trash and debris.

In addition, the base had a horse stable for pleasurable rides through the hills and a go-cart track for those seeking a little more speed and noise. It had bowling alleys, archery ranges, college courses and clubs for every level of officer, enlisted person, or civilian. In short, it had everything an American could want and most of the services were provided by the cheap labor of Filipinos.

Even the lowest ranking people living in base housing could afford maids and gardeners, some of whom lived with their American families. Life on the base was an exceedingly rare departure from the reality the enlisted members faced as working-class poor in the states.

Many of those young military wives, disdainful of life outside the gate and disgusted by what the "bargirls" did to get by, had no qualms at all about paying a maid a few dollars a day to clean her house, baby sit her children, wash her cloths, cook her meals, or change her baby's soiled diapers.

The money exchanged each month, paying for all the goods and services, was almost nothing to the Americans and almost everything to the Filipinos.

Shit River divided the two communities and was the source most people thought of first when they questioned the stench of the place. But there were also open gutters and drainage ditches throughout Olongapo which contributed to the overall smell assaulting the senses.

All of that awaited Roy Thompson. As he neared the far end of the bridge, Roy reveled in his relative ignorance of what awaited him. The thrill of exploring and experiencing a new liberty port was just as strong now as it had been when he was a Seaman Apprentice. At least now, he'd been able to gather some information before beginning the adventure

Don Bodicker, an acquaintance and fellow Chief Roy had known in Norfolk, loved Olongapo and filled him in on what to expect if he ever got there. As just about everyone in the Navy had, Roy heard stories about the P.I. since joining the Navy, but Don had been specific, telling him the lay of the city, the areas he should avoid and where he might find something interesting. Most of what Roy knew about Olongapo had been learned from Bodicker.

The bridge over Shit River led straight onto Magsaysay Drive. According to Don, that was the main strip which featured most of the loud and flashy nightclubs. It also had several movie theaters, restaurants and shops, but at night it was a pulsing jumble of neon signs, blaring music, honking cars and horny sailors.

To the left – and west – of Magsaysay was an area commonly referred to as the "jungle." The jungle also had the requisite bars and restaurants, but it catered to the black sailors and marines, almost exclusively. They, of course, were welcomed anywhere else in the city they chose to spend their money; however, if one wasn't black, one wasn't welcomed in the jungle. It wasn't official – there were no signs posted and no boundaries marked – but it was common knowledge among military people of all colors. The level of interracial violence which had been pretty high during the Viet Nam War had subsided considerably, but there was still trouble to be had if one ventured there unaware.

Magsaysay Drive intersected Rizal Avenue at Rizal Circle several blocks from the bridge. Rizal Avenue also had an extensive mix of bars and restaurants, but in addition, it had a high number of places meant only for the elite of Olongapo society. They were even supposed to be a few casinos along Rizal Avenue.

As a matter of fact, Roy hoped to check out all those places before leaving the island, but right now he was going to Gordon Avenue. Don swore that Gordon was the most laid-back part of the city and that if he wanted anything mellower, he would have to venture out to one of the barrios between there and Subic City. Gordon Avenue was the first city street on the right after coming off the bridge and Roy could see the intersection ahead.

Roy was surrounded by sailors, marines and civilians, each coming or going at their own pace. And at the end of the bridge, just as it became Magsaysay, Roy could see an outcrop of booths and small open bars lining the sidewalk on the right. Tee shirt vendors, barbecue stands and trinket shops were jammed side by side along the path so thickly that Roy was forced to walk in the street.

"Hey Joe, sell your watch?" Roy looked to his left and saw a young Filipino, perhaps twenty years old, pointing at his wrist.

"Sorry, don't have one," Roy replied, holding up his naked arm. The young man immediately turned away, looking for the next potential business partner crossing the river.

Roy shook his head slowly and continued walking toward the corner. He decided to not answer any of the other pleading voices which came from every direction, some laced with practiced despair, some with the drone of a litany.

"Hey Joe, buy barbecue?" asked a middle-aged woman from beside a smoking grill.

"Mister, buy gum," said a seven or eight-year-old girl, displaying a pack of Juicy-Fruit in her open palm.

"Hey man! Look at this," a young man held up a pewter key chain with two stooped, human figures on it. The vendor manipulated a lever and the male figure straightened, appearing to ram a huge penis into the female figure bent before it.

Roy looked straight ahead, to avoid eye contact with any of the vendors and found himself reading the tee-shirt of a sailor walking about two yards ahead. The faded silk-screened letters proclaimed, "1000 missions over Shit River....and still flying!"

And this is my first, he thought.

Interrupted Weekend

He continued through the bazaar and the voices, although never quieter, still faded further with each resolute step.

Chapter 6

Just past the bridge and to the left Columban Road followed the canal, but mostly residences and churches lay in that direction. Except for "the Jungle," which could be reached going that way, there was little reason for most liberty hounds to explore it. Straight ahead on Magsaysay is where they mostly wanted to go. After getting past the vendors, Gordon Avenue was the first street on which one could turn right. By the time Roy got there, the smells of Olongapo had already begun to meld into the background of his senses.

Just across from Gordon, First Street also lead west toward the Jungle. Turning right off of Magsaysay, Gordon Avenue started bending to the left after the first block and then kept curving off into the distance. It continued curving that way, through east Bajac-Bajac, until it eventually turned into a numbered street and intersected Rizal Avenue. At that end of the avenue were mostly residential neighborhoods, but true to the design of most cities outside military installations, the end closest to the base was packed with bars, massage parlors and cheap hotels, with the occasional restaurant, sari-sari store, barber shop and apartment thrown in for good measure. Most of the buildings on this part of Gordon were two stories, with a few that were either one or three stories tall.

The bar which Roy was looking for was supposed to be in one of the one story buildings, about halfway down the second block and on the left-hand side of the street. Don had told him about several bars and restaurants in Olongapo, while describing the different areas of the city, but this one sounded like the kind of place that might suit his purposes. No need to make this initial confrontation an all-out attack.

The next corner after Magsaysay was Sixth Street and it was swarming with tricycles. A tricycle was basically a two-passenger vehicle but carried as many paying bodies as it could hold. Fortunately for safety's sake, most "trikes" weren't equipped with engines powerful enough to haul very many. Prohibited by law from loitering on Magsaysay, these trikes congregated there at this time of day waiting for people getting off from work at the base.

Seeing no convenient way around them, Roy began to pick his way through.

Like the jeepneys, they were almost always garishly painted and covered with clever, little hand-lettered phrases. Additionally, they were usually festooned with plastic tassels and fringes just in case the reflectors and mirrors failed to catch the eye. It seemed that mufflers, working or otherwise, were seldom a part of their decor.

Roy weaved his way through them, having to stop and move sideways occasionally to avoid eager drivers who pulled up directly in his path. Sometimes a driver would say, "Ride, Joe?" But just as often, they would pull to within inches of him and say nothing, as if expecting him to climb aboard their trike, even though he had passed up twenty others before. Roy didn't get angry at their aggressive tactics; he simply walked around and ignored them as a beekeeper might work around pesky bees, eventually making it to the sidewalk.

During Don Bodicker's time, Gordon Avenue had had only small, jukebox joints which had catered to people actually stationed on the base, as opposed to the multitudes of sailors visiting the island on ships. They had been low-keyed and cheaper than the nightclubs on Magsaysay. Girls worked at them, but they didn't constantly hassle the customers to buy drinks for them and the music on the jukeboxes was for an older, perhaps mellower, crowd. As Roy looked around him, he saw that Gordon had seen some changes.

It appeared as if the bar owners had succumbed to the economic pressure to bring in the younger, more free-spending crowd and expanded their floor space to make room for live bands. Gordon Avenue now looked and sounded like a shorter, narrower version of Magsaysay Drive. Roy didn't know it yet, but the noise and music he heard now would only get louder after 8:00 PM, when most of the live bands fired up their amplifiers. It sounded plenty loud enough for Roy's taste already.

For whatever reason, a few establishments had decided to stay small and relatively quiet, and that is exactly what Roy wanted for his first night in the Philippines. A quiet bar in which to have a few beers and talk to some locals, seemed like the perfect place to get a feel for the city. And the fact that it was close to the base was even better if he needed to make a quick getaway. He hoped that the bar Don had recommended would be that place.

A faded, hand-painted sign proclaiming the location of Ace's Place dangled from the building's overhang and was almost lost amid a dozen similar ones marking the location of other establishments up and down the street. Ace's was located between another bar and what appeared to be a beauty salon. Roy looked around, taking a quick assessment of the street and headed for Ace's.

The bar front was fifteen or twenty feet wide but at its center was a metal-framed, glass door separating two large windows, each decorated with four aces fanned across its center. Both windows had "Ace's Place" painted in big red letters above the card design. The door was also decorated with painted lettering which read, "Ace's Place....Come on in and get lucky!!!" Curtains covered the windows and door, obscuring Roy's view of the inside, but he could make out the pulsing lights of the jukebox against one wall. Regardless of his luck, he opened the door and walked in.

Roy let the door go and waited for a few seconds to let his eyes get used to the dim light. As the door closed, he noted with some surprise how effective it was at cutting down the outside noise. Looking back over his shoulder, he could see out through the curtains much easier than he could see in.

"Hello, come in, have a sit." The words had a singsong, rhythmic quality and came from a girl behind the bar. Although, as Roy was beginning to see more clearly, the bar was really not much more than a Formica topped counter, fronted by four bar stools and the girl was a very attractive young woman. He seemed to be alone with her.

"You want beer?" she asked, with less singsong and more earnestness. The dim lighting hid some details, as the counter did most of her body, but neither hid her beauty.

"Sure, thanks," he said, walking toward the bar. He thought she smiled and as he got closer and he noted the deep luster of her long, straight hair, parted in the middle and black as a lawyer's heart. It swung freely as she turned and reached into the cooler and then returned to a smooth, flowing stream on either side of her face, ending at the top of her smallish breasts as she set the beer in front of him.

"Want a glass?" she said with the same earnestness as before and used her index fingers to slide her hair behind each ear.

"Okay," he said, vaguely remembering some sage advice, received long ago. The glasses were under the bar and Roy studied her as she bent to retrieve one.

She wore a simple, blue smock whose square neck highlighted a tiny crucifix dangling around her neck. The sleeveless blouse provided ample room for her thin and well-toned arms and complimented her white shorts, cut to just above mid-thigh and having one pocket in the back. Three keys hung from the pocket, evidently attached to some type of fob. She looked thin, athletic and nicely proportioned, but her hips seemed a bit wide, perhaps just appearing so because of the white shorts.

Still holding the glass, she put a cardboard coaster down and picked up the beer to pour.

"You like head?" she asked before pouring.

"A little bit," he said, trying to believe she was speaking only of the beer.

The girl tipped the glass and poured the beer slowly, creating a small head of foam. She wasn't smiling with her mouth, but her eyes seemed to be laughing while she watched the glass fill.

Even in the dimness, Roy could see she wore no makeup and had little need for it. Her fresh face was accented by dark, long eye lashes and full and even lips. He thought her to be in her late teens or early twenties.

She sat the full glass and the nearly empty bottle back on their respective coasters and now smiled with her lips and teeth and eyes. "Okay?" she asked.

"Okay," he replied, returning her smile with one of his own, although his teeth were not nearly so white or even. He had taken a ten-peso note from his wallet as she poured the beer and now laid it on the counter as he lifted the glass to his lips.

"*Salámat*," he said and took a drink.

"*Waláng anumán*. You speak Tagalog?" she asked, as if really interested.

"No, that's just one of the few words I got from my welcome aboard package."

"Oh, so you are new here in the Philippines?" she seemed more interested now as she made change. Luz had worked with American sailors long enough to know that a "welcome aboard package" was an information packet provided to new personnel, usually prior to transferring in.

"Well, not exactly new. I've been here all day now," he said.

"Oh, okay," she said. "What's your name?" she asked, stacking two, one-peso coins on the counter.

"My name's Roy." he said, "And yours?"

"I am Luz," she said. "Roy," she looked him squarely in the face. There was something strange about her eyes. "I need to ask a favor to you," she sounded as if he were her last hope on earth.

Roy's grin disappeared as he leaned toward her.

"Roy," she said, "can I have a peso for the jukebox?" She smiled as she said it, but it took Roy a few beats to figure it out.

"Oh, yeah, sure," he said.

She smiled radiantly again and picked up a coin. "Gotchu," she said, walking toward the jukebox. "What you think? I'm going to ask you for electric fan? I don't know you yet."

Roy watched from the corners of his eyes as she moved away. She walked confidently, but not seductively and again Roy sensed a fair amount of athleticism. A favorite image of Lisa walking naked into the bedroom flashed in his memory and a familiar pressure stirred ever-so-slightly in his crotch. The feelings of arousal immediately brought on another pang of guilt. He thought, not for the last time, that this was going to be more difficult than he at first believed.

Luz punched buttons on the jukebox without looking to verify which songs they corresponded to. She knew practically every song's number and the records weren't changed often enough to cause much confusion. She paused after punching in the second set of numbers only to decide the best song to end the set.

"So, now you know all about me, what's your story," Roy said, as the jukebox began playing a song by "Queen."

"I am the daughter of Ferdinand Marcos. I had to hide out in this bar when he leaves from the P.I. because they had no room on the plane," she said. She had pulled a stool up behind the counter and settled into it noisily, sipping on a glass of cola brought out from somewhere.

She looked at him helplessly and although Roy knew the story was bullshit, the sadness in her eyes had a tinge of genuineness. The sadness disappeared and she smiled again before Roy could think of a snappy come back.

"The lawyers are still making things straight. When they finish, I will go back to live in my *ano*, my penthouse, in New York." There was no sadness this time, only sarcasm. "Then I will only work in bars on weekends."

"I see," Roy said. "I hope I still know you then."

"No problem. I'll be the one to tell you when I go."

The volume of the jukebox was low enough to allow for an unstressed conversation and they continued to dance around verbally, getting little bits of real information from broad questions and silly answers.

What Roy suspected as being true about Luz was that she was from Manila and had a married sister living in Bremerton, Washington with her Navy husband. She had mentioned no other family except for various "aunties," which Roy suspected were merely older girl friends. She said she had worked at Ace's for about five years and before that, "somewhere on Rizal." He assumed that to be the street intersecting with Magsaysay Avenue. Also, she never said exactly what it was that she did. He further assumed she was a hooker.

Roy had not been much more revealing in his banter. She found out early on that he was single, although he didn't mention his marriage and divorce or Lisa. She also learned he was originally from Florida and was a Senior Chief, newly assigned to NAVMAG. Luz did not let on that she had heard about him earlier in the day from Scott and did not ask too much about what he did in the Navy. He, in turn, volunteered nothing about his work. He did ask if she knew Don Bodicker, but he must have patronized the place before her time.

Crosby, Stills, Nash and Young had just finished singing about Woodstock when the door burst in with raucous laughter. Roy looked back to see three women, all dressed in colored tee shirts, shorts and sandals, talking excitedly about something. They laughed and pointed at a fourth girl, probably no more than eighteen years old and clearly the youngest of the bunch, who trailed them through the door. She was also saying something in Tagalog, and it seemed to Roy she was trying to defend herself against some sort of ribbing.

Luz listened to the older women as they gathered round her and told an evidently hilarious story about the girl. They could barely finish it, for laughing so hard. Luz simply nodded and smiled, asking short questions of all the ladies, including the youngest one.

Finally, they all settled down a bit as Luz began talking to the youngest one in low, even tones. The two oldest of the girls disappeared through a plywood door next to the refrigerator as the third took up the stool Luz had just left.

"*Pogy naman*," she said looking at Roy and smiling. "What's your name?" She was in her late twenties and pretty, probably not really needing the heavy makeup she wore.

"Roy. And yours?" he said in a manner similar to the way he'd talked to Luz earlier.

"Royanyurs?" she asked. "I don't know that name before. What ship you off?"

"I'm not off a ship," he said. "I'm stationed here, and my name is Roy. Period."

"*'Sus, namon!*" she said. "Station *dito, kariput kano, namon!* Royperiod, can I have a peso for jukebox?"

"Sure, go ahead," Roy pointed toward the remaining coin and picked up his beer again. She picked it up and came around the bar smiling. She stepped up to him, pressing her breasts into his back and squeezed his right biceps gently.

"*Salamat po*," she whispered in his ear. "My name is Gloria." Then, dragging her fingernails lightly across his shoulders, she walked to the jukebox. The long nails left a tingling trail beneath his thin polo shirt and an itch longing for continued scratching. Almost as an afterthought, she pointed at the jukebox and said, "What you want?"

"I don't care. Whatever." Roy drained his glass of the warming beer just as Luz appeared before him again.

"Want another?" she said. All the girls except Gloria had disappeared into the back of the bar. Gloria swayed as she leaned against the jukebox.

"Sure," he said without thinking and dug in his pocket for more money.

As Luz came up with the beer, Roy gestured toward where the girls had disappeared and said, "What was that all about?"

"Oh, Lena is very new here. The other girls make fun of her. We all are new, sometimes. That's all," she said, stacking his change on the bar.

"You know what is *saput*?" Gloria said without turning from the jukebox. She went on without waiting for an answer, "Lena has a boyfriend for two weeks and she don't know he is *saput*." Gloria didn't laugh this time; she just shook her head slowly.

Roy turned to Luz for some explanation and saw that she had an amused, almost nostalgic, look on her face. Her eyes were downcast, and Roy got the feeling she was a bit embarrassed.

"You know when a man still has skin on his *ano*, his dick?" she said. She was looking at him now, but he still sensed embarrassment. "You know, like a baby?"

"Oh, you mean uncircumcised?" Roy asked.

"Yeah, yeah, like that," she seemed excited at learning a new word. "She didn't know he was like that until Amie told her today and the girls teased her." She internally repeating the word "uncircumcised" a few times to herself and then smiled.

"She don't want to give him blow job now," Gloria said and howled with laughter again. She had stopped behind Roy's stool and began massaging his neck and shoulders and speaking to Luz in Tagalog. Roy closed his eyes as her strong fingers untied the knots in his neck and he realized just how inadequate the afternoon nap had been. Still, he felt he could hold out for a couple more beers before succumbing to the jet lag.

Gloria was massaging the base of his skull with her left hand and his right biceps with the other until Roy had almost tuned out their voices altogether. In addition to a normal sleep pattern, his body hungered for the attention that Gloria was showing it and he leaned back into her hand, ready to turn control of his muscles over to her completely. He was nearly on the verge of dozing off when she stopped, reached around and pinched his nipple playfully through his shirt. Roy jerked forward, nearly out of the stool, causing both Gloria and Luz both to laugh.

"What you thinking of me?" Gloria said in a mocking tone. "You think I give you free sample?" She laughed again and pushed through the back door, singing along with the jukebox.

Gloria Lamdagan was not a woman who thought deeply about a lot of things, but she wasn't stupid. She was just disinterested in most things which didn't affect her or her livelihood. She was clear in her own mind about her motives and those of the people she knew. She liked money and she liked having fun, but she also wasn't one to put up with a lot of shit just to keep those things around her. That is why, after making a lot more money working the bigger nightclubs, she decided that life at a small, Gordon Avenue bar was a much better way for her to go. When she wanted, she could still talk her customers into taking her to the dance clubs or the nicer restaurants on Magsaysay or Rizal, but she didn't have to be there all the time. Additionally, she thought that the customers she encountered on Gordon were more laid back and fun than those that sought the sound and fury of the nightclubs.

Her thinking wasn't necessarily deep or profound, but they were ideas which had served her effectively for most of her life.

Shortly after her husband was killed by government forces in her home island of Mindanao, she heard that she could find fun and money and less hassle elsewhere. That happened just before their first anniversary. In her small village near Daang Lungsod beach, there was little opportunity for a nineteen-year-old widow other than to find another husband or stay with her family. She might have found some work in the modest tourism industry, but she was unwilling to put up with her parent's rules and tired of the constant harassment by her religious community. So, against the advice and wishes of nearly everyone she knew, Gloria gathered all the money she could borrow and told everyone she was moving to Manila to find work. As soon as possible after arriving in Manila by ferry, she boarded a bus to Olongapo and hadn't thought much about that part of her life since.

Her only thoughts now were to freshen up for the evening of work ahead of her.

Chapter 7

Roy's interest was piqued. He supposed his curiosity would keep him going for a little while longer, despite his fatigue, but he decided to start drinking Coca-Cola just in case. More beers on top of his recently screwed up sleep patterns were likely to cause a major crash and he didn't want that to happen while still on the beach.

At first, few other customers came through the door. Occasionally, an American would come in looking for someone else and then leave when they saw how deserted the place was. As far as he knew, no one was looking for Roy.

However, as the time grew later, the visitors appeared more frequently and began staying for beer. The two older girls, who had first fled to the back of the building, now emerged from there sporting clean dresses and freshly made faces. Eventually, Gloria and Lena joined them, also refreshed and beautified. Luz never changed clothing nor put on makeup.

Behind the bar, high on the wall above the beer cooler was the front of an air-conditioning unit. Roy hadn't noticed it before because of its inactivity, but it came to life when Luz punched its "On" button and began blowing gradually cooler air out over the bar. A fan at the end of the bar closest to the wall and a fan on a stand in one corner of the room were also doing duty. In between the occasional interruptions when Luz had to greet customers and serve beer, Roy learned a little more about Ace's Place and its crew.

Ace's got its name from the late husband of the owner. Erlinda Garcia had married a sailor, Asa Prescott, when she was quite young, following him around the globe until he eventually retired from the Navy as a First Class Petty Officer in 1969. Asa Prescott had been called "Ace" since the day his father had announced his birth. His last duty station was San Diego, where they decided to stay until their one and only son graduated from high school. Shortly thereafter, he enlisted in the army and was shipped off to Viet Nam, where he was killed within the first month. In 1971 they sold everything they owned in California and moved back to the P.I. where his meager retirement check went much farther. So much farther in fact, they found they had money left over to invest. With that and the little bit of capital remaining from the sale of their stateside home, Asa and Linda opened "Ace's Place."

In 1973 Mr. Prescott died. Some said he drank himself to death. More than a couple of folks said he came into contact with a toxic substance after Mrs. Prescott caught him sampling the services of the bar's employees one too many times. Luz had no opinion on the subject.

Regardless, the newly widowed Mrs. Prescott promptly turned over the operation of the bar to her brother Armando and his wife, Mama Nina, and returned to San Diego where she re-married and lives to this day.

According to Luz, she returns to the Philippines at least once a year to see how business is going. Her brother, a bus driver for Victory Liner, left the running of the business to his wife Nina, who evidently is a hell of a businessperson. Roy didn't see how the place could generate much revenue, but then again, he was nobody's businessperson himself.

The bar did well enough to stay afloat and had anywhere from three to ten girls working there at any one time. Luz said that there were now eight girls working there all together, but that three of them had "steady bar fines" and didn't normally come in to work. One of the three, Amie, had a "steady" who was stationed on a ship, so she sometimes worked when his ship was out of port.

The four that Roy had seen today, in addition to Luz, were Gloria, Lena, Amie and Lita. Amie and Lita were probably in their mid to late thirties and had been in the game for quite a while, working in several places around Olongapo. Lena was just starting, and Gloria had worked in two of the "Super Clubs" on Magsaysay before seeking a less stressful and less profitable life at Ace's. Luz remained somewhat of a mystery.

He knew she had worked here and one other place, but still was not sure in what capacity. She never talked about "boyfriends" or "customers" in relation to herself. And although the other girls would occasionally get a beer out of the cooler or make change, they usually left that to Luz while they spent time with the customers. Perhaps she was a cashier only.

"So, Luz, who's your boyfriend?" Roy asked. For some reason he felt reluctant to just come out and ask if she were a hooker.

"*Wala*," she said. "I don't have."

"Husband?"

"*Wala*."

"Fiancé?"

"*Wala*."

"Girlfriend?"

44

"*Wala*!" she said. "What you think of me? Like that?" Luz feigned anger well, but Roy saw a spark which intimated he may not want to witness her real anger firsthand. Again, he saw something strange in her eyes, or perhaps, about her eyes.

Roy smiled and said, "Gotchu."

"Ha, ha," she said flatly, just as Gloria came up to the bar with a hand full of twenty-peso notes. They spoke in Tagalog for a while and then Luz retrieved two beers and a pad of blank receipts from behind the bar. Gloria winked discreetly at Roy and then returned to her table with the beer and some change as Luz began writing something on the pad.

"What's that?" Roy asked.

Luz stopped writing and looked up. "You know… it's a night off paper; a bar fine." She smiled and continued to write information into the appropriate spaces. "This way the police know she is not a street walker and I…" – she paused for dramatic effect while ripping the paper from its stub – "…can do bookkeeping."

Roy nodded his head thoughtfully and raised his eyebrows as if to show that he knew exactly what she was talking about. She chuckled softly and returned the pad.

The beer and soda were starting to accumulate at near flood levels in Roy's bladder and he just started to ask Luz where he might relieve himself when the front door opened. He noted a subtle shift in her expression, so Roy swiveled around to see a young Filipino male, somewhere between thirty and forty years old, entering the bar. He had a sky-blue plastic satchel slung over his shoulder and was carrying several new billfolds.

He was dressed casually, but far better than what Roy considered the average for a street vendor. Instead of a tee shirt, shorts and flip-flops, he wore a button-down shirt, slacks and Nike cross training shoes. He waved his wallets at Luz and went to a table where two Americans sat drinking beer.

"Want to buy wallets?" he asked. He fanned his wares out in front of him like a winning poker hand. Both guys shook their heads and held up a hand as if to ward him off. Unfazed, he dug in his satchel and brought out two small plastics bags filled with whole peanuts.

"Want to buy peanuts?" he asked in the same hopeful voice. Again, the Americans declined.

His smile never faded as the vendor took his merchandise to the next table, where Gloria and her temporary boyfriend were drinking beer. Roy tuned him out at that point, because of more pressing matters which needed attending and turned back to Luz.

"Luz," he said, "please tell me there is a head close by. It's time to break the seal."

"Okay," she said. "It's through that door and on the right." She pointed at the same door the girls had used and smiled pleasantly.

He expected her to make a smart comment about his use of the word "head" to describe the toilet, in keeping with the way she had been bantering all afternoon. Her concise reply threw him off balance for a second, so he simply thanked her and got up to relieve himself.

He took a curious peek behind the bar counter as he passed by and noted that, in addition to the beer cooler/refrigerator, there was a small sink against the wall and a makeshift curtain covering a storage area under the counter.

The painted, plywood door leading to the back had a spring attached to make sure it closed completely, and it hid a dimly lit, short hall. It was only slightly less effective at hiding the smell of urine, stale beer and Pine-Sol that now filled his nostrils as he looked around for the toilet. The floor was bare cement and the plaster walls had been painted a dull turquoise color. A small, door-less closet on the left played home to a worn-out, short-handled broom and various other items Roy couldn't make out in the dim light. He could hear the noise of the air-conditioner and suspected it sat on a rack in there as well. He could feel the heat and humidity it was pumping into the air and hoped that sufficient ventilation would help with that. On the right were two, plywood doors, both painted black with white lettering and each with an empty thread spool nailed there as a handle. There was another, much sturdier door at the end of the short hall which had a real doorknob, a dead bolt and a peep hole at just about four feet above the floor. He suspected it protected some living quarters, but Roy didn't ponder the issue because what he really needed was behind the door that had "BOYS" hand-painted in three-inch letters. He pulled it open.

The room was dark, so Roy held the door ajar to let in as much light as possible. The urine odor was stronger in here, but not overpowering. It was far from being the worst place he had ever pissed. He was relieved to see a string dangling from the middle of the ceiling, attached to a light fixture, and was even more relieved to see the light come on when he pulled it. It revealed a five-by-five feet room containing a barren toilet bowl and a tiny sink with one faucet. The toilet wasn't excessively dirty, but it had no seat and no cover for its reservoir. The walls were the same flat blue as the hall. The door banged shut as Roy stepped before the toilet and unzipped his fly. He detected the faint hint of yet another aroma as the newly reprocessed San Miguel foamed in the toilet bowl. Ah, yes, Roy thought. Old vomit. All in all, it was not a place where he wanted to loiter.

Roy looked in vain for some sort of towel rack as he zipped up has pants, but saw only a small, empty shelf above the sink. He wondered if the faucet even worked and was mildly surprised when a narrow, slow stream of water came from its mouth after he turned the squeaky handle. He rubbed his hands quickly under the light flow of water and wiped them on his jeans, giving up on the idea of finding a towel. He turned off the water and took another quick glance around the room before pulling the string dangling from the light fixture. He saw no toilet paper and made a mental note to avoid taking a shit while on liberty, if at all possible.

Luz was speaking to the wallet vendor in Tagalog as Roy opened the door leading to the front. The vendor looked up and smiled at Roy as he came around to reclaim his stool.

"Want to buy wallet?" he said in the exact same, hopeful tone he had used earlier.

"No, I don't think so," Roy replied. "But I will take some of those peanuts. How much are they?"

"Fifty centavos," the vendor's smile widened.

"Okay, gimme two bags," Roy picked a peso off his stack on the bar and handed one to the man.

"I am Ben," he said, handing over two small plastic bags filled with shelled peanuts.

"Thanks, Ben," Roy didn't offer his name and eased himself back onto the bar stool. He ripped a bag open and spilled the contents into a neat pile on the bar. Picking up a couple of nuts, he looked at Luz and said, "Knock yourself out."

"*Ano yan?*" she asked.

"Help yourself," he said, pointing to the pile on the bar.

"Oh, okay, *salámat*," she said and picked up a couple of peanuts and popped them in her mouth.

"You want anything, you ask for Ben, okay?" Roy had forgotten the man still standing behind him.

"I get everything you want, I know everyone," Ben said, still smiling.

"Okay, I'll remember that when I need everything," Roy smiled back and drank some soda to wash down the salty nuts.

Luz said something quickly in Tagalog and Ben sat the wallets down on the bar. He pulled the satchel around, resting it on an empty bar stool and began rummaging through it. Beneath the bags of peanuts were other wallets, each enveloped in plastic sheaths and as Roy watched, Ben picked one out a plain black one and handed it to Luz. He returned the other wallets to the bottom of the bag and picked up his original samples. He spoke a few more

47

words of Tagalog to Luz, pointing first at the sink and then to her hands, before turning back to Roy.

"Don't forget, hah?" he said. "You want anything, I'll be the one, okay?"

"Sure, Ben. You'll be the one to be the one," Roy lifted his glass in a carbonated salute as Ben headed for the exit.

Just as he got to the door, it opened and a huge, muscular, black American man walked through. He was easily six and half feet tall, weighed over 250 pounds and the Hawaiian shirt he wore might have doubled for a shower curtain. He had a smile on his face and nodded as he walked by the peanut vendor, coming toward the bar.

Ben nodded back with his official smile and then hurried toward the door, off to hustle more sales. No one noticed his hesitation at the door.

Chapter 8

The black man approached the bar saying, "Gimme, gimme, gimme," his voice was a booming baritone, and he held his arms wide as if to embrace the world. Luz giggled like a little girl and said, "Denny, Denny, Denny," as she skipped from around the bar up to the man. Luz gave the man a hug, but he waited until Lita and Amie had joined her before closing his massive arms around them all, his face beaming. Lena and Gloria were busy with customers and gave him only a quick look and a smile.

"God, what a country!" he said rocking the girls gently from side to side.

He finally let them go and made a bee line for the back door. Lita and Amie chattered among themselves as they returned to their table in the corner and Luz went straight for the beer cooler.

"You know the score," he said to Luz and smiled as he disappeared into the back, ducking slightly, as if by habit. Luz had just begun to lift the lid on the cooler when he reappeared.

"Man, business must be slow! You don't even have the paper out yet," he said, winking at Roy.

"'Sus, namon! I forgot," Luz exclaimed as she abandoned the cooler to reach under the bar. She emerged with a slightly rumpled roll of toilet paper and a half-roll of paper towels and handed them both to the jolly stranger. He disappeared once more, smiling all the while.

"Do you know him?" Roy asked dryly.

"Sure, don't you?" she replied. "Oh, yeah," she said again, more to herself, as she remembered Roy's recent arrival.

"That is Master Chief Denny," she said, opening his beer. "He runs the whole Navy base. He's a nice guy." She had set out two more coasters next the Roy and was pouring the beer into a glass when the Master Chief emerged from the back.

"God, I feel like a new man," he said, as if announcing it to the world. He pulled a ten-peso note from his front pocket, tossed it on the bar and sat on the stool next to Roy.

"My name's Dennis Boggs," he said, extending a hand to Roy. "Who am I talking to?"

"He is Roy," Luz said before he could reply. "He is a new Senior Chief on the base." She ignored his money on the bar.

"Roy, nice to meet you," he said, smiling even larger as his hand engulfed Roy's. "You can call me Denny." His was a well-practiced handshake, firm and dry and aware of the power it possessed. "I didn't know you were coming. Where are you working?" he asked.

"I'm going to be working over at the NAVMAG," he said. "I just got in this morning, but I've finished most of my check-in. What's your rating?" he said, retrieving his hand.

"Oh, I'm a Boats'n by trade, but I've been the Command Master Chief here for the last year and a half or so and did the same thing on the Kitty Hawk before this. I haven't tied a knot in years!" He took a small sip from his beer. "That explains why I didn't know you were coming, though. I don't hear about new arrivals on the Cubi side very often. Got any idea what they got you slated to do over there?" he asked.

"Physical security," Roy said. "I'm an 'MA,' so I'll be in the Master-at-Arms shop... maybe Security Officer. I've never been at a NAVMAG before though, so it should be a learning experience."

"Well, it looks like you made a good start, Roy," Denny said, placing his beer gently on the bar. "I always feel secure when I come to Ace's Place and there is no better place to get physical. Ain't that right, Luz?" He bellowed laughter at his own joke winked at her, but she said nothing, returning only a thin-lipped smile as she opened beers for other customers. "I'm impressed with your sense of direction," he said with a nod.

Roy smiled and told him a quick version of how Don Bodicker had filled him in on Olongapo in general and Gordon Avenue specifically.

Other customers came and left the bar as the two spoke, keeping Luz busy for a while. Finally, when she had the chance, she said, "Denny, I don't see you for a long time on Friday. How come?"

"You know I live in the barrio," he said plaintively, as if her understanding were paramount. "It's just easier to go out the Kalaklan Gate and here lately, by Friday I just want to get home and rest. This 'getting old' shit is hell!" he chuckled. Roy thought even his chuckles sounded bigger than normal.

"One of the folks in the office is going back to the States next week," he continued, "so we had a little going away lunch at 'Spooner's Pizza'." He took another small sip of beer while looking at his watch.

"Ha!" he barked. "That was one long-assed lunch! Those "Nooners" at

Spooner's just keep getting longer. God, I love this country!" He chuckled again and shook his head slowly.

"So, Roy," he said more soberly. "I guess you haven't had a chance to meet the senior enlisted at the NAVMAG yet, huh?" Roy shook his head.

"Well, he's an old Aviation Ordnanceman and meaner'n hell, but he's a good man," Denny said. Then, lowering the volume, but not the power of his voice, he said, "He gives a shit 'bout his troops and that's gettin' harder and harder to come by these days. I tell ya, I've seen more politicking in the enlisted ranks over the last couple of years, than I ever thought possible." He stopped and took another sip of beer.

"But… hey, you don't want to hear the Reverend Boggs' sermon on your first night in the P.I., right?" he said on a more upbeat note.

Denny put his right hand on Roy's shoulder and gave a good, quick squeeze as he stood from his stool and then extended the same hand for another shake. "Roy, it was nice meeting you," he said, smiling. "Only next time, don't do so damn much talking, okay?"

"Sure thing," Roy replied, again accepting the hand for one light squeeze. "Good meeting you too."

"Hey, listen," turning a bit more serious. "There are some security issues that we might be talking about over the next couple of weeks, but I'm not gonna burden them with you now. There will be plenty of time after you get fully checked in at NAVMAG."

He fell back into the happy uncle persona without missing a beat. "Luz, I just stopped in 'cause I knew ya missed me. Now I gotta get back to my home turf. I'll see ya later," he said and turned for the door.

"Bye, bye, Denny," Luz said, which seemed to ignite the two girls at their corner table.

"Bye, bye, Denny," they sang together. Then Lita said, "*Ba balik*, okay?"

"*Siguru mamaya*," he said, waving. "Bye now."

After he walked through the door, Roy could still see him faintly through the thin curtains. He walked to the curb and climbed into a scratched and dented jeep, ostensibly green under the dried mud and dust.

"He seems like a happy guy," Roy said to Luz as he swiveled back around on his stool.

"Yeah, he's funny too," she replied. She picked up the near-empty bottle and mostly full glass left by the Master Chief. She emptied them both in the sink next to the wall and left the glass there, returning the bottle to a green, plastic crate.

"Always the same when he comes to here," she said. "He always acts like drunk, but he never drinks a whole beer. He always gives me money and never takes change. And you know what?" she continued. "I don't even touch his money now and he still leaves it!" She smiled and shook her head slowly, "He's nice guy, that guy."

She took the money off the countertop and said, "I used to think he's Benny Boy, you know? But he's got a girl friend from the base. I hear from my friend there in Barreto," she said it as if Roy might not believe her.

"I think it's a secret, but they meet there sometimes," she said. "You know, there in Barreto, in the 'Half Moon Bar'."

Roy could understand why a Command Master Chief would want to keep any romance quiet, especially if she were in the military. A CMC is the most senior of all the enlisted people on the base and any kind of personal relationship with him would more than likely be considered fraternization and punishable under the Uniform Code of Military Justice. Roy was normally quite strict about rules and regulations, but the fraternization policy of the Navy was a whole different animal.

Designed to codify the long-standing tradition of separation between officers and enlisted people, the fraternization policy also restricted how certain enlisted people could relate to each other. Anything that could be considered "unduly familiar" was forbidden, but quite a bit of leeway was given to individual commanders to enforce the rules as they saw fit. The intention was to protect against junior people being sexually harassed or some others getting preferential treatment because of a personal relationship they might have with an officer or senior enlisted person. However, depending on the size and mission of the command, the effect could just about kill the social life of a single senior person and Command Master Chief is nearly as senior as an enlisted person can get. Because of that, Roy would never rat on anyone for fraternization unless someone was obviously taking advantage of the situation.

"Well," Roy said, "I hope it stays a secret, for his sake."

Roy finished his soda and Luz asked him if he wanted another when, as if on cue, a huge yawn racked him, and he stretched his arms above his head to try and squeeze it all out.

"No thanks," he said when he was able. "I think there is only a Navy bunk in my immediate future." He continued the stretch as he got off the bar stool.

"Okay," Luz said. "When will you be back?"

"Oh, I imagine you'll be seeing me again before I transfer," Roy said, smiling. "Say, how do you say, "good night" in Filipino?" he asked.

"*Magandang gabi*," Luz said. "That's how you say in Tagalog."

Roy thought about it for a second, decided not to attempt to reproduce the sound in his jet-lagged condition and said, "Well, good night, Luz. It was nice meeting you," and headed for the door.

"Bye, bye," she said. "See you never."

He turned at the door to look at her, wondering what she meant by that remark. She was smiling sweetly and waving. Lita and Amie were busy with two new arrivals, Lena was leaning over the jukebox, picking out a song and waiting for her "saput" boyfriend and Gloria had already left to go barhopping with her "temporary" one.

"Yeah, see ya," he said and left the bar.

The trip back to the base and to the barracks was much the same as when he first ventured out, only louder and darker.

He arrived in his room just past 7:00 PM and was in his bunk less than ten minutes later, but the fatigue that pinned him to his mattress was a terrible teaser. It beckoned, it urged, it taunted, but it would not let him sleep.

Since leaving the bar, the bulk of his mental activity had centered around how good the bed would feel, how he would prepare for bed, what he might do in the morning and again, how good the bed would feel. But as he lay there, eyes closed, waiting for the kiss of Morpheus, his thoughts turned to Luz and Lisa. Their images appeared so simultaneously that he could not tell if one had led to the other. Almost as quickly, feelings of desire and guilt also started competing for center stage, chasing sleep further into the future. It seemed the shaper of dreams was working without the support of slumber.

While Luz was clearly an attractive and desirable young woman, there was something more about her that commanded his attention. Her wit, her apparent curiosity, or perhaps it was just the way the other in the bar seemed to show such respect to an obviously younger woman that had captured him. Whatever quality it was, it was powerful enough to hold its own against the force of nature that had been Lisa Bartow.

Many of the happier memories of Lisa had already diminished to the point where he was left with only her smile, green eyes and red hair, wrapped in the golden glow of joy he experienced in her company. Unfortunately, the end of their relationship was still crystal clear.

After angering a senior officer in Norfolk, he had been abruptly transferred to Iceland. A visit back to Virginia confirmed that he needed her to be in his life permanently, so he decided to ask her to marry him. He wanted every word to be just right, and he wanted to have a good counter-argument ready in case she balked, so he spent two weeks figuring out how best to make the proposal. They had talked a couple of times since his decision, but he had always been unable to put his thoughts and feelings into words. Finally, his emotions translated, his lines set to memory and his resolve bolstered by just enough cheap bourbon, he called Lisa's house.

Her phone rang four times before the machine answered. The voice on it wasn't Lisa's. There were similarities, but this voice was tired and tentative and tense and completely Appalachian. It said simply, "Please leave a message at the tone."

Roy was sure he had dialed the right number, but as the long tone played out, he decided to leave a message and then dial the number again.

"Hi, this is Roy Thompson," he said. "I am trying to get a hold of Lisa Bartow, so I guess I'll..." The answering machine clicked faintly.

"Roy?" it was the same tired voice on the recording. "This is Gina Farmer, I'm Lisa's older sister?" She said it as if pleading for recognition. He recognized the name and a chill crept down his spine like a hairy spider.

"Where's Lisa?" he said, sounding much calmer than he felt.

"Roy, Lisa told me all about you guys, you know?" Gina's voice was more tired and bit shaky now.

"Uh huh, and where is she?" The calmness was leaving his voice.

"Roy... she's dead, Roy," Gina said, her words drained and faint.

"Uh, uh," Roy felt like a fool but was unable to form that thought coherently. "I... I mean, how? What happened?" The investigator rose up in him.

"She killed herself, Roy, she just killed herself," her voice was pure weariness now and she began to cry softly.

During the rest of that conversation, Roy was unable to get much else from Gina that would shed light on Lisa's death. Only that she had been depressed and had died in her jeep. Eventually Roy was able to pull out the information about Lisa's funeral and immediately arranged to go. After receiving leave approval from the X.O. and the last flight reservation was made Roy finished the rest of his bourbon.

After what seemed like the longest flight of all time, Roy arrived on the East coast. He rented a car, drove straight from Dulles airport and arrived in rural West Virginia, where Lisa was born and raised, with only minutes to spare before her interment. With Roy standing quietly in the background and a small group of mourners looking on, Lisa was laid to rest in a quaint family plot, next to a church on a hill. Roy guessed their identities during the ceremony and at its conclusion he introduced himself to Gina.

He was received warmly by Lisa's family, a close knit and loving group of people, but the only person who seemed able to talk about her death was Gina's husband. He told Roy that Lisa had called her sister and simply said there was a note in her house explaining why she was killing herself and where they could find her body. She then climbed into her faithful old jeep and drove it into the hills.

Gina called the police as soon as she got off the phone and drove with her husband as fast as she could to Lisa's house in Virginia. When they arrived, the police had already found Lisa and were waiting at the house. Gina and her husband were still there two days after her death, trying to take care of things when Roy had called.

When Roy first heard that Lisa had died in her car, he assumed she had crashed into something. The suicide scenario seemed so totally out of character for her that Roy used it to hold on to some glimmering spark of hope that she might not really be dead. What he learned however, was that Lisa had driven into the countryside and parked overlooking her favorite valley. Once there, she took a nearly full bottle of prescription sedatives and then slit her wrists.

Another thing Roy learned from Gina's husband, was that Lisa had a history of bipolar disorder. She had been on a drug regimen for quite some time and was very functional, so he had always assumed her robust energy was a consistent trait. He now recognized that she was just "slightly" manic a lot of the time.

The drugs normally kept her on a fairly even keel, but they were gradually losing their effectiveness and Lisa had been trying different concoctions to get back to a more functional state. It was when she started feeling better that she was hit with the devastating diagnoses of an HIV infection. It could not have come at a worse time.

The note was still in the custody of the Virginia police, but the gist of it was that she had tested positive for HIV and couldn't bear to think that she might have passed it on to Roy. What none of them knew was that the day after Roy's last visit she had been contacted by a former lover who had AIDS and thought she should be tested. When her positive result had been confirmed twice, she wrote the note, called her sister and climbed into her beloved Jeep for one last drive.

The memory had flashed through his mind in seconds and activated every possible human emotion in its path, a process which was entirely too familiar to Roy. However, this hypnogogic version of events included visions of a beautiful, young Filipina popping up at inappropriate times. Finally, mercifully, sleep came.

Chapter 9

The murderer's mind was racing. How much longer must I stay here, he thought. His schedule was flexible, but he did have other tasks to complete, other commitments. After all, he had a life. He prayed his target would come. He needed to come soon. The murderer had to go.

Evidently the car he had heard some time ago just used the driveway to turn around. Since that time there had been some traffic on the street, but no one else had approached the house.

When the last car left, the murderer had stayed behind the door for a full twenty minutes before finally allowing his guard to come down. He had held his knife for the entire time, passing it now more comfortably between his rubber-enclosed fingers. Finally, he folded the knife and slipped it back into his pocket. He had cleaned and dried the gloves earlier but now his fingers had begun to sweat inside them. He briefly considered taking them off just long enough to let his hands dry out and breath but decided against it when he remembered his frustration putting them on in the first place. Instead, he explored just a bit more of the small house.

A quick tour of the home revealed little of interest except a plain, black, rotary-dial telephone in the main bedroom. They were expensive on the Philippine economy and the murderer suspected whoever would go through the trouble and expense of acquiring one, must be of some importance.

The wall opposite the foot of the bed had some plaques and letters hanging a little above eye level, ranging in shape, size and color. The one thing they all had in common was a name. He was not a highly educated man, but the murderer could read Tagalog and English. He leaned close to the wall to read in the rapidly dimming light the name of his next victim.

*   *   *

Dennis Boggs was a happy man. He could think of nothing to be unhappy about. As he drove past the cemetery on National Highway, his most serious thought was whether or not he needed to worry about anything.

He concluded with a mental smile that, no, there was nothing.

He was at the top of his chosen career field, admired by his peers and trusted by subordinates and superiors alike. He loved his job. And it didn't really matter what they gave him to do or where he had to do it, he just loved it. God, what a life!

Denny had terrific relationships with his three adult children and his ex-wife, and they kept in contact as much as their busy lives would allow. As far as he knew, they were all as happy as he.

The one area in his life that held the potential for grief was his current love interest. He smiled thinking about her and, despite the possible problems related to fraternization, was still content with their arrangement.

Winnie was a mustang lieutenant who had started out as a non-designated seaman recruit who had worked her way up through the ranks. She reported for duty as the Administrative Officer just months earlier and the two hit it off immediately. After she moved to a neighborhood just a mile from his house in the barrio, there was no keeping them apart. "Plain, old, fat-assed fate has plopped her butt down at our table," is how Winnie liked to put it.

They spent much of their private time at each other's places, but other times, they just needed to get out of the house and be together in some out-of-the-way, low-profile place. The "Half Moon Bar" was about as low and out-of-the-way as they came and was really more of a private residence than a public bar. Denny's favorite part of its décor was a wooden plank emblazoned with their motto: "We don't give a shit and don't know anybody else who might." Tonight, at 8:00 PM it would once again serve as their rendezvous point.

After exiting the "zigzags" and coming into Barrio Barreto, he found himself whistling a song called "Any Day Now." He liked Chuck Jackson's original version of the song from the sixties but enjoyed Ronnie Milsap's recent version even more after Winnie had turned him on to it. He never realized he whistled it so much until Winnie had started doing it too.

The thought of her made him smile again. She had told him to expect a surprise this weekend and he was looking forward to the prospect, although he hadn't a clue of what it might be. With her, it could be anything.

The local Philippine Constabulary Station was coming up on the right and as he approached it, Denny slowed the old jeep to turn onto Rizal Street which led to his small, rented house. As was his habit when he neared home, he glanced at his wristwatch. It was nearly 7:00 PM.

*   *   *

The murderer made a decision. One dead American is as good as any other, he thought. He decided to stay in the house for another thirty minutes and if his original target didn't come to roost before then, too bad. He had been hired for one killing and one had been done he rationalized, so anything more was just a bonus for his employer.

He checked the time on one of the clocks in the master bedroom: 6:55 PM. He considered setting on the bed or the living room furniture while he waited for Dennis Boggs, but then nixed the idea. He didn't want to be too relaxed when the American returned home. Instead, he opted to squat in his familiar position behind the spare bedroom door. From there he could see the glowing red digits of the clock in the master bedroom across the hall. When they displayed the numbers 7:30, he would leave out the kitchen door and the only sign that he had been there at all would be a sealed envelope and the lifeless body of Winnie Jackson.

He didn't know exactly what was in the envelope and really didn't care. However, one thing he could figure out for himself was that it had something to do with the Americans being there in his country. Although his employer was not one to discuss motives and politics with the likes of him, the intruder could tell that he hated their presence more than anything else in the world. His reflexive smile flashed again as he recalled the lather his employer would get into when the subject came up. But the smile faded as he realized how those episodes of agitation seemed to be coming more and more often.

He rose lightly to his feet, retrieved the butterfly knife from his pocket and then squatted and leaned back against the wall once more. The knife danced gracefully between his fingers as he twirled it skillfully back and forth, now slowed by the rubber gloves. He looked at the body of Winnie Jackson, nearly invisible in the fading light, and wondered who she was to this Dennis Boggs: friend, lover, daughter, wife, mother, sister, maid? Perhaps she was none of those to him and all of those to others. Perhaps she was just a gift to the murderer from his god. Whatever she had been, he knew from now on she would be a memory and little more. She would become an immediate statistic and a picture in a crime lab and then, briefly, a news story. And finally, when the excitement subsided and the tears dried, she would be just a name and a number in some official file and some personal memories. Even the memories would eventually fade until she was barely more than what he saw before him now, a vague shadow in the corner. What she had been was no more and what she was now was what everyone would become eventually, nourishment for the earth.

"If he fails to heed the call,

Man becomes the food of all."

The jingle caused an unconscious grin to flash across his face once again. Had she heeded the call? Did it really matter? He didn't think so. What he thought was that everything eventually becomes food for something else, no matter what. And what really mattered was whether or not one appreciated the food when it was delivered. He again thanked his god for letting him take the life of the woman in the corner and began to whistle her tune.

*   *   *

As Denny turned the corner, he saw an old and grizzled white man standing next to a beat up, '77 Ford Maverick parked in front of the "Bad, Good and Ugly" bar. Though the car wasn't nearly as old as the man, it was obvious they both had traveled many hard miles and neither had been particularly well cared for. The man wore baggy, khaki shorts and a tattered, grey tee shirt and stood in a pair of flip-flops possibly stolen from MacArthur upon his celebrated return to the Philippines. The car, once the color of a new penny, had rusted and faded to a dirty brown. When he saw Denny, the old man waved and yelled, "Park your ugly butt over here. You owe me big time."

Denny dutifully complied and pulled his jeep next to the ancient mariner. He left his engine running.

"Hello, Marvin," Denny said. He always called him Marvin – although everyone else referred to him as "Marv" – because Marvin insisted on calling him Dennis. "I see your missus has left the gate open again. God damn! Do you naturally get uglier every day, or does Minda beat you with an ugly stick when you get home at night?"

"Neither, my friend," Marv said. "I have carefully cultivated this appearance for years and it is only now, in the prime of my life, that I approach the perfection which few can achieve." Marvin Turnbull was a retired Chief and obviously full of shit.

He lived with Minda, his wife of five years, near Subic City. However, any night of the week his battered vehicle could be seen parked along National Highway somewhere, in front of one or another of the many bars between Subic City and Olongapo. Minda was never with him, which led more than one acquaintance to suspect she was only a myth. Denny knew her, but it was true she didn't get out much. He felt that if Marvin ever went any place other than cheap hooker bars, she might be more inclined to be seen in public with him.

Marvin's longish hair was mostly grey but retained a few patches of the original black and it lay limply above a gaunt, weather-worn face, which seemed to display one deep crease for each beer he had ever drunk. A near skeletal physique made his 5'11" seem much taller and he resembled nothing so much as a Calcutta street beggar. He was barely sixty years old.

"So why dontcha cut that engine and come in and buy me a cold one," Marvin said. "I have lies to tell and favors to ask. Now surely, you've received no better offer for this Friday night. Have you?" Marvin knew Denny met with Winnie almost every Friday night, but he still hoped to prod Denny into sharing at least a little bar time. He didn't mind drinking alone, but drinking with someone whose company he enjoyed, was infinitely more pleasurable.

Without killing his engine, Denny said, "You know I've got to get home and change. Can't hit the beach in uniform."

"What uniform?" Marvin responded. "It appears to me that you are in the appropriate civilian attire for shooting pool and drinking beer."

Denny looked down to the bright flower-print shirt he had forgotten about and smiled. He wasn't supposed to wear his khaki uniform on liberty, so when he decided at the last minute to attend the going away luncheon, he went to the exchange and bought this shirt rather than go all the way home to change. He had simply taken off his khaki shirt and put this one on over his white tee shirt. He thought it didn't look all that bad with his khaki trousers and black shoes, although he knew Winnie would disagree. His uniform shirt was rolled up in the same plastic bag the exchange had given him with the Hawaiian shirt and stuffed beneath the driver's seat.

Trying to change the subject, he said, "What's this shit about me owing you big time?"

"Oh, that is a lengthy tale of greed and corruption, and you know my throat gets very dry around this time of day."

"Uh huh," Denny said flatly, giving in to the inevitable. He switched off the jeep's ignition and climbed out. "Okay, but you know I don't have all night.

"Sure, sure," Marvin said. "Now come and hear a story about greed and corruption and... did I say that already? And sex... corrupt sex at that."

"God," Denny said with an immense sigh. "What a country."

*   *   *

Tucked away at the end of a short driveway, surrounded by high fences and undisturbed jungle foliage, sat a smallish, nondescript house. Its windows were barred, and its doors were locked tightly against the threat of thieves and intruders and its interior was shielded from prying eyes by dusty green and yellow curtains.

Inside the house, other colors faded, and the red numbers of an electric digital clock grew more pronounced while sunlight deserted the place as the sun receded into the west. All was silent except a faint dripping sound coming from the refrigerator.

In one corner of a spare bedroom, Winnie Jackson's body sat, her head reclined against the wall as if she were resting from a hard day's labor. A plain, white envelope was tucked between her hands as they lay folded on her lap. It stood out against her faded denim shorts and scarlet tee shirt. It reflected the red of her shirt and the feeble red light of the clock from the next room and appeared to radiate a subtle rose color.

The clock glowed the time as 7:32.

Chapter 10

"Whomp, whomp, whomp, whomp," was the overriding sound in the club. The bass notes were giant, convulsive balloons on which every other sound rode, like specks of confetti. There was a melody somewhere, perhaps even a harmony, but Scott could only imagine them mixed in with the other high frequency sounds fighting to be heard. He picked up his beer bottle, still cold but empty, and sat it back on the table.

He craned his neck around in a search for his waiter. Disco lights swirled with various colors which reflected off every surface, adding to the power of the rock and roll music and go-go dancers gyrated on their perches, precariously close to the giant speakers which threatened to blow them onto the crowded dance floor. Nearly every table had either a hostess or a customer at it, with their empty chairs belonging to people now dancing and waiters scurried around clearing empty bottles and glasses and delivering ladies' drinks. Scott saw Tony standing toward the back of the club with his hands crossed behind him, as if at parade rest, looking out over the sea of bodies. Scott held up his empty bottle until Tony saw him and then put it down again when Tony nodded and turned to go to the bar.

Across the table, Billy sat facing a hostess named Tessie and was saying something directly into her ear. His left hand was cupped around his mouth and was a fraction of an inch from her head, which bobbed and weaved along with the music. His right arm rested on the back of Tessie's chair and his hand was jumping and pointing, stressing points to a non-existent audience. If Tessie was listening, it wasn't evident. She was slowly mixing her drink with one long, painted fingernail and watching the newest steps of her co-workers on the dance floor. Her other hand, which had been resting on Billy's crotch, rose absently to her breast and caressed her new, oval name tag. Her fingers traced the white letters and number exposed by the engraver's tools, lingering on the new number "2." That number was up from the "12" she had worn the previous month and represented a substantial amount of time rubbing sailor's dicks and coaxing overpriced ladies' drinks from them.

Although Scott could hear nothing being said, Billy was emphatically arguing his point. He stopped talking and looked at Tessie expectantly about three beats before the band stopped on a staccato note. The sudden silence left a void which seemed to physically suck energy from the room. The other sounds gradually became recognizable again and Billy took the opportunity to push his agenda.

"Well, meet me later?" he said.

"You pay first," Tessie replied, as if already bored five seconds into the band's break. Then said, "I'll be back," as she stood and walked toward the women's powder room.

"Man, I gotta get outta here," Scott said. "You gonna pay her bar fine, or what?"

"I don't pay bar fines," Billy replied, contemptuous of the idea. "If she won't meet me after she gets off, I'll find someone who will."

"Well, either way," Scott said as Tony approached with a fresh beer, "I'm going back over to Gordon when I finish this one. And then I'll probably head on home. I won't wait up."

Scott handed Tony a twenty peso note and said, "Thanks, Tony. I'm heading out after this one, so I'll see you later, okay?"

"Okay, Scott," Tony said, raising the money in a salute. "Thanks, hah?" The waiter walked again to the back of the bar, stuffing the money into his shirt pocket.

"You keep giving tips like that and you'll be broke when Judy gets back from the province," Billy said.

"It's play money, man. Besides, what did it work out to? A couple of bucks?" Scott said. He picked up the San Miquel and drank almost half in four quick gulps.

"Not the point," Billy replied, swiveling around in his chair, searching the bar. "Not the fuckin' point."

The next band was beginning to make warm-up noises as Scott saw Tessie sit down at a table with three marines.

"She's over there, man," Scott told Billy. "I think she's making too much money to leave early tonight. Looks like she wants to be number one."

"Oh, well," he said, turning back around. He picked up his rum and coke and took a sip. "There's a couple of new good lookers up at the "Zanzibar." Want to go?"

"No, I told you, I gotta get back over to Ace's." He finished the beer with several more gulps, leaving just about a half inch in the bottom of the bottle. "Besides, this fuckin' place is making me deaf," he said and released a tremendous belch.

Before the fresh band could drown him out, Scott raised his hand and said, "Gotta go, Billy Jo. Later."

Out on the sidewalk, the band inside the Pearl Club became just another part, albeit a slightly louder part, of the cacophony that filled Magsaysay. Smoothing his thin blond hair back against his head, Scott turned resolutely toward Gordon Avenue and began dodging people like a salmon going up stream.

As he fought the early evening crowd, the image of Judy dominated his mind and his thoughts about her crowded out the noise of the street. He had been thinking about her a lot this last week, while she was off visiting family in the province. They were anguished thoughts. She was beautiful and smart and kind and funny and terrific in bed and a huge, huge problem. And he didn't know what he was going to do about her.

Scott was now a Yeoman Second Class, working more or less as the CO's writer at the U.S. Naval Magazine and was pretty much locked into that for the next six months. However, he was conflicted about what to do next. He had aspirations which exceeded those of taking notes and fetching coffee for officers. Those aspirations were never very clear, but dreams about being on Broadway or starring in action movies or touring with a rock band helped make his Navy life a bit more bearable. However amorphous those dreams had been, they never included a wife before now and he wasn't sure he wanted them to.

As he turned the corner at Gordon and Magsaysay, he heard the click, click, click of pesos being tapped on the Formica counters of the money changer girls. As he walked by, Scott smiled and waved casually as if he knew each girl personally. None acknowledged his gesture, staring stolidly through their glass cages, but continued tapping their coins in hopes of attracting real customers.

Judy, Judy, Judy, Cary Grant's voice echoed in his head, what to do about Judy?

Judy wasn't really a hooker. At least she wasn't in the sense that she worked in a bar and screwed different guys for money every day. She had certainly worked in a bar and even Scott couldn't deny she had slept with different men. What made her different from the rest in his mind was that he didn't think she liked it as much as the others might.

Like many of the girls in Olongapo, she was where she was because of problems at home. She had become pregnant by a boy from her hometown of Tarlac and was sent by her family to live with an aunt in Angeles City, outside of Clark AFB. She suffered a miscarriage there but stayed with her aunt and was eventually introduced to an American sailor stationed on the

Air Force base. She moved in with him after a time and followed him to Olongapo when he was transferred there. After two years as a live-in girlfriend, her American transferred again. Only this time, he transferred stateside and left her where she was, with an apartment full of cheap furniture and just enough money for two month's rent.

She had met many other girls in those two years, girlfriends of American sailors and marines, who had at one time worked in Olongapo or who still did. They helped feed her for a while and then helped her find work at Ace's Place, where she met Scott on her first day on the job.

She wouldn't go over night with Scott right off, which was probably the first, and deepest, hook sunk into his jaw. She made him wait a week before taking him to her apartment. An apartment filled with cheap furniture and one week from the rent being due. It was the first and only week she worked at Ace's.

Scott couldn't tell you how many lines were cast, or how many hooks were set before he was reeled in and landed. He could tell you only that he had been landed, stuffed and mounted like a prize big-mouth bass and he loved it. At least, he was pretty sure he loved it, just like he was pretty sure he loved her.

He moved in with Judy the day after having first slept with her and began giving her money for rent and food and whatever else she wanted. Billy, who was a YN1 working at Cubi Point, offered to pay half the cost of rent and utilities if they would let him stay in the extra bedroom. He moved in almost a month after Scott had.

Now, a few months later, here they were… one big, happy family. Judy was visiting Tarlac, Billy was bringing home a different hooker nearly every night and Scott was six months away from getting out of the Navy. He was no closer to a decision as he approached Ace's Place.

The jukebox was blaring as Scott stepped into the bar and walked to his favorite spot. He climbed into the barstool and only then noticed that no one was behind the bar. Amie sat at a corner table, laughing with an American who appeared to be in his fifties and Lena was standing at the jukebox, pushing buttons.

Before Scott could formulate a question, Luz pushed through the back door, carrying a case of beer. He jumped off the stool and hurried around to help her, taking the case from her and hauling it the extra two yards it needed to go.

"Thanks," she said with a sarcastic grin. "Where you are for the last two cases I am bringing?"

"I am not the one to be being here, like 'dis and like 'dat," he replied in his best comic Filipino accent. "I am *doon*." And then switching back to his normal voice, "Hey, are any of those cold yet?"

"Is it mattering to you?" Luz asked, purposefully distorting her own English.

"*Hinde! Sige Na! Gusto ko!*" he said in his own broken Tagalog, trying to sound like one of those excited announcers he heard on television. "You know it don't matter to me! Just bring it on!"

"Sure," Luz laughed as she retrieved a cold one from the cooler. "Hey. I see your new Senior Chief today. He left a little while ago. He is *mabait*, I think."

"So you think he's nice?" Scott asked. "Sometimes the nicest guys out here in town, are the biggest assholes at work. Oh, well," he said, performing the ritual cleaning of his beer bottle, "I guess I'll see for sure next week."

"But you know," more to himself than anyone else before taking a gulp, "Just the fact that he came out here at all, especially after spending all that time on the plane, might say something good."

Luz knew better than to say anything when Scott was debating with himself. She waited and listened for any point/counterpoint of interest. However, Scott remained silent, taking little sips from his beer as he stared at the strips of plastic billowing from the face of the air-conditioner. Luz resumed stocking the cooler.

In a sharp and clear voice, completely free of any Oklahoma accent, Scott began to sing short portions of a song playing on the jukebox. "...Open the door and got that look on his face...He's got a dream about buying some land...some quiet little town and forget about everything...."

"I gotta learn that song one of these days," he said, putting his empty bottle on the bar. "Hey, I gotta go, honey-ko. See ya later." He slid off the stool and turned for the door.

"Wait," Luz said. "Ben gave this for you." She reached under the bar and retrieved a wallet, black and wrapped in a clear, plastic sleeve. "He says to pay him Monday."

The wallet was a simple bill fold with no decorative hand-tooling like some that Ben offered. It was basic black and made from carabao hide with a few compartments and no plastic picture holders. Scott smiled. It was to be his Dad's birthday gift and he felt confident that his dad would be the only person in Enid, Oklahoma with a genuine carabao hide wallet, made in the Philippines. His dad didn't necessarily care for fancy stuff, but he did like exclusivity.

"Thanks, Luz," he said, taking the package from her. "I'll give the devil his due on Monday. See ya."

"Bye, bye, you," Luz called as he walked out the door.

Scott walked to the tricycles waiting at the corner wondering how his dad would like a Filipina daughter-in-law for Christmas.

Chapter 11

"Shit," he said. He had meant only to think it, but the word escaped his lips, nonetheless. He had immersed himself so deeply into this sewer, that now even his cursing was done in English. But why not, he thought. The language exists only to express the curses and oppression they would visit on those less able to defend themselves. I'll use it against them, he reasoned, fuck them all and damn them to hell. But the silent cursing did nothing to lessen the churning in his gut.

The American was still alive, and Ben didn't know what would happen now. The American always went home after work on Friday and should have been home by now. Ben had witnessed it himself – or had others confirm it – for over two months. That was his routine. That was his norm. That was what he should have done tonight. He knew the American had some concubine he saw on the weekends, but the information he got was that she and he hooked up only on Saturdays and Sundays. He hoped that he would get to his house in Barrio Barretto before Nestor left.

But yet, here he was, frolicking on Gordon Avenue. He was smiling and throwing around his American money in that disgusting, glad-handing, American manner which seemed to scream, "Why shouldn't I be happy? I run the world!" Why couldn't the others see this? Were they all sheep? Did he belong to a nation of lap dogs, anxious to roll over and have their bellies scratched by whom ever gave them the biggest bone?

He trusted Nestor. That is, he trusted him to be at the American's house on time and to carry out the assignment they agreed upon. But he wasn't sure how long the assassin would wait if the American didn't show up when expected. They both understood that the longer he stayed at the house, the greater were his chances of being discovered. All Ben could do was trust that the single mindedness and pride that Nestor had shown in previous assignments would help him adjust to the new wrinkle. Their next meeting was to take place at Sunday afternoon mass, and he didn't expect there would be a reaction from the Americans until either his girlfriend found his body or he failed to show up for work. Depending upon the outcome of tonight's operation in Barretto, Ben would have a few hours to adjust his plans, if need be, and go to the next phase.

He knew that an officer's death would likely get more press coverage than that of an enlisted man, but he hoped that the death of the popular and influential Command Master Chief would initiate a collapse in morale among the American enlisted men in the Philippines. The bombastic American Master Chief represented the success that an oppressed minority could still achieve in the U. S. military system and Ben wanted to dishearten the Americans as a first step towards chasing them out. In his own mind, his countrymen were blind to the way the American presence was poisoning their future potential as a sovereign nation. He believed deeply and rigidly that Filipinos around the world would come to see the truth in his vision and that they would eventually support him and his party's position on the American presence. When that happened, he would be recognized for his patriotism, for his...

"Excuse me?" the man said. He didn't say it as if he were apologizing.

"What?" Ben asked. He had completely tuned out his surroundings, a highly unusual and upsetting lapse in his normal behavior. He quickly remembered he was in the front room of Sunny's Bar and standing by a table which hosted two white Americans. They didn't look particularly friendly.

Getting back into character, Ben said, "Oh, sorry, want to buy wallet?"

"Not if your selling shit; that's what I heard you say... shit. Isn't that what you heard, Stevo?" the man said to his friend across the table.

"Sounded like shit to me, Jimbo. And those wallets look like shit, too," Stevo said.

"Want to buy peanuts?" Ben said, reaching in his bag. He tried to infuse his professional smile with some semblance of warmth.

"Are they shit too?" the one called Stevo said. "I don't know Jimbo, do we want some fucking Flip trying to sell us shit?"

"I don't think so, Stevo," the one called Jimbo said. And then to Ben, he said, "You wouldn't try to sell us shit, now would you, Joe? I didn't think so," he continued, expecting no reply. "Now why don't you take that shit in your purse, stick it up your shitty, pansy ass and get the rest of your shitty, Flip body out of my bar before I do it for ya?"

"I'm sorry, I go, I go," Ben said through his wide and, he hoped, contrite looking smile.

Backing toward the door, he took a quick inventory of the people in the bar. In addition to the two assholes he had just met, there were three other unrecognized Americans at a table on the far wall, several prostitutes scattered about the front bar and several more customers and staff in the back room. All the Americans and some of the prostitutes in the front watched him backing away like a scared puppy, while those in the back continued partying, oblivious to his humiliation. The Americans in the back bar – regular customers who had grown to look on Ben as a kind of mascot – might well come to his defense if they knew he was being harassed. But he quickly decided against drawing any more attention to himself than he already had. This was no time for confrontation.

By the time he reached the door, the two who had suggested he leave were laughing and the others in the bar had returned to their previous entertainment. Ben opened the door to leave, but then stopped and looked directly at the sailor called Jimbo. He finally looked up, and when their eyes locked, Ben slowly relaxed the timid and painful smile that burned his face. It melted away and was replaced by an expression which felt immanently more comfortable, completely natural and caused the laughter in Jimbo's throat to stop with surprising abruptness.

Ben's disgust and hatred shown with complete veracity for only a moment before being replaced by another smile, just as false as the first one, but of a completely different timbre. Ben blew a kiss to the ugly American, turned slowly and walked out the door in a calm and casual manner, confident the vile creatures he left behind lacked both the courage and energy to accept his challenge.

He picked his way through the traffic on Gordon and turned left on 6th Street, toward Shit River. Humiliation rose like bile in his throat as he fought to keep it buried with the similar emotions simmering and stirring within. His face was now a mask of utter indifference and the stiffness in his walk could have been interpreted as sore muscles if anyone were to spot him on the unlighted street. He turned left on Perimeter Road and walked to his small apartment, hoping his thoughts would clear before he arrived. There was, in the back of his mind, a faint but urgent voice interfering with the process of clarity.

Successfully quieting that voice for the moment, he resolved to think more clearly, put this ugly little episode at Sunny's Bar in perspective. He wouldn't purge the incident from his memory, rather he would roll it into a tight little ball and pack it into some cool, dry place in his psyche. From time to time he would wrap himself around it and feed from it slowly, letting the humiliation and anger fuel his hatred for the Americans. Their vulgar displays would serve for him as samples of the greater contempt with which their government viewed his country. His mask of indifference cracked as a small grin creased Ben's face and slowly the grin became a smile as he thought how this lap dog would soon have his day. He could feel that small voice in his mind also smiling. It expected to also have its day.

Despite the small hitch caused by the apparent delay of the black American's death, the arrival of the new American might prove very fruitful. He had been unable to garner much information from Luz, but he did find out the new American was a senior enlisted person and was going to work at the Naval Magazine, perhaps dealing with security. Luz had been unclear, but he suspected Thompson was more than just military police. If he really were going to be in security, his rank indicated that he would be dealing at the "nuts and bolts" working level, but still be in a position to understand the big picture of how it worked on his new base. Ben viewed this as an excellent opportunity to gather intelligence about the ammunition dump where he would work.

That would be his next goal, Ben determined, as he reached his small, three-room apartment and unlocked the deadbolt of his front door. However, he knew there were challenging obstacles, and his mind began working unconsciously on ways around them even before he closed his door and securing the deadbolt.

Ben had gone home earlier than usual because of the minor confrontation, but even on a normal night he would not have stayed out much longer, without having a specific purpose in mind. Information gathering was much more fruitful in the first three hours after the Americans began to drink, when they were happy to be off work and still complaining about whatever injustices they might have suffered that day. Shop talk abounded during this time and the Americans made things easier by frequenting the same bars and traveling in work related cliques. Ben lingered around those groups, when he could do so without being noticed, and often complained loudly about the heat while sipping sodas in their presence, as if taking a break from the arduous task of bar-to-bar sales. Most of the talk which took place later in the evening, it seemed to him, usually involved the debauchery of Filipinas. Occasionally a drunk American would utter something of interest, something Ben might be able to use, but for the most part they were useless inconveniences.

The girls themselves were an excellent source of secondary intelligence. He worked hard at keeping his relationships with them as friendly as possible and many, like Luz, owed him favors. He would engage them in friendly chatter about their customers, mentally taking notes about traits and characteristics which might later prove useful. It seemed that many bar girls knew future ship's movements better than most sailors and they would have been surprised at just how much useful intelligence they heard on a daily basis. It was his strategy to encourage them to continue their learning, without them finding out they knew anything.

He took pains to not appear too eager for the information. After more than a decade of working the streets of Olongapo, he had developed an extremely smooth style and charm that served him well. During his last several years of membership in the New People's Army, his ability to detect and catalog important information had also been finely honed. He often did favors for the girls, even occasionally loaning them money and when problems did occur – like with the two at Sunny's tonight – he always reacted as the sheepish, non-aggressive victim, which only ingratiated him more with the prostitutes.

Ben switched on the lights to both sides of the apartment and quickly surveyed the remainder of the home to ensure nothing had been disturbed. His front door opened into one room which served as both living room and kitchen. This room, like the bedroom, had one window which was heavily draped and almost never opened. The room contained one padded chair tucked away to the right of the entrance, accompanied by a small table and lamp. The "kitchen" part of the room was really only an "L" shaped counter in the far-right corner supporting a built-in sink with running cold water. A propane, two-burner cook stove sat next to it. There was a space allocated for a standard sized refrigerator, but it was empty. A couple of open shelves, holding a modicum of dishes and glasses, completed the room.

To the left of the front door, separated from the remainder of the apartment by only an open archway, was a small bedroom containing a single bed and a nightstand with a lamp. Along the wall opposite the window was a single door which hid a small toilet room, adjacent to an open closet space.

Satisfied that everything was intact, he took off his outer garments and hung them neatly in the small bedroom closet before donning gym shorts and a tee shirt. After sliding the hanging clothing to the right side of the closet, he knelt at the bottom of the wall separating it from the toilet. Even though he had thoroughly checked and locked the apartment, he reflexively glanced over his shoulder and felt for the familiar fabric tab about a foot above the floor. He pulled it gingerly and a ten-inch by ten-inch piece of sheet rock separated from the rest of the wall. The seams were invisible in the dimness and nearly so in full light. After carefully placing the cubby hole cover on the floor, he retrieved a green ledger. Returning to his bed, he switched on the table lamp and to record the relevant information while it was still fresh in his memory.

He opened the ledger to a section identified only with the capitol letter "A." At the top of that page, written in small, tight letters was the English word "assets." He first learned the word in school, but only after joining the cause, was he taught to apply it to people who could be used. Ben liked the brevity of it and how it sounded. He flipped through a few pages listing Filipino and American names and at the bottom of wrote:

"Tomson, Roy - Senior enlisted – Weapons – Security?" and then, after a slight hesitation, he drew another dash and wrote, "Luz."

Ben looked over his latest entry and then skimmed quickly over some previous ones. Before closing the book, he drew a "?" in the margin next to Roy's name.

The first obstacle to overcome with any asset was to achieve some level of trust and his limited dealings with this new American already showed that task would be considerable. Roy Thompson was no child needing to prove his importance by talking endlessly about his responsibilities. Ben had seen in his eyes maturity, intelligence and wariness; unfortunate qualities in someone you hope to exploit.

There was, however, something else in Thompson's face. Maybe sadness, maybe loneliness, but definitely interest in Luz. Ben thought – in fact he knew – knew that Luz would be the best way around that obstacle. Perhaps she could be the best way around several obstacles.

Ben closed the ledger and returned to the closet. Kneeling, he repeated a ritual that no longer even registered in his conscious mind. Before replacing the ledger, he reached into the void and casually caressed the leather covered handle of a sheathed Ka-Bar fighting knife. The knife was the only item he still owned which had belonged to his father and it had rested at the bottom of this nook since Ben first created the space.

His father had cherished the knife but didn't talk much about how he obtained it. Ben knew that Ninoy de Guzman was involved in some capacity with helping the Americans during the world war, but just as it was with many returning American soldiers and sailors after the war, he refused to elaborate on anything he might have witnessed or participated in. With the exception of an old blood stain on the leather handle, it was in remarkable condition. After his father's death, Ben cleaned, sharpened and oiled the blade and then returned it to its sheath, where it remained until now.

After securing his treasures, he went to bed. A familiar parade of Filipino heroes marched quickly through his mind and there among them, was Benito "Ben" de Guzman. The intercranial voice, perhaps a bit louder than normal, cheered for them all. A reflexive smile curled his lips and he fell asleep quickly.

Chapter 12

Luz turned the thumb latch on the dead bolt and then reached up to slide the top latch into its socket at the very top of the door jamb. She used the occasion to stretch her back muscles and peek out through the curtains at the still bustling activity on Gordon Avenue. Some other bars had also begun to close, and tricycles were zipping around vying for the late-night passengers. Streetwalkers lingered around the corner, trying to attract servicemen still looking for something they hadn't found in the bars. A few servicemen were still trying to find just the right hooker or the perfect place to drink, but most had either already paired up with someone or were going back to their ships and barracks alone. Shore patrol trucks and vans had also picked up their activity, cruising slowly up and down the streets, searching for potential problems and making their presence known to all.

The ringing engines of the trikes, for the most part, drowned out the bands in the clubs and the evening negotiations being waged between off-duty hostesses and their potential customers. To Luz, they were the discordant melodies of too many different songs and locking the door against them provided her an unusual comfort. It was comforting in the way her sister, sleeping with spoon-like snugness beside her, had partially shielded her from the snores and bony knees of her grandmother.

Today would have been the twenty-seventh birthday of her older sister. And while she thought less and less about her sister as the years passed, she still remembered the date. She had celebrated her fifteenth birthday just days before leaving Manila, which was the last time Luz saw her alive.

The beer cooler had been restocked, the plug had been pulled on everything else except the hanging lamp and the few dirty glasses had been washed and stored away. She remembered the rubber gloves that Ben had mentioned bringing later and wondered how they would feel as she washed dishes. All that remained was to take the cash box back to her room and count the receipts for the day. She wasn't always shackled to such responsibilities, but the other girls shared them infrequently and they had become an almost welcomed routine to Luz. She had earned the trust of

Mama Nina – a sizable task in itself – and thus a lion's share of the responsibility. Besides, even when the others were out overnight, she seldom went out with a customer and almost always returned to sleep alone in her room in back of the bar. She walked to that room now, stopping to gather up the cash box and unplug the hanging lamp.

Mama Nina had two nephews, both in their mid-twenties, who would come around the bar one or more times a day to complete minor maintenance or to help the girls with heavy lifting. They would also usually stick around on the busier nights to help secure the bar, but since there were no customers when they dropped by this evening, they did not feel obliged to help her close. Ace's tended to have a familiar and low-keyed clientele which allowed operations to usually run smoothly and without drama.

Walking by the rest rooms, Luz glanced in to double-check that the lights were out and free of residual customers and then unlocked the door at the end of the short hall. From inside the door, she switched off the hall light and switched on the one lighting the bar storage and common areas of their apartments. Then she closed and locked the door behind her and peeked through the peephole into the darkness. It was part of the ritual that she always followed after locking up, whether she was alone or not. With all the other girls having been bought out of the bar, she would be alone tonight.

Every girl working at Ace's had a bed in a windowless room behind the bar, even those whose steady bar fines had been paid and who were living in rented apartments with their boyfriends. Each room could accommodate two girls and were situated along a short hall beginning just opposite the entrance. Each of their rooms had solid doors equipped with dead bolts and at the very end of that hallway was a door leading to a small alley. It was also secured with a dead bolt and sliding lock. The toilet and shower stall were on the right side of the entrance. The toilet was in a small room with a sink and door that actually locked from the inside, while the shower was little more than a cubbyhole with a drain in the floor and a water spigot protruding from one wall. This served also as their laundry. The only hot water available was what they heated on the stove.

A minimum of bar provisions, including a couple of full beer cases and some paper products, were stacked around the minimally appointed kitchen.

By virtue of the years she had worked there, Luz occupied the largest room directly behind the kitchen area. And although it was by no means a penthouse, she didn't have to share it with any of the other girls. In addition to a bed and small bureau, Luz's room had space enough left over for a tiny closet and a set of shelves on which she kept private stores of food and a few personal items. Secured on nails and strung across two of the room's corners, were wires for hanging additional clothing. Luz had little, but most girls had less.

Luz left the kitchen light burning as she unlocked her door, pulled the chain on her own room's light socket and placed the cash box on her bed. The small volume and simplicity of the business ensured Luz's bookkeeping remained a minimal chore and within minutes the books were done and stored with the cash box on an old and neatly folded canvas bag adjacent to three pairs of shoes along a bottom shelf. She absently stroked the bag like a sleeping pet and straightened it by habit.

She disrobed, slipped on her comfortable old, rubber sandals and wrapped herself in a huge multi-colored beach towel, but stopped before going to the "shower." She pulled out the top drawer in her bureau, retrieved a small mirror and propped it on one of the shelves. With a feeling approaching embarrassment, she pulled apart the towel and draped it on the bed and then adjusted the mirror to get a better view of her breasts. They were firm and round with dark, brown nipples tilting ever-so-slightly toward the ceiling. They were not large by anyone's standards, but she felt as if they were her best feature. She looked down at her slender body and noted, with some misplaced shame, the hundreds of tiny scars on her legs which told the story of her childhood in the trash heaps of Manila. However, her twenty-two-year-old belly was unmarred and still flat. Wispy, black hair barely covered her pubic mound. Looking back at the mirror, Luz twisted from side to side and glanced at the indentations made by her bra. She casually rubbed her finger over one, as if to press it even with the rest of her skin. She slowly dragged her fingernail across the top of one nipple, which hardened quickly and ignited a bolt coursing through her body. Luz closed her eyes and cupped both breasts in a reflexive move and then quickly snatched up the towel, wrapping herself once more in its comforting warmth. She suppressed one more chill before digging out a half-used bar of soap and walking out for her evening bath.

Hanging the towel on a nail, Luz turned on the spigot and squatted in front of it to wash her face with soap and water. Next, she used a small, plastic bowl to pour the cold water over the rest of her body before scrubbing her arms, legs and torso with a rounded, porous rock. Luz's legs were tanned halfway up her thighs and her arms were tanned just to her shoulders. She thought the tan might actually highlight the little scars that she found so ugly. She couldn't remember the last time she had been to a beach, but that had never been a priority for her. Despite the blemishes, her skin was smooth and supple and clean and that was good enough. After another dousing of water, Luz lathered with her soap and scrubbed once again with a cloth before a final rinsing. She never washed her hair at night.

Luz was always relaxed after this nightly ritual and tonight was no different, although there was a nagging, little something, dancing in the back of her mind. Something she couldn't pin down about the day that just wasn't quite right. She tried to dismiss it as she closed her door and slid the bolt into place, but it wouldn't go.

Picking up the mirror, Luz brought it close to her face. She stared into her beautiful, brown eyes and then gently pulled the bottom lid of her left eye down to reveal the bottom of her prosthesis. The artificial eye was so realistic that only a couple of people knew about it and Ben was the only one of those who still lived in Olongapo. She inspected it and its socket with her one good eye and decided that it didn't need to be removed and cleaned on this night. She would remove and clean the artificial eye every day or two, depending on how many irritants she may have picked up during the day. Occasionally, she would also check in the morning to see what may have accumulated during the night's sleep. Some things in her life were better accomplished through a ritualistic behavior, but she had always approached the care of her false eye as a continuous adjustment to circumstances. Satisfied, she readjusted her eye lid, smoothed her eyebrows and replaced the mirror in the drawer.

Dry and snug in her over-sized towel, Luz settled back on a pillow propped against the headboard of her modest single bed and pulled a magazine from the stack on the floor. She wasn't really all that interested in the lives of Filipino movie stars, but it was all that remained unread in her old magazines, and she needed something to finish up this relaxation ritual.

She was bored after only one page of the pap from Manila and her mind drifted darkly back to reality. The memory of her sister's birthday often stirred a mix of emotions in Luz and while there were a few bright moments in her childhood, they were mostly of fear and anger. Unfortunately, those memories also brought with them memory of her grandmother's death.

*   *   *

Jun Rojas hadn't seen the old woman and her little girl since early the day before. The sun was now approaching its zenith and their shack was quieter than he could ever remember. The recently added door was standing slightly ajar and would probably have blown completely open, had it not hung so poorly from its hinges. A rusting corner of the corrugated tin roof squeaked sporadically, its curled-up corner heroically resisting the persistent breeze coming from Manila Bay. Jun hoped against all hope that it was abandoned and that he was the first one to notice the vacancy. He looked around casually for witnesses to his discovery and seeing none, approached the door. His first tentative raps on the door produced no response but he did not follow them up with louder knocking; instead, he pulled it open as quietly as possible and peered into the relative darkness.

The old woman lay still on a blanket to one side of the small enclosure. Sitting cross-legged next to her on the floor, back to the door, was the young girl rocking almost imperceptibly back and forth. Jun crossed himself before taking another small step forward and said, "*Ateh*? Luz?"

Luz stopped moving immediately and Jun watched curiously as she began to breath heavily. She suddenly burst into ear-piercing screams, shrill and primal. Jun literally jumped out of his shoes, leaving one of his sandals upside-down on the floor and rammed his back painfully into the door jam. The shack shook violently and left an indentation in his shoulder which would turn into a three-week long bruise. Retrieving his flip-flop as quickly as possible, Jun ran back to his own hovel, unaware and unconcerned with the surprised looks of his neighbors.

Some of the others eventually went to check out the cacophony and found that Luz had finally succumbed to the sobs Jun had expected. They comforted her as they could and determined that her grandmother was dead. They could tell from the temperature and stiffness of the body that Carmelita had been dead for some time, probably from the night before. Yollie, whose bossiness was acknowledged and accepted by nearly everyone in the community, convinced the others that Luz should be protected from the government. The police didn't care much about what happened in these shanty towns, but they would have to be summoned to take the body of the old woman and if an unaccompanied child were present, she would almost assuredly be consumed by the broken machine that was the Philippine's child welfare system. As much as Carmelita had worshiped Imelda Marcos, Yollie hated and distrusted anything having to do with the Marcos regime, including the Council for the Welfare of Children.

Before anyone was sent to retrieve a police officer, they all agreed that no mention would be made of Luz. She would be adopted by the rest of the group. Jun was informed about their decision and reminded that he had been seen fleeing the hut, an action which would be described to the police if he said anything about Luz. And, while many police cared nothing about the welfare of the people populating the trash heaps, they cared even less about things like due process and human rights. Jun would be quiet, and Luz would definitely be safer with them.

Yollie's plan was to move Luz's things into her own place until after the police had taken the body and then to move them both back into the slightly larger and more sturdy structure. Slowly, as if in a trance, Luz gathered her meager belongings stuffing them into a canvas bag she had scavenged only months before. In the meantime, Yollie moved some of her things in and gathered anything of value that had belonged to Carmelita. If the police asked, she would tell them that she had lived with the older woman. Those few things of limited value that she found were put into the canvas bag which hung from Luz's shoulder. She directed another woman to lead Luz back to her place and then started combing over the rest of Carmelita's former home to find any possible treasures which might have been hidden. By the time the police arrived, there was nothing left they might have wanted for themselves.

Luz said nothing while being herded around by her well-meaning neighbors. She said nothing as those same well-wishers talked around and over her, discussing what was to become of her. She said nothing while peering at the police from the safety of Yollie's hut. In fact, she had said nothing since first discovering her grandmother cold and unresponsive early that morning.

Since her first realization of *Impo's* death, Luz had been planning what to do. She knew she was going to Olongapo to find her sister and was finalizing a strategy to do it. The very first part of the plan was to retrieve the small stash of money they had saved and wrap it in an old tee shirt. The planning had been a way to not think about the corpse that had been her beloved grandmother. It had served as a tight lid on the simmering pot holding in her emotions, roiling just under the surface. When Jun had called to her, that lid was flipped and all of the fear, anger and grief boiled over into the shrieks that sent him running back to his own hell.

Now, trudging through the motions of relocation directed by Yollie, Luz's planning turned back to how she would get to Olongapo and find her sister. She knew on some unconscious level that she needed to move quickly to successfully extricate herself from the only world in which she could remember living. Despite having no experience of a different reality, she had memorized the stories of her grandmother, had listened intently to any description proffered by her neighbors. Along with those, her fertile imagination, bolstered by occasional glimpses outside the trash heaps in which she lived, had scripted a host of beautiful possibilities. Somehow, she knew with certainty that her life would get better and that it would begin today.

Left alone for the moment, she shrugged the canvas bag from her shoulder. Double-checking for witnesses, she returned to the bag and retrieved a few items which had belonged to *Impó*. Some she placed on the floor next to Yollie's sleeping area and buried a few others more deeply into the bag. She then slipped into her cleanest and newest dress. Finally, while looking warily through the door, she wriggled her fingers into the folds of the tee shirt left by her older sister. She felt the small roll of peso notes and some coins which they had been collectively saving since having first fled the scene of her parent's death. She removed a couple of bills and a few coins, clenching them tightly in her trembling fist.

She took a last look at the others either watching the police fulfill their duties or attending to their own survival. Luz moved slowly through the door and edged along to the corner of the hut with her back to its wall. Satisfied in her preadolescent mind that no one was currently watching, she clutched the bag a bit tighter and turned to make her escape.

"Watch out, little one," the uniformed policeman had nearly run her over as he strode toward the clutch of people gathered around her former home. Hoping they had not drawn the attention of others in the camp, Luz looked up at the beefy officer and said, "I, I think someone died over there." She glanced over her shoulder hoping to find no curious faces. Fortunately, she saw only the backs of heads.

"We'll see," he said. "In the meantime, go home and stay out of the way." He skirted around her with no further concern and Luz continued through the gate to one of the noisy jeepney's idling in the street.

While Luz had never seen the inside of a school building, she could nonetheless read both English and Tagalog at a rudimentary level. Her grandmother had never intended for them to live the remainder of their lives in the garbage heaps of Manila and had taken every opportunity to teach both girls everything she knew about reading, writing and arithmetic. Carmelita had not been very well educated herself, but she had always valued education and knew that it was probably their only path to a better existence.

For her part, Luz had always been a curious and clever girl. She took the miniscule bits of knowledge provided by her grandmother and in her spare time tried to use them to gather more. Almost every scrap of paper found with writing had been taken back to their hut for examination and interpretation. However, the basic aspects of math had come to her much easier and the constant pressure to collect centavos and pesos had impressed upon her the importance of such skills. Hours spent sitting around on the bamboo mat of their bed, counting the little bits of money they were able to scrape together, instilled in both girls the value and virtues of money.

Luz used the complete set of skills she had acquired to navigate her way first to the Victory Liner station in Manila, then to Olongapo and finally to the restaurant where Emmy was supposed to have worked. Once there, her plans collapsed.

* * *

Luz reread the paragraph about Rico Puno's latest song for the fifth or sixth time and decided she was ready for sleep. She traded her towel for a clean tee shirt and panties and crawled between the thin sheets of her lonely bed.

Luz slipped into sleep quickly, as was normal, but she did not rest quietly. She dreamed of her sister and Ben.

Saturday

Chapter 13

The clock alarm buzzed like a ten-pound bumblebee. No sound could possibly be more annoying. He reached through the fog of his deep sleep, groping for relief in the form of a snooze bar and found it. He fell back into slumber even before his hand had returned beneath the sheets.

Again, an alarm arose, and he again reached for the snooze bar, pressing the comforting spring-loaded button with the warm anticipation that his misery would soon end. No change. The alarm continued and the sleep-fog began to clear, revealing a blinding, burning light which melted away the cocoon protecting him from the waking world.

Roy mustered all his concentration and peered at the glowing numbers of the clock in his hand, which blinked dimly each time he pressed the snooze bar. The noise continued. Only then did he remember the new irritant came from the desk across the room and was a totally different sound. Rather than a constant, flat-toned, annoying buzz, this was an annoying, flat-toned, electronic chirp. If it had been designed to make the waking experience a more pleasant one, its designers had failed magnificently. On the other hand, if it had been designed to encourage the newly awakened sleeper to hate all things electronic, it had succeeded beyond all possible predictions.

Roy swung his feet to the floor and looked around the room to pinpoint the source of noise before shoving his body in its general direction. He trudged across the floor to the desk and was awake enough by the time he got there to locate the off button and disable the small travel clock before its irritating alarm drove him to violence.

He yawned as he looked around the room and re-acquainted himself with his new home. It was a large room by Navy standards, probably 12 by 15 feet. It was appointed with two stand-up lockers separated by a sink, fitted into a cabinet beneath a 1 ½ by 2 feet mirror and light fixture. A nightstand made from fiber board, a single gray, metal bunk, a desk and a chair completed the furniture décor. There was also one lamp on the nightstand and a single row of florescent lights on the ceiling.

Opposite the entrance were two jalousie windows covered with tan colored drapes which more or less accented the cream-colored paint covering the bare, cinder-block walls. In one far corner was a door which led to the toilet and shower Roy would have shared with a next-door neighbor – if he'd had one – and a neutral tan colored linoleum tile covered the floor. It was similar to every room Roy had ever occupied while in the Navy and provided a pleasing level of comfort.

It was a few minutes past 7:00 AM. Roy vaguely remembered setting the alarms the previous night in hopes that by starting off the day early he might get over his jet lag a little easier. Setting two clocks, with the second one being as far away from the bed as possible, was a survival tactic he learned early in his career, when tardiness meant punishment. Roy had never been an "early bird" and getting up early had been a chore for him since childhood. It was one of many concessions he made for a Navy career.

After a quick shave, Roy indulged in a long, "Hollywood" styled shower. He enjoyed the high-pressure spray, letting it drum on his scalp as he watched the water swirl down the drain. It was easy for his mind to drift at such times, and it now wandered back to his lost love and his lost enthusiasm for the Navy career that was nearing its end.

Usually, Roy's focus seldom drifted, and he knew his current place in his career was a direct result of that trait. As a Navy Master-At-Arms he had provided security and investigative services at several bases and ships during his career and had done a good job. He usually enjoyed the challenge of the work, and he enjoyed the pace that it usually kept him going. There were boring moments, like in any job, but the days were never the same and Roy had discovered that boredom comes in many varying degrees. He'd had other jobs in the Navy and tried to approach each new assignment with a fresh perspective.

Since leaving his first command, he went to every new duty station hoping to disprove something he had heard as a young third class petty officer. An old chief (probably all of 35 years old) had once told him, "There are only two good duty stations in a sailor's career; the one he just left and the one he's going to." And although Roy had forgotten the chief's name, he had never forgotten those words. He hoped to end his career having had all good duty and, for the most part, he had.

He had been hungry for adventure as a young man and decided soon after graduating high school in 1972 that there wasn't much of that, or work, to be found in the Florida panhandle town of Pensacola. A shrewd recruiter told him he could find both in one shot, so he joined the Navy one month after his graduation and went straight to boot camp in San Diego.

Like most kids, he had no idea about where to point his life, so when he was offered the chance to go back to Pensacola for more training after boot camp, he jumped at it. He would be able to spend a little time at home with money in his pocket; an attractive idea to any 18-year-old with friends to impress. That chance also involved him going to a class "A" school to become a Communications Technician, "R" Branch.

Roy didn't really have much of a clue about what a "CTR" was or what they did. He had been told that it was a very secret kind of job and that sounded like excitement to him. He knew only that he would get to go home for a while and that he would learn about radios and that was enough for the time being.

Shortly after reporting for school, Roy was shown into a huge room, filled with several rows of individually sectioned carrels, reminding him of booths found in a library. At each station was a typewriter with a small console built into the wall behind it. Antique headphones, called "tin-cans" by the old salts at school, were plugged into the console and lay beside the typewriter. He could hear the faint sound of "dits" and "dahs" emanating from them as the instructor explained the various dials, knobs and switches with which Roy would become intimate. After being told that a "ditty chaser" was someone who searched for and intercepted manual Morse code communications, his meager introduction was complete.

Much to his amazement, Roy discovered he picked up very easily the trick of copying code. He was able to copy it at a rapid pace, too. He was getting so fast at receiving it, he began to wonder when he would learn to send it as well. It was about that time that he found out what a CTR really did and that he didn't need to learn to talk; he was going to be a listener.

He liked being a listener and he liked the Navy. He liked it so much in fact, that when he finished his school and was granted a Top Secret clearance, he extended his original four-year enlistment for two more years and was promoted to the rank of CTR3. In March of 1973, Roy became an "Instant Petty Officer" and was given orders to report to Hawaii.

His first duty station was Naval Communication Area Master Station, Eastern Pacific, or "NAVCAMS EASTPAC," and it was located in the middle of a pineapple field, northwest of Honolulu on Oahu, Hawaii. While there Roy learned a lot more about being a CTR and about being a sailor. He also learned how to get into the bars on Hotel Street – usually with a group of friends – and what to do once he got there.

After about two years in Hawaii, two momentous events happened. First, he passed the rating exam required for promotion to second class petty officer and second, he met and married Kim Sung Ye, a Korean woman working as a bar "hostess." Because she was not a U.S. citizen, and had family members living in Korea, the high clearance needed in order for Roy to perform his job was temporarily suspended. While waiting for a security background check to be completed on his new wife, Roy was assigned to the Master-At-Arms office. For a while he given a few "gopher" jobs, but eventually he was offered a choice between some other, more permanent jobs he could do temporarily on the base.

In the meantime, there was considerable debate along Roy's chain of command about whether or not to allow him to receive the promotion to CTR2. Eventually, it was decided that Roy's clearance would most likely be reinstated fairly quickly so they allowed him to be frocked to the new rank. That meant he would be recognized at the higher rank, with the exception of the pay. He sewed the second class rating badge on his uniform, reflecting a crossed spark and quill, two chevrons and the silhouette of the American eagle.

With this new "crow" on his arm Roy worked in the galley checking I.D. cards or in the barracks making sure women and men stayed out of each other's rooms. Also, he was offered the opportunity to get a bit more involved in the "real" work of Master-At-Arms, including security and investigation. This seemed to him to be the most interesting choice by far.

Of course, he wasn't THE Master-At-Arms. That was a job held by a chief Boatswain's Mate, stationed at a shore command for only the second time in his career. Instead, Roy worked for the MAA as an assistant, kind of like a full-time shore patrol. He made sure the club was emptied on time every night and helped gather evidence during criminal investigations. He never before realized how many sailors got drunk and then got angry and then put their fists through one of the Navy's walls. Every time something like that happened, an investigation was required. And although the sequence of events didn't always go in that order, the outcomes of those events were eerily common.

While Roy was waiting to get his clearance back, he was also finding that married life wasn't all that he had hoped it would be. In June of 1975, Roy ended his childless marriage to Sung Ye, paving the way for the return of his clearance. However, just when Roy was about ready to resume duty as a CTR, the divine hands of providence formed a time-out sign.

The Navy had recently revived the enlisted rating of Master-At-Arms, due to a finding that the service did not have adequately trained and prepared law enforcement personnel in the field. After some race riots on a couple of ships near the end of the Viet Nam war highlighted the need for a more positive response to such problems, the Navy resurrected the traditional rating. This new and improved MA rating was screaming for anyone with experience, while at the same time, the CTR rating was becoming over-manned. Faced with an option, Roy decided he liked being an "investigator" much more than being a "listener." And so, with high praise and ringing endorsements from his superiors, Roy was shipped to a school, re-designated an MA2 and ordered to the USS Kennedy home-ported on the east coast of the U.S.

He was promoted to MA1 prior to transferring from there and then had tours of duty at Naval Station Norfolk, Virginia, NAS Bermuda, the USS Mount Whitney. After earning a promotion to Chief Petty Officer, he was ordered back to Naval Station Norfolk again in 1987.

Around Christmas, time routines on stateside bases slow down considerably, so one day Roy made a decision to let a junior sailor leave early from work. When he was asked by a senior officer to provide a person to chauffer his wife around Christmas shopping, he said he didn't have one to spare and then made an offhand remark about how unfortunate it was that an Admiral's wife couldn't afford a taxi.

Roy had used smarter words in the past, and would again in the future, but this time they abandoned him. He got to spend New Year's with the folks in Pensacola that year, but he had to be in Iceland by the fifth of January. Courts-martial or Captain's masts take time, money and legal precedent, but to get someone where they live, so to speak, a shit-hole transfer is just a phone call away. This is especially true for a well-connected senior officer.

By far the worst thing about the transfer was that he would have to leave Lisa Bartow. He visited her in the spring and again in the fall when their time would be filled with long country drives, delicious home-cooked meals and passionate love making before a mellow, stone hearth fire at her rural Virginia home.

Roy was shining professionally in Iceland and aching personally for the red-haired beauty in Virginia. It was after being promoted to Senior Chief Petty Officer that he started thinking seriously about making Lisa his wife.

After her death, he attacked his work. He neglected his feelings and avoided thinking about Lisa until eventually the pain subsided and the self-directed anger became a low-level depression. He had tested negatively for HIV since then but was unwilling to pursue another relationship.

When his tour in Iceland was up, Roy accepted the first set of orders offered to him, not caring where he was sent. He left Keflavik with a Meritorious Service Medal and a performance evaluation in the top one percent of his peers. He was in a good position for a promotion but didn't seem to care much about that now. He wasn't sure he wanted anything anymore.

Despite the painful memories, Roy felt considerably more refreshed and awake as he toweled off and almost human when someone rapped loudly on his door.

"Just a minute," Roy called. He wrapped the towel around his waist and stood behind the door as he pulled it open.

"Yeah?" he said, peering around the edge of the door.

Bill Eikleberger stood at the door wearing red and black, plaid Bermuda shorts and a tight yellow tee shirt which had the words "Balut Vendor's Union" stenciled across its front. He also had a worried look on his face, which kept Roy from laughing out loud, but couldn't keep him from smiling.

"Hey Bill, what's up," he said.

"Hi Roy," Bill said. "I called earlier but the desk boy said you didn't answer your door, so I came over to get you. You, uh, decent?" he said and gestured as if he wanted to be invited in.

Roy stepped back and opened the door wide enough for Bill to come through. "Come on in."

Roy retrieved a pair of skivvies from one of the lockers and pulled them on beneath the towel, before looking through the few items hung there for something else to wear.

"I say again: what's up?" Roy asked again as he took a pair of Levi's off their wire hanger.

"Well, I'm not sure. I got a call from the XO this morning and he wants to see you real bad. He said to get you down to OPM as soon as I could."

Roy didn't question the request and started to put his jeans back on the hanger when Bill stopped him. "He said not to worry about a uniform, I guess he wants you there quick."

Roy pulled on the Levi's but didn't say anything as he wondered what could cause the XO to call him in on a Saturday. And why OPM and not the NAVMAG?

"Guess I don't have time for breakfast, huh?" he said before tugging a plain blue tee shirt over his head.

"I don't think so," Bill said, looking more disappointed than Roy felt.

In another three minutes they were in Bill's small Chevy pick-up, headed for the main gate. Bill repeated that he didn't know what was going on. All he knew was that he had been awakened by a phone call from the XO looking for Roy. It was the first time in a long time that Bill had been awakened by anything other than his kids and it rattled him a little.

"Is that why you dressed that way?" Roy said.

"What do you mean?" Bill countered. He seemed truly unaware that his clothing made an unflattering fashion statement.

"Nothing," Roy said. "I just thought you dressed in a hurry."

"Yeah, I did. I got this shirt from my yard-boy and I usually just wear it around the house. Hey, if you want, I can get you one."

"No thanks," Roy said. He figured he would probably collect a lot of tee shirts while he was there, but he didn't want to start right then and certainly not with that one.

Roy spent the rest of the ride in relative silence, listening to Bill describe, in excruciating detail, first his daughter's ongoing ear infections and then his son's recent circumcision. Guess they won't be calling him "*saput*," Roy thought.

A little after 8:00 they reached the main gate which was experiencing considerably less foot traffic than it had the night before. Mostly it looked to be sailors returning from their night on the town. His view of the gate was obscured when Bill pulled his truck into a parking space behind the building of the Office of the Provost Marshall and Roy noted with interest the presence of several Navy vehicles. According to their tags, one belonged to the CO of Naval Station and another to the CO of the NAVMAG. He didn't know what to expect inside, but he didn't think he was going to like it much.

They stepped from the relative calm of a humid tropical morning into an oddly mixed atmosphere of quiet tension and murmuring expectation. The large, open office nonetheless seemed cramped and was crowded with battered furniture. The air buzzed like a high intensity streetlamp as several people stood around desks talking in guarded tones. There was a mix of civilians and military of both nationalities, though no one seemed to pay any attention as the two entered. Bill closed the door and pointed ahead with a crooked finger to indicate they should turn to the right at the end of the wall.

A U. S. marine guard and what appeared to be a Filipino Army enlisted person stood at parade rest, protecting a door at the end of the hall and eyed the two chiefs suspiciously as they approached. Bill removed an overstuffed wallet from his back pocket and dug for his I.D. card. Roy pulled a thin I.D. folder out of his front pocket and held it up for the guard as he came up to the door.

"I think I'm supposed to be here," he said, waiting for the marine's response.

"Senior Chief Thompson?" the guard asked as he came to attention. He leaned forward and looked closely at the black and white picture as his fingers traced Roy's name across the bottom of the card like a blind man reading Braille. He glanced up at Roy's face and then back to the card again before stepping aside and opening the door. As Roy walked through, he heard the marine tell Bill he would have to wait outside.

The room Roy stepped into turned out to be a reception area. Just inside the door and to the left was a nice leather sofa with matching chair arranged for informality. Directly across from the door was a huge secretary's desk, neat and meticulous. It was a modular unit with built in shelves, lamp and plenty of surface area for three telephones, a Wang word processor and IBM electric typewriter. Several live plants were strategically placed around, providing warmth and comfort under the stark florescent lights.

On the left side of this reception area were two smaller and separate spaces. The first was a cramped room containing a conference table behind a large window through which Roy took a quick inventory. He saw several Navy officers and two Filipino officers sitting around the table. They were speaking earnestly, though Roy could hear only muffled voices through the closed door.

As the outer door closed behind Roy, the door to the second smaller office opened and a petite figure backed out of it. She carried an aluminum coffee urn which seemed almost as big as she, and Roy's first thought was of a child. However, as she turned around, Roy could see she was a fully-grown Filipina, or at least as fully grown as she would ever be. She could have been thirty-five or fifty-five, as far as he could tell, but she was a grown woman and tiny, no more than four feet. She was primly dressed in a long traditional Filipina dress with large, arching ridged shoulder pads over its short sleeves. She was as neat and meticulous as her desk. She smiled and said with the faintest of accents, "May I help you?"

"I'm Senior Chief Thompson," he said plainly.

"Okay," she said. "Please wait." As she said the words, she simultaneously looked at the sofa, kind of pointed her chin at it and raised her eyebrows. It was a gesture he had witnessed several times the night before. She lowered the urn to the floor and turned toward the conference room, but before she could reach for the door, Roy saw one of the Captains motioning for him to enter. The lady, whatever her capacity, saw the gesture and opened the door for Roy.

The Captain who had called him in stepped from around the table as Roy entered and extended his hand.

"I'm Captain Johnson, NAVSTA C.O. Are you Senior Chief Thompson?"

"Yes sir."

Going around the table, Johnson introduced three senior Navy officers, one Marine Corp Lieutenant Colonel and two Filipino officers assigned to OPM. The only name he recognized was that of his new Executive Officer, Lieutenant Commander Pillsbury. Each acknowledged him with a nodded head or curt hello as they were introduced.

"Commander Pillsbury recommended we invited you to listen in on this, Senior Chief," Johnson said as he leaned back in his chair. "We're waiting for someone from the PC." Gesturing toward the back wall, the Captains said, "Go ahead and take a seat." Sitting there in folding chairs, invisible from the reception area, were a Master Chief, a Senior Chief, two Chiefs and another Filipino dressed in civilian clothes. None were introduced, but as Roy made his way to an open chair, he felt incredibly out of place in his own jeans and polo shirt.

Chapter 14

"Holy shit," Scott said. He took in a mouth full of San Miguel and held it for a few seconds before swallowing. Then he took a deep breath and said, "holy shit," one more time for good measure.

"That's what I heard," said Gloria. "And I heard he is arrested there on base and that he will be sent back *doon*, to the states." She poured a little more Pepsi in her glass and waited while the foam subsided. "*Yelo*, eh?" she said, pushing the glass toward Luz for some ice.

The buzz of an electric fan sitting at one end of the bar seemed to be the only sound Scott could distinguish as he twirled the brown beer bottle with his thumb and forefinger, keeping it within its own sweat ring. The fan blew Luz's hair into her eyes temporarily and then sent the thick aromas of Gloria's perfume past Scott's face as it oscillated back toward the center of the room. Scott stared at the small puddle at the base of his bottle and thought 'holy shit' again but did not voice it.

Luz said something to Gloria in Tagalog as she plopped two large chunks of ice into her soda glass. She then took the bottle from Scott, wiped the countertop with a rag and replaced the beer on a cardboard coaster.

"*Oo, talaga*!" Gloria continued, reading the look on Scott's face. "*Ateh* Julie is the one to know what is going onto there!" She seemed adamant that her sources were correct in this latest revelation, although Scott – and it seemed perhaps Luz too – had some reservations about its reliability.

Scott really didn't know Master Chief Boggs all that well but what he knew of him, he liked. They had met out in town several times and, of course, Scott knew he was the Command Master Chief at the NAVSTA, but they weren't really friends. Regardless, he couldn't believe the Master Chief was capable of murder, especially of his own girlfriend. He had always seemed happy and friendly when Scott had run into him and didn't fit any kind of a profile Scott could imagine for a killer.

Going in to work on this Saturday morning would never have occurred to him until now. His CO was at some meeting of the minds in Hawaii and the XO was filling in for the week. And even though Scott knew the duty officer would have a handle on the situation, he also suspected the XO would be called in and might need his help with things. He didn't know what kinds of things, but he felt he needed to be helpful.

Gloria was talking to Luz about the movie she was on her way to see that morning. Scott picked out enough Tagalog words to know that Gloria was excited about seeing it and could read Luz well enough to know that she didn't care at all.

"*Isa pa nga?*" Luz asked as Scott looked vacantly at the last half-inch of beer in his bottle.

"No thanks," he said. "I better go up and see what's what." Scott slid from his stool and absently plunked a few pesos on the bar. "*Mamaya,*" he said walking toward the door.

"I'll see you never," Gloria said just as Scott opened the door. He didn't turn to give a snappy reply; he didn't smile. The man who made a habit of hearing everything wasn't listening.

"Julia is talk too much," Luz said, still speaking her broken English.

"*Hinde*! She didn't want to talk at all! That's why I think she has it right," Gloria stated seriously. She was speaking in the curious mix of dialects that many of the girls spoke. "When I saw her this morning, I could tell she was upset but she wouldn't say anything at first." A hint of a smile came to her as she said, "I knew she was upset when she smoked two of her own cigarettes before thinking about asking me for one."

"Did she say where she heard it?"

"One of her cousins works somewhere on Cubi Point and she told her. Maybe on the Quarterdeck?" Gloria really had no idea where Julia's cousin worked, but she knew it was somewhere on the air station. All of the girls who had been in Olongapo for more than a month knew the difference between a Quarterdeck and the Administrative Office. In fact, many knew where they were located on base, in addition to the Bachelor Officer's Quarters, the Bachelor Enlisted Quarters, the galley, sickbay, the Officer's Club, the Enlisted Club and especially the Base Exchange.

"Anyway, I think she is close to right. I don't think Denny would murder anyone either, but his girlfriend is, *ano*, dead." Gloria spoke the English word "dead" because she thought it sounded so much more final than the words other Filipinas might use.

Chapter 15

The gathering of brass at the OPM had nearly dissipated by the time Scott came through the main gate and there was not much to suggest that a high-profile murder had just taken place. However, Scott thought he noticed just a few more guards on the vehicle gate than usual. Did they always have four guys in the shack? He might have detected just a bit more interest on the part of the marines who checked him on the way in. Did they always look twice at his face and I.D. card before waving him through? He chided himself for not being more observant prior to this and made a mental note to do better in the future. As he walked over to the bus stand to wait for the one that would take him to Cubi Point, Scott mused about what else he might have missed since arriving in country.

As Scott waited for the bus, Roy Thompson and LCDR Pillsbury were walking out of the meeting at the OPM. The Naval Magazine personnel had been brought into the meeting only because of a manifesto found at the murder scene made vague references to the possibility of sabotage or infiltration at that command. Roy would not be involved in the investigation of the murder but did need to know about the threat level escalation at his new command.

As for the murder itself, Philippine and American officials had already completed the process of gathering evidence at Boggs' and Jackson's separate homes. The Naval Investigative Services Office had secured the offices of Dennis Boggs and Winnie Jackson and agents from every involved organization were gathering whatever evidence they might find.

Roy learned from the morning's briefing that LT Winifred Jackson had been murdered the night before in the rented bungalow of Command Master Chief, Dennis Boggs. They worked in the same building and, evidently, had a personal relationship off-duty that was unknown to anyone in the chain of command. Roy remember what Luz had said about Boggs' "girlfriend" the night before.

The letter left with the body indicated Boggs himself had been the original target of the murder. Mixed in with the rambling diatribe about the

U.S. presence in the Philippines and the escalating revolt against imperialist forces, was an allusion to the Naval Magazine being a possible future target. That had been the reason for Roy being called to an otherwise high pay-grade meeting.

Pillsbury and Roy stepped aside at the entrance to OPM, allowing others to file out first.

"I'm sorry this is the way that you were welcomed to the command, Senior Chief." Pillsbury said. "No one should ever have such a shitty first weekend at a new command... especially in this country." Roy said nothing.

"And believe me, I don't want to fuck up the whole weekend for you, but I do have a few more things I'd like you to do before Monday morning. I know Chief Eikleberger showed you around a bit of Cubi Point and the NAVMAG yesterday but get him to take you around the Naval Station before you go on liberty today. Maybe the Quarterdeck, PSD, COMNAVPHIL's office. Also have him take you by the NIS office before noon today. You met Commander Pillotero this morning and he is headed to his office from here. He has a preliminary copy of the report from last night's incident, and I asked him to let you go through it privately in his office. He told me that he'll be there until 12:30 or so. Couldn't hurt."

"Yes sir," Roy said, looking around the room for Bill Eikleberger.

"Did Eikleberger stick around?"

"I don't see him here, but he might be out by his truck in the back."

"Well, if he's gone, I'll take you back up to the command and have the duty driver to run you around."

He retrieved a business card from a breast pocket and handed it to Roy before pulling his piss-cutter hat from under his belt and squaring it on his head. "If you have any problems or questions about anything before Monday, give me a call. My home number is written on the back of that card. And even though my wife will bitch about it, don't hesitate to call me at home if you have to."

He took a set of aviator sunglasses from his other breast pocket and settle them on his face before pushing open the door.

Eikleberger was in the parking lot, his yellow tee shirt glowing in the sunlight. While Roy had been in the meeting, he had found a red ball cap and bulky sunglasses to guard against the sun. The hat had a logo that Roy couldn't quite place and the sunshades were the type meant to be worn over prescription glasses. He had been leaning against his little white truck with his arms crossed over his belly and his head bowed but must have glanced up just in time to see Pillsbury and Roy emerge from OPM. He straightened abruptly, almost snapping to attention, and once again Roy had to suppress a smile at the Chief's unique blend of fashion and decorum.

"Again, Senior Chief, I'm sorry you had to get this dumped on you the first day, but there never really is a good time for this kind of crap."

The two shook hands and Roy said, "They warned me it was 'more than a job' when I enlisted and they didn't lie," he said.

As it turned out, Bill Eikleberger was more than happy to drive Roy around the base. And as they pulled away from the OPM, Roy related the minimum possible information about why he had been called down.

"There was an American killed somewhere in the barrio last night," he said. "There might be some fallout effecting the NAVMAG and the Commander wants me to get up to speed and get a little more familiar with the Naval Station's layout also."

Bill decided to first take him through the shipyard and then down to the administrative building, COMNAVPHIL headquarters building and then NIS. Roy was running the morning briefing back through his memory and was more or less silent through the quick shipyard tour. Bill, uncomfortable with the lull in conversation, started talking about the next thing that came to his mind.

"I don't know as much about this base as I do about Cubi and the NAVMAG, but I know where the Chief's Club is. As a matter of fact, I think it's not far from Building 255, where we're going next." Bill hesitated a few seconds between each sentence in case Roy had wanted to interject anything or if he had any questions. Roy just looked out the window and Bill couldn't think of anything else to say.

"How long has my billet been gapped?" Roy said.

"Uh, lemme see... maybe a month or two?" Bill said, happy the silence had ended. "Maybe longer. Chambers – the guy that was here before you – retired unexpectedly and I guess they couldn't find anyone who wanted to come here. I can't imagine why, myself. You know my wife and I have saved a pretty good chunk of change since we got here. Chambers was married too, I think, but I never met his family or anything." Bill chattered as if dreading the quiet and Roy let him. Finally, they stopped in front of a two-story Admin building, one building removed from the water's edge.

"I thought we could go inside, and I'd point out a couple of offices," Bill said. "Most of the personnel support stuff is in here and a lot of admin stuff. Chaplain, Command Master Chief, things like that."

Roy hadn't told him who was murdered or her connection to Boggs because he knew the rumor mill would grind it down to Bill, and everyone else, eventually. Roy thought me might need to clarify things later, but for now his silence was frustrating Eikleberger, so Bill just kept talking.

The first floor of the building 255 was split in the middle by a large quarterdeck. The western end of the building was occupied by the offices of some tenant commands on the bottom floor, with the second-floor housing the offices of the Naval Station Commanding Officer, Executive Officer and Command Master Chief. The bottom floor of the eastern end contained the Subic NAVSTA personnel offices and the office of the Chaplain. The whole of the second floor in that wing held the headquarters of the Marine Corp contingent. Mostly, the building was referred to as just "admin."

A high counter guarded one corner of the quarterdeck and Roy saw a civilian and a second class petty officer sitting quietly behind it. Both seemed lost in their own thoughts and didn't acknowledge the two as they entered. They hadn't yet received an official notification of the death of their Divisions Officer, but the rumor mill was active and engaged. Roy glanced at the tenants list and noticed a listing for "Naval Security Group Detachment, Subic" to his right.

"What's up"? Bill must have noticed some hesitation on Roy's part as they looked around.

"Nothing important," Roy replied. "It's just that I was a CT in a previous life and was wondering if I knew anyone down there," nodding to the western end of the building.

The Admin offices were separated from the quarterdeck by double, glass doors which led into a rather small lobby area. There was considerably more activity in there than Bill would have expected for a Saturday morning.

"I guess murdering an American gets everyone riled up, doesn't it?" he said.

"Looks like," was all Roy would say.

There were glass double-doors leading out of the building opposite from the point where they entered and Bill pointed through them saying, "The other offices the XO wants you to see are in the CNP building over there."

Roy pushed through the doors and from the outside, building 229 looked almost identical to the one they just left.

Once at the Naval Investigative Services Office, the Duty Petty Officer checked their ID cards and asked them to wait while he notified Commander Pillotero. He returned quickly and asked Roy to follow him to the Commander's office, but Bill was asked, again, to wait in the lobby.

Pillotero was at his desk reading from an aluminum briefing folder but looked up when the duty Petty Officer wrapped his knuckles on the door jam.

"Senior Chief, take a seat. Petty Officer Higgins, close the door please."

Pillotero closed the folder and retrieved a plain manila folder from his top desk drawer. The rest of the office décor was typical of an officer-in-charge and Roy sat at the end of an over-stuffed sofa to the side of Pillotero's desk.

"This is a preliminary report from the OPM after they went through the Master Chief's house," Pillotero said. "I don't think you got to see this earlier. Let me know what you think."

The folder contained a three-page summary of the initial team's inspection of the premises, a copy of the murderer's letter and an envelope containing color polaroid pictures of the victim and the rest of the house. The summary contained a short synopsis of Boggs' initial statement and description of the scene. In it, he explained that his maid, Rosalita Tiangco, was visiting a sister in Leyte and was supposed to return on Saturday or Sunday. Roy glanced through it quickly and saw that an addendum had been paper-clipped at the back stating that Boggs' maid would be deposed when she returned.

Then he removed the snap shots from the envelope. He was struck with the relative serenity of the scene. There was no blood on the floor that he could see and little other evidence of the violence with which the murder had taken place. Lieutenant Jackson might have been taking a nap, for all the photos showed. The envelope left by the murderer was clearly visible on Jackson's lap and he could make out a symmetrical stain on her shorts. He quickly shuffled through a few more pictures before he came across a close-up shot of the fan-shaped blood stains. Pillotero was watching him closely and anticipated Roy's first question before he could voice it.

"I know we discussed the New People's Army involvement in this murder at the meeting, but do you know much about them?"

Roy responded that he had heard about the organization and read as much about them as he could find after receiving orders to the NAVMAG, but emphasized he was no expert.

"Well, this isn't their typical assassination MO and we have no reports of a similar one occurring like this," Pillotero said. "But while this could just be the work of a local nut job, it's most likely the work of the NPA." Roy seemed to remember that their typical assassination involved an execution-styled bullet to the head.

Roy looked through a few more pictures until he came across one of a cement slab, on which lay a door mat and a single, yellow glove. It was the type intended to protect the hands of anyone doing cleaning around the house. He turned it clockwise and viewed it from each angle before looking at the next picture. It showed the same items, but this wider perspective also showed that the slab was a porch in front of a narrow door. A note written on the white margin beneath the picture read, "outside kitchen door."

Roy quickly scanned the few remaining pictures and then put them back in the envelope. As he started to hand it back to the Commander, Pillotero said, "So, have you got it solved yet?"

"Sorry, Commander?" Roy asked, not sure where he was coming from.

"Just messing with you," he replied. "I know you're mainly concerned with NAVMAG security, but I am glad to have another set of eyes looking at this shit. Especially a set of eyes that haven't been looking at things here in the P.I. for very long."

"I was kind of wondering why Commander Pillsbury wanted me to drop by, but..." Roy rubbed the back of his neck and started to say more about what he might be able to help with but instead said, "I didn't see much blood in those pictures. I see very little on the floor, victim or the glove. I take it they are testing the glove?"

"Yes. The locals have most of the items of interest, we have the lieutenant's body for autopsy. And you're right, there wasn't much blood, but the on-sight guys found a couple wads of blood-stained tissue stashed behind the body. We're assuming it belongs only to the victim, but it will be checked. Since the killer had enough time for some clean-up, he – or she – was probably in no big hurry to leave. So, what do you think?"

"Not much, I'm afraid," Roy rubbed the back of his neck again. "I know that rebel groups have murdered others before but from what I heard about that manifesto this morning, this one seemed more personal." By this time, the rubbing of his neck was becoming a habit.

"I agree," the Commander said. "There is a copy of it in that package somewhere and it's not that long if you want to take a look at it."

Roy retrieved it and leaned back into the lush cushions of the sofa for a detailed reading of the killer's manifesto. Pillotero took the opportunity to finish reviewing his briefing folder. Both men read in silence until Roy quietly slipped the pages back into the manila folder.

He gazed with disinterest at the wall opposite him and then closed his eyes slowly. When he opened them again, he happened upon a faded color photograph of a small group of men standing before a dusty tent in some jungle clearing. As his focus cleared, he recognized a very much younger Pillotero, dressed in the familiar and ubiquitous olive drab fatigues worn by the thousands of troops who served in Viet Nam, smiling back at him. At the center of the five men posing there, a lone Vietnamese face registered an obviously less enthusiastic smile for the camera. He too was dressed in the casual attire of a soldier standing down between missions, but his weary features didn't reflect the joy of a man who had survived the last fight. His was the look of a man still engaged in fighting. His was the smile one found painted on a well-worn mask, but his eyes were those of a captive tiger looking for any opening through the bars of its cage.

"Do you mind if I ask where you served in 'Nam, Commander?"

"Not at all. It's a short list." He followed Roy's gaze to the picture, and he took on a slightly less official demeanor. "That was in early '72 at Ben Het Camp. I was a cherry grunt, still shitting bootcamp chow and thought I could win the war in a week or two. We started taking fire a few hours after that picture was snapped. The ARVN ranger in the middle took a round between the eyes and I got enough shrapnel for a free ride to Okinawa. We called that kid 'Ronnie,' although I don't think I ever heard what his real name was." He closed the briefing folder again and leaned back in his chair.

"I never really got back into the shit after that and finished my Army days cleaning latrines and buffing decks. I realized that I had never seen an officer doing either of those and I didn't see too many squids in the jungle. So, when I got back home, I enrolled in the University of Kansas and got into their Navy ROTC program. I keep that picture as a reminder of my exceedingly good luck and the incredible stupidity of youth."

"Good things to keep in mind, for sure," Roy said. He started to rub his neck again, but scratched the back of his head instead, saying, "I was just thinking, after reading that letter again, that whoever wrote it might be closer to the intended victim than your typical NPA operative might be. I happened to meet Master Chief Boggs on Gordon Avenue last night and he seemed to be, well, outgoing."

"I've worked with the Master Chief for quite a while now and I can tell you that 'outgoing' is an understatement," Pillotero said.

"I can't point to anything specifically, but that diatribe seems to have the feel of someone who really, really doesn't like Americans – especially really outgoing Americans – as opposed to someone who just has a political axe to grind. I don't know, maybe I'm not over my jet-lag yet."

Roy's stomach rumbled.

"Or, maybe I'm just hungry," Roy grinned. "There was one other thing in there that I thought was a little curious. There was a lot of talk in here about the Naval Magazine and some about Cubi Point, but I don't remember seeing anything about the Naval Station."

Pillotero reached out for the folder and Roy handed it over. He pulled out the letter and started to go over it again as well, reading through it quickly and then glancing back and forth between a couple of different pages.

"Well, you might still be jet-lagged and hungry, but I see your point. Curious."

Roy looked at his wristwatch and leaned forward in the comfortable sofa.

"You are right about my not having experienced the P.I. for very long. Maybe I ought to go out and look at it just a bit longer."

Pillotero smiled at that and said, "Maybe you should, Senior Chief." As he stood up from his desk, Pillotero nonchalantly twisted his hips to the left until Roy heard a quiet pop. It was a well-practiced move that seemed so automatic that he may have been doing it since his days in an Okinawa Army evac hospital.

He extended his hand to Roy and said, "Thanks for coming in Senior Chief. Try to enjoy the rest of your weekend and if there are any developments, I will notify you and Lieutenant Commander Pillsbury on Monday."

When Roy came out of Pillotero's office he saw Bill leafing through a week-old Navy Times. He had already been through the Stars and Stripes newspaper.

"Anything good in there?" Roy said.

"Looks like there might be tropical storm coming through," Bill said.

"Have you ridden out any Typhoons since you've been here?"

"We had a couple last year, I guess but there wasn't much to them. Everyone was told to batten down the hatches, but they were duds, I guess. They always try to make these things bigger than they are, you know?"

Roy didn't know that. In fact, Roy knew just the opposite. People almost always give too little thought to the massive destruction than can happen from good old mother earth. At least they do until it is too late. A hundred clichés and platitudes have addressed such short sightedness and they would no doubt proliferate once again, should something happen.

"Did you learn anything good in there," Bill said, nodding toward the back of the office?"

Roy wasn't going to be part of the main investigation. He wasn't going to be needed at the NAVMAG until Monday. However, he felt he needed to do something, even if that something was just hitting the town again to snoop around. For now, his stomach was grumbling at him about having missed breakfast and he believed Bill wouldn't mind joining him for a meal.

"Just that I think I'm ready for that lunch now," Roy said.

"Great!" Bill said. "Did I mention that I know where the CPO Club is?"

Chapter 16

Ben had been busy since waking, around 5:00 AM. Walking around the market on his normal morning routine was usually time well spent gathering intelligence. He didn't ask prying questions. He didn't take notes or do anything else which might be interpreted as unduly curious. Just his typical banter and exchange of social pleasantries usually yielded something he could use to his advantage. To a casual observer Ben was just another entrepreneur building networks, haggling over prices, buying and selling the things he thought would bring him the best return. A more studious observation would have revealed that most of the vendors with whom Ben spent his time, had a common connection to the base. Ernesto had a sister that worked at the shipyard. Maribel had business connections with the Navy Exchange. Esther had a brother who did gardening for the Public Works department on base. There were many, many more in his network and it was extensive because there was so much money to be made from dealing with the Americans. None of them suspected that Ben's motive was anything other than theirs. They could not have been more mistaken.

Ben loathed the idea of making money from these interlopers, these occupying forces. He felt that business connections were exactly the things which needed to be severed in order for the Philippines to rise to its full potential. His country was dependent on the crumbs which fell from the table of America, and he knew that those crumbs would always be tightly controlled in order to keep his country on the leash. He pitied some of those in his network but mostly he hated their complacency, and he hated their compliance with the status quo. He especially hated that most, if not all, of the people to whom he smiled so charmingly, would gladly give up their place in the Philippines to go to America. They would jump at the chance to pursue the American dream, while never once considering a Filipino dream.

His own Filipino dream included a change in government, and he was sworn to do whatever was needed in order to bring that about. The New People's Army, to which he had sworn allegiance, was the fighting unit of the Communist Party of the Philippines and he had been drafted early into both.

Benito de Guzman was born to a hard-working family in Olongapo some 35 years ago. They had owned two sari-sari stores on the east side of the city and lived in a modest apartment located between the two, also close to where Ben attended school. Without siblings, he was doted on by his mother and became a good student. No matter how much he studied though, he could never reconcile the disparity between the apparent wealth enjoyed by the Americans on the base and the growing awareness of his family's own relative poverty.

In his teens, Ben's mother died suddenly leaving he and his father to run the small business. That was when he discovered his mom had been the main business brain in the family. By the time Ben was done with schooling, his father had run both stores into the ground. His mother had left him little but an extensive network of contacts and Ben was able to keep their diminished family in their rented apartment by doing odd jobs and running errands for other businesses in his neighborhood. Before his father also passed away, Ben started his vending business and had become enmeshed in the politics which ushered him into adulthood.

When he still harbored dreams of going to college, Ben had learned all about Philippine history and especially reveled in the stories about José Rizal. He fantasized that both he and Rizal had descended from the same Chinese immigrant who had landed on the shores of Luzon generations before, although he had no basis for such a connection. Nonetheless, this imaginary affiliation had strengthened during his adolescence, and he became enamored of the communist movement within the country. He viewed himself as a future Filipino hero who would eventually be recognized as having picked up where Rizal left off a century earlier. Rizal had used his keen intelligence and rhetoric to spark the nationalistic pride of his people and rebuke the Spanish conquerors. Ben hoped to use intelligence gathering and espionage to rid the country of what he considered the current colonizers. He believed his country was far from being the free and independent nation he had been taught about in school. He viewed it now as being just another American outpost, rented from whatever corrupt, capitalist officials should happen to occupy Malacañang Palace. He, Ben de Guzman, would be server of their final eviction notice.

His network of information this morning was tingling, if not abuzz. Rumors had already begun circulating about a murder in Barrio Barreto and the versions he heard so far ran the gamut from Boggs being murdered to Boggs murdering a family of six. He was not surprised by the variety of stories, since the first rumors seldom produced accurate information, but he was excited to hear that someone had died. He hadn't yet spoken to Nestor and feared he might have left the American's bungalow before completing the mission. Now, at least, he had some hope that Boggs had returned home after leaving Ace's last night and met his fate at Nestor's hand. Nonetheless, he held his excitement in check for the time being. He needed confirmation.

It was too early for the bars to have customers he could exploit, but there were a few girls that he might speak to later in the morning. For now, he wandered through the marketplace, his familiar blue bag over his shoulder, buying and talking and feigning surprise and dismay at all the right times. Gradually, he worked his way back to Esther's table.

Esther Dimasalang sold sandals. She sold all kinds of sandals and she had lots of them, but she also had a brother and Ben was in no market for sandals.

Ester sat on a short wooden stool with her feet resting on its cross brace. Her long green skirt, faded by years of hand washing, covered her knees and hung to just above her ankles. She wore the cheapest version of the rubber flip-flops offered at her table. They had once been bright red but were now a shallow shade of pink. Completing her wardrobe was a white, button down, short-sleeved shirt, turned gray by at least as many washings as the dress. The shirt had been made for wear by a male, but Ben never noticed those kinds of fashion statements and didn't care. Before her was a three-by-five-foot folding table, covered completely by the sandals she hoped would be gone before the end of the day. Behind her were four more boxes holding additional sandals in the off chance she was successful.

Hoping to make a sale, her near-toothless grin broadened as Ben approached her table again. Her face crinkled into an asymmetrical map of tiny lines and her long gray hair, twisted tightly and tied into a bun on the top of her head, twitched. When she saw that Ben was in no buying mood, her hand came up from behind back holding a filter-less, smoldering cigarette and she took a drag. She didn't lose her smile as she puffed, and Ben could never remember a time seeing her without both a cigarette and a smile. Perhaps it wasn't always a smile that he saw, but rather an amused look, as if remembering a good joke. A joke on everyone but her.

"You've come back, my friend," she said. "Have you changed your mind about your feet?"

"No, no *ateh*. I just forgot to ask you about Nestor. Have you seen him lately?"

"He came home later than normal last night, but we didn't speak. And then, he was up very early for mass, so we still didn't talk." She shifted slightly on the stool and waved lazily at a persistent fly. "I think they work him too hard there!" She cackled as if her comment was the funniest thing ever and then settled quickly back into her enigmatic grin.

Ben wasn't sure if she was talking about the Americans or the Catholic church, but by now he was used to the woman's slightly off-center perspective of life, so he plowed through.

"I need to see him today, if I can. Will you let him know?"

"I will, I will." Never losing her smile. "Maybe you work him too hard too, hah?" There was no laughter this time, but the grin was steady.

Ben flashed a smile of his own as he thanked her and turned to go but did not address her remark. Not for the first time, he wondered how much Nestor told his sister about their mutual business agreement, but once again brushed off the idea. Her remark was indicative of her personality quirks and nothing more. He could wait until their scheduled meeting the next morning if he had to, but he really wanted to find out what had happened in the barrio sooner, rather than later.

Chapter 17

The refrigerated air of the Chief's Club welcomed Roy and Bill with a swoosh as they walked through the second set of double doors. The subdued lighting was also a welcomed change from the blazing sun outside, and as Roy's eyes continued to adjust, Bill strode confidently toward the restaurant section of the club.

The dining area was well separated from the bar, but it was easy to see that there were many more patrons there for lunch than were there for just drinking. Approximately twenty patrons were in various stages of their dining experience, but none seemed to be waiting to order. Like nearly every military facility which allowed dependents to live on them, this club had an excellent dining section with an extended menu and plenty of servers. As Bill looked around for a table toward the middle of the room, Roy noticed a white board mounted on an aluminum easel. The day's specials were advertised as being spaghetti with meat balls and sweet and sour pork, but only a smudge of grease pencil shown beneath the "Soup of the Day" heading. There might have been a hostess seating guests later in the day, but for now a short sign next to the easel asking the hungry to "Please Seat Yourself" was facing the entrance.

Roy looked around to see Bill waving him toward one of the square tables surrounded by four padded, metal chairs. There was already a young woman standing next to him holding a couple of menus and smiling brightly. She was one of four identically dressed servers currently on the floor and, for the time being, the only one who was not bustling around the room. As he moved toward them, Roy could see the other tables were pretty much split between small groups of sailors in uniform and couples. Two tables had been pulled together to accommodate a young family of six.

Piped in music from the sixties emanated quietly from some unseen speakers as the waitress passed out the lunch menus and took their drink orders. While she went off in search of their iced tea, Roy took the neatly folded linen napkin from the table and spread it on his lap. It was only then that the tantalizing smells from the kitchen hit him, and he realized how hungry he had become.

"This is a treat for me," Bill said. "I don't get down here often and when I do, I usually have the family along. Feli can't bitch about my diet if she can't see me." He smiled and started rearranging the soy sauce and hot sauce bottles to align with the salt and pepper shakers.

"How's the chow here," Roy asked.

"I've never had a bad meal," Bill replied. "But then, I guess I like just about everything. You may have noticed I'm not shy about food." He rubbed his belly and his smile faded to a slightly sadder shade. "But," he said as his smile brightened once more, "I'm not worrying about it today."

Neither talked much as they devoured their lunch. Bill had plowed through a double-bacon cheeseburger with ease and was just polishing off the last of his French fries. Roy had opted for the sweet and sour pork and was considering downing the little pile of remaining white rice as he reached for the pitcher of iced tea to refill his glass.

"Bill," Roy said. "My streak has begun. I've never had a bad meal here either, so far." He suppressed a small burp as he wiped his mouth and decided against the rice.

He was just settling back into his seat, when a voice from his left said, "Well, I'll be dipped in shit! What the fuck are you doing here?"

Roy looked around, thinking the slight southern drawl in the voice was familiar but certainly not addressing him. He saw a trim, tanned white man dressed in blue jeans, a green polo shirt and white Nike sneakers. He was in his mid-forties, but his once-black hair, now mostly gray, was cut in a "high and tight" fashion which made him look at least ten years older. He was wearing gold-toned, wire rimmed glasses which did not disguise his identity from Roy.

"I could ask you the same," Roy said. "Aren't you supposed to be dead"?

"Naw! It turns out her husband and I had more in common than just her."

Bill was absently dragging the last remnant of a French fry through ketchup as he tried to figure out what was happening.

Frank Burkholdt extended his hand as Roy got up to shake it and said, "I always wondered if you stayed in. Did you come back to the SECGRU or are you still doing Operation Golden Flow?"

"I haven't had to collect any urine samples for a while now," Roy said. "But I'm still a Master at Arms."

"And you haven't shrunk any either," Frank said, looking up. He was 5' 8" and felt that if he brought up height issues first, others would move on without commenting on it. He was usually right.

Putting his left hand on Frank's shoulder, Roy turned and said, "Bill, this is my sea daddy from my previous life as a CT, Frank Burkholdt. He took me to Waikiki for the first time and introduced me to my first big mistake."

"Hey, don't try to pin that shit on me, amigo! I just gave you a ride to that bar. No one told you to fall in love with the first hogger to grab your dick."

"Frank, this is Bill Eikleberger, my sponsor at the NAVMAG."

"Pleased to meet'cha," Bill said. He wiped his hands on his shorts before standing to extend one to Frank.

"We were just finishing up here, but do you want to sit and have a beer and tell a few lies? I haven't heard any really good bullshit in a long time." Roy said.

"Well, I was just heading out to the barrio, but I don't mind having another expensive one, especially if you're buying."

Their waitress was at the table before Frank could pull out his chair and Roy said, "Bill, you want a beer"?

"Better not," he replied. He looked like he wanted to say more but reached for the iced tea pitcher instead.

"Two San Magoo's," Frank told the waitress before Roy could.

"Put those on my bill," Roy said. "And both of these lunches, too."

The server smiled quickly and disappeared into the back of the room.

Before the beers were halfway gone, Bill had learned that Frank had been Roy's first Watch Section Supervisor at the Naval Communications Station at Wahiawa, Hawaii. Roy had been right out of "A" school and Frank had been a First Class Petty Officer. He also learned about the histories, locations, trials and tribulations of at least twenty people whom he did not know and would never meet. Although contributing nothing to the conversation, Bill was nonetheless fascinated with the network of people shared by the two old friends. Two things he never did learn at that table is what Frank and Roy did when they were in Hawaii, nor what Frank was currently doing.

By the time those beers were empty, Bill had also learned where both men had been stationed over the past fifteen or so years and a bit more about their personal lives. Roy spoke about his short-lived marriage and how it had led to his becoming a Master at Arms. He never mentioned Lisa Bartow. Frank spoke briefly about his first three wives in those intervening years as well as the one currently, according to Frank, "breaking his balls" from the comfort of their home in Sonoma, California.

"Anyway, I decided I would hang around long enough for one more shot at Senior Chief before I turn in my papers. June didn't want to come here so she is baby-sitting her grandkids in Napa and keeping the wineries in business," Frank said. "I'm staying at the Chief's barracks and saving a peso or two."

Roy relayed a short version of how he been sent to Keflavik and an even shorter version of what he had been doing in the last twenty-four hours. Again, Lisa wasn't mentioned and the only thing he related about the murder of Winifred Jackson was that "some shit went down in town last night which might effect security at the NAVMAG."

"Hey," Frank said. "Once you get settled in, come on down to the DET and I'll introduce you to our OIC. Did you ever meet an "I" brancher named Helms? He was mainly in the Atlantic but picked up LDO and was recently selected for Lieutenant Commander. He won't be here much longer."

"The name isn't familiar, but I really haven't heard much about anyone in the SECGRU lately."

Bill had been listening intently to the two reminisce but understood only part of what was being said. He knew that "OIC" meant Officer in Charge and he understood that "LDO" meant Limited Duty Officer but had no inkling that "SECGRU" was shorthand for the "Naval Security Group," that "DET" referred to the detachment where he currently served, or that the letter "I" represented the interpretive branch of those sailors within the Naval Security Group.

"So, what are you doing for the rest of the day," Frank asked.

Roy glanced over at Bill, who was checking his watch.

"I thought I would checkout some of the other places on Gordon and then turn in early again. This jet lag's a bitch."

Frank looked at Bill and said, "Why don't you guys come out to the barrio with me? I have plenty of room in the boat and I promise I'll have you back and tucked in before you can get into trouble." The "boat" was what he called his 1975 Chevy Impala.

"No thanks," Bill said, almost immediately. "In fact, I guess I need to get back home pretty soon."

Bill started to take out his wallet to leave a tip, but Roy waved him off. "Hey, I got it," Roy said. "Thanks for running me around. And I'm sure I'll need some more of it before I get settled."

Before making his goodbyes, Bill made sure that Roy still had his phone numbers. And even though he indicated that he might be able to go out with them sometime in the future, he didn't really seem that interested.

"So, I can drop you off on Gordon if you want, but I really think you would like Barrio Barretto better," Frank said. "And, besides that, I know of at least one girl who might let you buy her a drink... or an air-conditioned Honda."

"Yeah, well I'm not falling for that line again," Roy grinned. He liked the idea of spending a few hours drinking beer and catching up more with his old supervisor, but still felt a bit of apprehension in the pit of his stomach. He knew he would eventually move on from Lisa's death but for the time being, held on to his grief like a security blanket.

"Okay, I'll take your tour. Can you get me back to Gordon Avenue fairly early?"

"Have you already found a sweet thing?" Frank seemed genuinely surprised.

"No. Nothing like that, but I really only got to one place last night and I kind of wanted to see what else they had. Might even check out Magsaysay." But as soon as Frank had made the crack about a sweet thing, Luz came to him in a flash and once again a twinge of guilt pecked at his gut.

"I am not shitting you here," Frank bowed his head a bit to look sternly over the rim of his glasses. It was a gesture and phrase that Roy remembered well from his days on the receiving end of Frank's sea daddy lessons in Hawaii. What Roy found most peculiar about it was how Frank would employ the technique, whether explaining a highly technical intercept procedure or recounting the firmness and smoothness of a stripper's breasts.

"I heard about a DIRSUPer in San Miguel back in the day who was one of the first guys to keep his clearance because of compelling need," Frank continued. "It seems he was in a shorthanded Direct Support shop and had been rotating in and out of 'Nam on back-to-back-to-back trips in country, with hardly any liberty in between. He had just got back from one when they told him to pack his sea bag again and to be ready to go within 48 hours. So, he decided the only way to avoid it was to lose his clearance. He walked down to the crossroads and asked the first hooker he met to marry him and took her right on base to start the paper work."

Frank picked up his empty bottle and tilted it to see that no beer remained. "Short story long," he continued, "they told him, 'congratulations, we have a compelling need for you to go back, so see you in a couple of months.' Fucked himself big time."

"Nice story, but what's your point? I haven't had that kind of clearance in over a decade and there is no danger of being sent into a war zone." Roy glanced down at his own empty beer bottle and thought about ordering another.

"Not just a story, amigo. It's a fucking *loooove* story," Frank drew out "love" in comic fashion and batted his eyes. "Legend has it that they are still married and have five grand kids. Danger lurks for young lovers in the P.I."

Frank looked around for their waitress and made a gesture of writing on his hand when she saw him.

"Let's go find you someone to take your mind off of whoever broke your heart last," Frank said as the waitress started toward them. He didn't notice Roy tighten slightly at that last comment. "I, on the other hand, will find someone to take my mind off of my wife breaking my balls from the other side of the planet."

Frank started extolling the virtues of Barrio Barretto as soon as they left the club and by the time his dull yellow Impala had exited Kalaklan gate, Roy had already heard about seven or eight of Frank's favorite bars. Most of his praise was saved for "My Other Place," "Bad, Good and the Ugly," "Cutie's" and "Lucy's Hideaway." The criteria for making Frank's favorites list included the coldness of the beer, the number of girls employed at each place and the personal relationship he had cultivated with the owner/mama-san/manager of each establishment. The latter criterion was based partly on how many free drinks and/or discounted prostitution rates Frank was likely to receive because, of course, there was virtually no differences between the normal costs of beer or services.

Roy was not at all surprised to see that Frank was still cheap and lascivious. He had been married to his second wife when they worked together in Hawaii and was cheating on her then. He was honest about these flaws, but he wasn't necessarily ashamed of them. Frank had that enigmatic understanding of the opposite sex that other men envied, and he welded it skillfully like an invisible butterfly net in the hands of a master lepidopterist.

A large cemetery dominated the hillside to Roy's right as they drove the zigzag highway to the barrio and Subic Bay was a glistening, open expanse to their left. A few small bangkas were still visible on the water as their crew's cast fishing nets, but most had already returned to sell their catch.

A painted wooden sign announced the "Grass Hut" bar and grill coming up on their right and as Roy glanced up the hill to see the tall, thatched roof of the establishment, Frank casually said, "So, did you know that a lieutenant was murdered out here last night." The comment caught Roy off guard because he hadn't mentioned the murder, much less the victim.

"I stopped into the shop to look over the message board this morning and heard about it," he said. "It sure doesn't take long for shit to spread." Roy didn't say anything right away, so Frank continued, "I didn't see the actual CASREP, but the "O" brancher on duty had already heard about it from the mid-watch. I guess those guys can't talk about all the top-secret communications they process, so they kind of gossip about the confidential crap. At any rate, it sounds like a really fucked up deal."

"Pretty fucked up," Roy agreed.

"Master Chief Boggs is a great guy, and that lieutenant was sharp as a tack. Sounds to me like the fucking Huks are up to their old tricks." He was referring the *Hukbalahap* forces which had originally formed as a peasant insurgency against occupying Japanese troops during the second world war. After the war, they continued to fight against the Philippine government and were considered to be aligned with communist ideology. They had actually dissolved around the middle of the 1950s, but reports persisted of individuals who identified with the defunct group continuing to harass the population into the 1960s.

"The last I heard," Roy said, "they weren't interested in fucking with Americans so much. Maybe the NPA doesn't have such qualms about fucking with us though."

"Maybe not," Frank said.

Frank slowed the Impala down a little to navigate around a couple of Jeepneys which had stopped on the side of the road and kept his speed down as the pedestrian traffic seemed to increase. They were also just passing the Philippine Constabulary station, which was never a good place to press one's luck.

"First stop: the 'BGU'." Frank angled the Chevy onto the dirt parking lot of the Bad, Good and Ugly bar and shut off the engine. There were already four vehicles parked in front of the place and Roy could hear the juke box playing within.

"You're gonna like this place," he said. "It's owned by an American who also works on base. He's got cold beer and his girls are clean and friendly... and you don't have to worry about getting ripped off."

Chapter 18

Ben waited until Luz hung the wet bar towel under the counter and took a drink from her Pepsi and then said, "So that new guy in here last night, that Thompson… is he married?"

"He said no, but… you know," she left the rest unsaid. Roy would not have been the first American to lie about marital status. She had no reason other than experience to suspect he was lying about it, but she nonetheless believed he was being truthful.

"You know, I have said before that you need to find a steady. A guy like that seems like he might be mature enough for you and I know how important that is."

"Well, maybe. But he might be so mature he isn't interested in me," she said.

"He's an American and you are a pretty, young Filipina. Unless he is a Benny Boy, he is interested. I saw him look at you and I don't think he is a Benny Boy."

Luz felt the slightest of flushes rise in her cheeks, perhaps because she was not used to having this type of conversation with Ben. Or, it might have been because she was also already interested in Roy.

"Plus, he is new here and you could help him settle in, maybe. If nothing else, you could find out if he is a *paruparo*," he said.

"I don't think he is like a butterfly, but that will become obvious pretty quickly," she said, already warming to the idea. "Maybe if he comes back tonight, I can… well…" her words faded out as her thoughts became clearer. She had not allowed herself to even think about having that type of relationship in a long time and the fact her mind went to that place so freely, was more than a little frightening, especially since they had just met. She chided herself for thinking like a schoolgirl and quickly defaulted to her comic-belligerent mode.

"I think I might marry him tonight," she said. "And if he's a bum fuck, I'll divorce him in the morning."

Ben smiled but did not react with the laugh Luz expected. "Have you ever had a boyfriend who was stationed where he is?" Ben knew that Luz had never had a "steady boyfriend" or "long-term repeat customer" since coming to Olongapo, but she had gone out with Americans on occasion. He preferred the term boyfriend, instead of the more accurate "long-term repeat customer," mainly because he detested so much all of the economic entanglements the U.S. had with the Philippines and Filipinos. It was a silly distinction, but one that was important to him for some reason.

"Never," she replied. She was sobered by the fact that the idea took on an attraction she did not expect.

"It doesn't really matter, I guess. I just thought if you had, you might be able to judge what kind of person that place attracts." Ben did not want to overplay his hand, but he also didn't want her to forget the idea that Thompson might be worth her time.

"What ever happened with that guy from Clark Air Force Base?" Ben asked. "Didn't you like him?"

"He was *bastós*," Luz crinkled her nose at the mention of that particular customer. "And he is also *karipot*." She turned to the beer cooler when she saw Amie coming with two empty bottles and some pesos.

Ben had eavesdropped on the American in question one day while they were both at Sunny's Bar and already knew he was married. He also knew that she had gone overnight with him at least once and would have been smart enough to pick up on the clues. Even if she hadn't figured out his marital status, she wouldn't like him. It wasn't that she had any particular qualms about sleeping with a married man, but she did not like liars, and she had a highly refined bullshit detector.

Luz made change for Amie and then put the two empty bottles into a waiting case.

"Well," Ben went on, "Maybe Scott can help that Thompson guy find the right Filipina. But hopefully, not until after you have divorced him."

Luz shot a puzzled look at Ben and then grinned as she remembered her own earlier joke. She started to make another comment but stopped when Scott entered the bar.

Scott walked into Ace's to find a few familiar American faces drinking beer and Ben talking quietly to Luz at the bar. Luz glanced quickly up at Scott and then returned her gaze to Ben who had suddenly gone silent. Scott walked quietly to the bar and lifted himself up onto a stool. His demeanor was uncharacteristic but understandable to Luz, who knew he had been trying to find out more about the possible murder.

"Hey, Ben. Hey, Luz," Scott said, leaning his elbows on the bar.

He was looking vacantly at the silent air conditioner, when Luz said,

"You want beer?"

"Oh, sure," he said and then looked at the Ben's blue bag sitting on the floor. "What's the balance on that wallet, Ben?" There was no hint of a fake accent. No witty repartee. No rhyming sentences. His voice carried just the faint Oklahoma drawl that sometimes crept back in when he wasn't guarding against it.

"Fifty pesos, my friend, but I can wait to Monday if you need." Ben's voice was in salesman mode as he asked, "What you think? Your dad like, yeah?"

"Oh sure, it's fine. He'll be impressed." Scott removed his own wallet and dug a few bills out for Ben and another for Luz.

Luz sat the cold bottle on a cardboard coaster and felt a strange sensation of embarrassment, as if she were trapped in an awkward encounter between rival salesmen. When either of these men were around, the conversations were usually boisterous and inane. Now it seemed as if Scott were carrying the burdensome secrets of the universe and Ben was waiting to be enlightened about them, perhaps anticipating some important information to come forth. Maybe Ben had already heard something about the murder and thought Scott knew more details.

Luz had seen Ben slip into this character from time to time, but as she thought about it, she realized that usually occurred when two or more Americans were talking. He would fade into the background and listen intently without interruption. She had always assumed it was part of his sales model to find out what his potential customers might want and to wait for an opportune time to make a pitch. Now, after the conversation that she and Ben was having when Scott came in, she wasn't so sure. That feeling of embarrassment she had felt earlier was now turning into something else. She couldn't put her finger on it, but it was uncomfortable and unpleasant and had a lingering air of deceit.

What Scott was contemplating had nothing to do with the mysteries of the universe but were true mysteries to be sure. He didn't hear anything official about the possible murder while at his office, but he did find out from the Duty Petty Officer that the XO had been called to a high-level meeting at OPM. Additionally, the DPO had to call Chief Eikleberger to find Senior Chief Thompson and take him to the same meeting.

"Scott, did you find out anything about last night?" Luz asked in an attempt to clear the discomfort she was feeling.

"Uh, not much," he said. "But something big definitely went down."

Ben made a show of picking up his bag and noisily shuffling through his goods.

"I've got to go," Ben said while scratching his head. He was hoping to impart the impression that he needed to restock his satchel, but actually felt a renewed urgency in his need to speak to Nestor. In Tagalog, he said to Luz, "Think about what I said, okay?" Then to both, he said, "*Mamaya*, hah?" Luz watched him until he was through the door, still thinking about what he had suggested before Scott's entrance.

Meanwhile, Scott was still mulling the issue of an American death.

"Whoever did it was probably after the Master Chief," he said. And in an even lower voice, "Maybe a sparrow attack."

Luz's attention snapped back to the present. She had heard of the infamous assassin squads associated with rebellious groups but like many people, thought it was only a problem for others, perhaps in the most southern provinces of Mindanao or the highlands of Luzon. And, like humans everywhere, her distance from a problem was directly related to the level of concern she was likely to have with it. If there actually had been an American murdered around the Subic area, it was now in her own yard.

Both remained quiet for several minutes, a spell broken only by Lita retrieving two beers for a couple of sailors. Eventually, tired of the silence and wanting to change the subject, Scott asked, "So, did Senior Chief Thompson make it in here last night?"

"*Oo*, I told you that last night when you asked."

"That's right, that's right, sorry! I'm just having a brain fart. So, are you going to take him home tonight?"

"I don't know. He might..." Then, in anticipation of their normal repartee, she continued, "Maybe I will, because he was too tired last night, but when he takes me, I will get air-conditioned jeepney. He said I was the biggest *magandang babae dito* and he might even take me to the exchange!"

"He said you were the *biggest* beautiful girl in Ace's?" he said with raised eye brows. "You mean the "mostest?""

"You know what I am meaning," Luz replied. "The 'most'."

Scott was starting to get on her nerves with his constant ribbing and it showed in her response because Scott said, "Okay, okay. I know you know."

Before they could enter into another contemplative silence, Luz said, "Can I have peso for the jukebox?"

"Sure."

As the sound of golden oldies started to fill the bar, a different type of silence came between them. Scott's mind careened from what might happen at work, to what might happen with Judy, to what might happen off base, to what might happen to U.S. and Philippine relations. That last item was not a topic that Scott was used to devoting much brain power to and it unnerved him that it even appeared among the jumbled mix of his thoughts. He took another sip of beer and sighed audibly.

Luz busied herself rearranging beer bottles in the refrigerator and hummed along with the music. However, she was also struggling to manage her own thoughts and the questions which started to arise around the whole scene unfolding from the barrio. Perhaps one of the most troubling of these questions had to do with a possible connection between Roy Thompson, Ben De Guzman and whatever happened in Barretto. There had been no inkling of any connection between those things until something that Scott had just said. After that, the fuzzy edges of the different stories began to slowly intertwine.

Chapter 19

The pungent odor of *bagoong* pricked Roy's nostrils as they walked through the front door of the Bad, Good and Ugly Bar and he could hear the clicking of billiard balls over the relatively quiet juke box. The powerful shrimp paste was ubiquitous, but Roy didn't think he would ever get used the smell.

The entrance was to the right of the building and a long counter, accommodating eight rattan barstools, faced the door and the street. A dark young male of fifteen or so, with frizzy hair, looked up and smiled broadly as they came in.

"Mister Frank!" he said. "You want beer?" Frank's name sounded like "Pronk," coming from the young bar tender, but the amusing accent didn't seem to faze him.

"Larry, set us up with two." Frank moved to the far right of the counter and moved a barstool around so he could face the door when he sat.

"Where's the pisser?" Roy said, noting there was no doors close to the end of the bar where they were sitting.

Frank pointed to the large area taking up the entirety of the north end of the building and said, "just to the right of that far pool table. Follow the signs."

Roy didn't spend a lot of time looking over the place, but he did notice that both pool tables were occupied. Two Americans in their twenties looked quite serious as they surveyed the newly busted rack of balls on the table closest to the street, while the table closest to the restrooms was being systematically cleared by a youngish looking Filipina dressed in cut-off Levi's and a flimsy halter top. A middle-aged white man with a short, gray ponytail and holding a half empty beer, leaned against the wall and watched while the young woman glided around the green felt, plinking solid ball after solid ball into the leather pockets.

"Bitch is kicking my ass," he said as Roy approached.

The woman never stopped stalking her targets as she said matter-of-factly, "you like."

"Yeah, okay. You got me," he replied, smiling at Roy.

Roy grinned back but did not slow his pace in search of the head. He glanced up at the "Restrooms" sign above the door near to where the man was leaning and entered. He found a scene not unlike the facilities he had used at Ace's Place the night before. Before him lay a short hallway leading farther into the back, divided by several unmarked doors and on his right were two doors labeled "Hers" and "His". However, he was pleasantly surprised to find the restroom was better appointed than the one on Gordon Avenue and that this one actually sported a light switch, a toilet seat and the appropriate paper products.

Coming back into the pool room, Roy once again was hit by the sour smell of some local delicacy and noticed that three girls were eating at a table between the restrooms and the bar area. They were all in their late twenties or early thirties and were dressed casually. A pot of rice sat in the middle of the round table and a steaming bowl of some sort of vegetable dish was next to it. Each of the girls had a pink, plastic plate in front of them, piled with rice and vegetables and none were distracted by his presence as they ate their lunch.

Ponytail and the pool shark were about to start another game of eight-ball as he was racking the balls and she was chalking her cue. The two on the other table appeared to be fighting the same battle he had seen going in and seemed just as serious as before. Jalousie windows lined the northern and western walls of the pool room and the jukebox sat against a solid part of the western wall between them and the front entrance. The kid who had gotten their beers was leaning on it, looking for some tunes to play.

Frank had already drunk about half of his beer when Roy sidled up on his own barstool.

"So, what are you doing here?" Roy asked. "COMSEC? Direct support?"

"We have those missions here, but I'm just kind of babysitting the ops." He took another deep drink and said, "We have a good crew and I just kind of coordinate the tasking. Kind of boring." Switching gears quickly, he interjected, "You know that lieutenant was killed just down the road from here, right?"

Roy had forgotten about Frank's tendency to hop around different topics but hesitated only momentarily before replying. He pulled from his own beer and said, "No, but I knew it was out here somewhere. Do you know them well? Boggs and Jackson?"

"Fairly well. They both lived out here and it's a small place. They were pretty careful not to be seen together out here much, but it was an open secret that they were hooking up."

One of the girls who had been eating walked up and put her right arm around Frank's neck, pulling his ear down to her mouth and resting her left hand on his crotch. Instead of whispering to him, as Roy at first suspected she might, she licked Frank's ear lobe and blew gently into his ear.

"Pronk," she whined. "I love you no shit. You play jukebox."

"Larry just stoked it, Josie."

"Pronk! Play jukebox!"

Frank's left hand had cupped her left butt cheek by that time, and he squeezed it firmly. "Hit up Roy, here," he said. "He's a soft touch and a cherry-boy."

Josie let loose of Frank and latched onto Roy in one fluid motion, but instead of grabbing his crotch, she merely rubbed his shoulder and knee while leaning against his side.

"Roy, I love you no shit. Play jukebox?"

Her breath was warm and still smelled of the bitter melon and shrimp sauce that had been her lunch. Somehow it wasn't so offensive, accompanied as it was by the soft warmth of her lean body. At this proximity Roy could see soft crinkles around her eyes and mouth that he imagined were more related to a lifetime of laughing than the passing of years. After collecting a peso from Roy, Josie shuffled to the jukebox in quick, short steps, dragging her flip-flops along the painted cement floor.

"Cutie," Roy said.

"Hey! Don't fall in love just yet… you haven't even finished your first beer. Besides, she will chew you up and spit you out. She may look sweet and innocent, but she can suck your bladder right out through your pee hole."

"Charming. I should start writing mom right now with the good news of our pending nuptials."

Frank barked a quick laugh and held up his empty bottle in the direction of Larry who turned immediately to the beer cooler. Roy thought for just a moment about draining his own beer, so as to keep up with Frank, but quickly decided against it. As far as partying went, he had been out of practice for some time and expected a long night ahead. Nonetheless, Larry sat a cold beer in front of him on his way to deliver Frank's.

"Drink it, or wear it, Royboy," Frank said with a smile.

"Shit! I haven't been called that in a while."

"Get me a beer!" came a voice from the pool room. A cadaver dressed in a gray tee shirt and khaki shorts had emerged from the back of the bar and made his way toward the counter. A Filipina walked behind him, adjusting her bra strap and talking to the ladies still eating their lunch. She sat at the table and began to dish up her own lunch while the ancient looking American continued to the front. No one else seemed at all put off by the vision of a walking corpse demanding beer, so Roy returned to his own without comment.

"Roy, meet Marv Turnbull. Marv, this is Roy Thompson," Frank said. "Royboy here used to work for me at EastPac before he got religion and joined the GENSER Navy. He's an MA at the NAVMAG now." And then to Roy, "Marv is a retired matman, but I don't hold it against him, generally."

Roy had known several cryptologic maintenance technicians from his early days in the SECGRU, but couldn't imagine any of them being old enough to have served with Turnbull.

Marv shook his hand before settling into the bar stool next to Roy. "You have my condolences, if you had to work for this prick," Marv nodded toward Frank as he spoke. "Nice to meet you."

"Same. Could be worse though," Roy replied. "I could still work for him."

"Bite me. The both of ya."

Frank leaned forward as Marv was reaching for his beer. "Did you hear that Winnie was killed last night?"

Marv hesitated for just a fraction of a second and then his jaw dropped, "Get the fuck out! What happened?"

"Evidently, someone murdered her at Denny's place before he got home," Frank kept his voice low. "Roy here probably knows more."

Marv froze with his hand still reaching for the cold beer, his mind reviewing his interception of Denny last night and their subsequent bullshit session. When his fingers finally reached the bottle, they grasped it tightly, more for an anchor than for a thirst quencher.

"That's some fucked up shit, right there," was all he could think to say. "Fucked. Up."

"Before anyone gets too excited, I am not part of the investigation, but I couldn't really say more than what Frank has already told anyway." Roy drank the rest of his first beer and reached for the next bottle. "But I can say that Master Chief Boggs isn't a suspect."

"And that doesn't need to be said, certainly not for anyone here," Marv said. "He was with me – right at this very bar – until about 8:00 last night. Can you say how it happened?"

"Well, no, but like Frank said, her body was found in his house and that is about all I'm comfortable talking about now," Roy replied.

"Super fucked up," Frank echoed the prevailing opinion.

The three sat without talking for a few moments, sipping from their bottles, until Marv finally sighed heavily and downed the rest of his beer. "I need to get home and get cleaned up. I have to let Minda know and then get on base and see if I can talk to Dennis. I'm sure they made him leave home and is on some kind of legal hold, but I still know enough people there who can steer me to his location."

"I didn't see him, but he's probably in the Chief's barracks," Frank spoke without giving Roy a chance to weigh whether or not to answer. Roy lifted his bottle silently to eye level and then took a swig, as if to support the assertion.

"Marv, you might want to clean up a bit more here before you go home. You've got Lola's fuck-smell all over you and I'm sure Minda doesn't want to know what you've been up to."

Marv drew himself up from the barstool and assumed an air of indignation. "You wound me, sir! You wound me!"

"Uh huh, well, suit yourself," Frank said before downing the rest of his own beer.

"I...," Marv lifted one arm and started to make another melodramatic comment about his innocence. But instead, perhaps remembering the gravity of the news he had just received, he pushed in the barstool and said, "She doesn't much care anymore, I don't think. But, if I wake up dead one of these days, I'll know I was wrong. Roy, am I correct in assuming you just got to our illustrious island?"

"That's right, got here yesterday," he said.

"I'd say that is a pretty fucked up welcome aboard, but I'm sure you know that already. Gentleman." He slapped a twenty peso note onto the bar counter and yelled at Larry to, "Get these yahoos another beer, Nathan." His walk to the car was not as spry as his emergence from the back of the bar had been, but he still seemed to have purpose.

"I thought this kid's name was Larry," Roy said.

"That's what I call him. He reminds me of one of the Three Stooges," Frank smiled at Nathan/Larry as the beers were delivered. It appeared that their bartender didn't care what he was called. "Let's finish these off and get down the road a bit."

*   *   *

The sound of a muted trumpet played slowly was the saddest, most lonely sound that he could imagine. Every time he heard it, he envisioned black and white scenes of deserted city streets, yesterday's newspaper blowing in a blustery breeze, windows shuttered against the cold and heartless world. He couldn't remember how he had come to such a correlation, how he had come to associate that haunting sound with that haunted vision of aloneness. Perhaps it was a snippet of a long-forgotten movie or even a music video but regardless of its origins, the image materialized like a ghost ship from a fog when that music played. However, this time it competed with the horrific memory of his lover, lifeless, propped in the corner of a stark room like an unwanted carnival doll.

The hours between when he had returned home till now were a muddy blur. After the initial shock of discovering Winnie's body, he first called the Command Duty Officer and then the home number of his Commanding Officer. Knowing that the CDO would notify Philippine authorities, he relayed who he was, what he had found and where he lived.

The conversation with his CO had been much more detailed and painful. They had a close relationship and the CO had even given the affair tacit approval, with the stipulation that it remain low-keyed and confidential. Along with the considerable power Commanding Officers had, they also had significant flexibility in how they administered their commands. They were all adults and aware of the consequences, but no one had imagined this contingency.

It seemed most of his night and all of his Saturday morning had been spent answering countless questions from Filipino and American investigators. He had been assigned this room in the Chief's quarters late Friday night, but he couldn't swear he had slept at all.

The portable CD player, along with a few CDs, were among the limited items he was allowed to take from his house. Dennis switched the playback mode to "shuffle" so that Davis' incredible combo might shift from "Blue in Green" to "So What" to "All Blues." As he sat in the room, alternately staring at the blank stationary before him and the music player's speakers, he struggled to put together any thoughts which might help him make sense of what had happened the night before. He was trying to describe the loss he had suffered to his ex-wife, who was still his best friend and who had known about Winnie since the beginning, but no words would come to him. Miles Davis played on the stereo, a small refrigerator hummed in the background and his mind could not move past the image of Winnie dead in his spare bedroom.

Finally, a small word formed and grew in intensity: fuck, FUCK, **FUCK**! He was generally friendly and gregarious, but today he was angry, sad and fearful and those powerful, base emotions would allow no other words to pass into the critical thinking chambers of his brain. He knew at some level that his life would eventually return to a semblance of normalcy, but for now it endured a raw, painful itch that he could not scratch. He wanted to scream but would not.

Although undeniably beyond suspicion for Winnie's death, he might still be looking at USMJ charges for fraternization, regardless of his relationship with the CO. He also already considered himself to be on a Philippine legal hold, but none of those things meant anything to him at this moment. For now, there was only this incredible pain and the nascent seed of retaliation. Somehow, someway, some vengeance.

Chapter 20

Scott remained distracted with his thoughts as he sipped absently at his beer. Eventually, he sighed heavily and slipped off the barstool, uncharacteristically leaving a half-full beer bottle on the counter.

"I'm heading home to get ready for Judy next week," he said. "See you later." His solemnity, while completely understandable to Luz, was nonetheless disturbing.

"Oh," Scott said, pushing the barstool back up to the bar, "There's a storm coming in… might be here tonight, so be sure to bring your undies in off the line."

"*Ano?*" she said.

"Never mind. Just an expression I remember from home. *Mamaya.*"

As he left the bar, a shudder went through Luz. There had been too many quakes shaking her world in the last twenty-four hours, and she felt unsettled. Some were major jolts, and some were mere tremors, but the fact that they were rippling across the lives of several people within her circle was not lost on her. The realization of that connection crept into her consciousness, pushing and pulling at the identity she had assumed over the years.

Luz had grappled with that identity since arriving in Olongapo, even if the struggle went largely unacknowledged in her usual day-to-day battle for survival. For all her early life, she had only her grandmother and sister and never really felt connected to anyone else. They were the only family she had ever known and when she first arrived in Olongapo they were both gone.

The other garbage dwellers had constituted a type of family, but *Impó* never really trusted anyone after discovering the bodies of Luz's parents. Luz and Emmy had been mostly protected from any personal interaction outside of their own little family and discouraged from forming closer ties with anyone else. It was a formative experience for Luz. Perhaps Emmy's slightly greater experience in the outside world had created the hunger for some belonging outside of their trio but Luz was more comfortable with practical, even shallow relationships. She didn't mind being around other people and, occasionally, even enjoyed the interactions she had with them, but she never felt compelled to connect on any deeper, more meaningful manner. Other events, which happened within the first year of her arrival in Olongapo, had made deep personal connections with others even more difficult to imagine. That kind of aloofness had served her well, until now.

A detachment from strong social ties freed her from the tyranny of peer pressure and allowed her the time to learn even more about the world in which she lived. The importance of things she learned was not immediately evident, but a good memory and agile intellect ensured that what could be useful, would be useful, at the right time.

However, from the very first time she stepped into the restaurant in which she and Ben had first met, the urge to connect more intimately with other began to grow. She started to like being associated with others she admired. The seed of a group identity outside her sister and grandmother had germinated. Gradually she began to see others as being important to her, whether or not they shared business or work ties. Perhaps more importantly, she began to see herself as a true friend to others. The process of existing in a world where one cared for others, and where those others cared for her, continued to gain importance in her life. In short, the concept of being a part of her community grew on her.

Certainly, the negative aspects of that connectedness also became a part of her life. At this moment she felt both hopelessly enmeshed in the drama swirling around Dennis Boggs and almost as desperately alone as when she discovered the cold body of her grandmother. That history of tenuous and fragile social life reached a crossroads in Ace's Place. This turmoil was the catalyst for her current emotional instability.

*   *   *

"The Mabuhay Restaurant" was her only clue to Emmy's location. A friend of *ateh* Mari had told Luz and her grandmother that was the name of the restaurant which promised employment for Emmy and Minda when they left Manila. Fortunately, it wasn't far from the victory Liner station and the tricycle driver charged Luz only a few precious centavos for the short ride. Standing there now, her canvas bag clutched tightly to her breast, Luz read and re-read the hand painted sign above the entrance. She was finally here! It had seemed an eternity since she last saw her sister and now Luz found herself almost too afraid to enter.

Business for the evening meal had begun to pick up and Luz became an obstruction to hungry patrons. She stepped away from the door while

132

trying to recall how she had planned this reunification. Still slightly confused by the novelty of her situation, she finally forced herself to walk into the restaurant behind an American serviceman and a young Filipina. As that couple was led to their seats by the hostess, Luz stepped aside so as not to block the coming and going of other customers.

The hostess, who appeared only slightly older than Luz, returned to the door and came to an abrupt halt. She looked Luz up and down, noticeably wincing when she saw her sunken and withered left eye socket. Finally, she asked, "Can I help you?"

"I'm, uh, I'm looking for my sister. Her name is Emmy Ballesteros. She came here a little over a year ago in May. She is supposed to work here." The words came out in a rush and carried only a pinch of the desperation which filled Luz's heart.

"I don't know her, but I've been here only a few months," the hostess said. "Maybe *ateh* Lucinda can help you. She has been the manager here for a long time, I think. Please wait here."

Luz gaped unapologetically at the fancy wood carvings and colorful pictures decorating the walls of the restaurant as the young girl walked to the kitchen. Five of the dozen or so tables were currently occupied but most would be full by the time Luz was done speaking with the manager. She was aware that some music was playing in the background somewhere, but it was soft and indistinguishable, just another unseen pretty picture. Four ceiling fans whirled lazily over the heads of the growing crowd and stirred the tantalizing aromas coming from the kitchen with the sparse refrigerated air which also emanated from the back of the restaurant. Roasted pork, pineapple, fried rice and a hundred other unrecognized fragrances passed through her nostrils and stabbed her empty stomach like a rogue serving fork. The mango that Luz had eaten while waiting for the bus to leave Manila was a faded memory and the smells swirling around brought her hunger front and center.

The whole experience was an assault on her senses. This was a fantasy palace ballroom from some long-ago story related by her grandmother. It was the finest room she had ever seen, and she wanted never to leave. She envied her sister for having experienced such grandeur for over a year and closed her eyes, imagining the adventures which Emmy must have experienced.

When she opened her eyes, Luz saw a tall, graceful woman walking towards her. She was wearing an amused smile on her lightly complexioned face which seemed to complement her long, Chinese inspired gown.

"You must be Luz," she said. "You look so much like Emmy when she came to me! Please, please come where we can talk."

Luz lit up with the mentioning of her sister's name. The fact that this elegant woman, of such obvious importance, knew her name and that of her sister, lifted her to new heights. Her hope had been rewarded.

Placing her hand lightly on Luz's back, Lucinda ushered the young girl toward the kitchen, automatically surveyed the customer's tables as she went. It was only then, walking through the splendor, passing by well-dressed customers capable of buying any meal on the menu, that Luz remembered her own poverty. She had washed herself as best she could before finding her dead grandmother and she had donned her best dress before leaving Yollie's shanty. Now she was being led through this nearly unimaginable opulence like a carabao through Malacañang Palace. It withered her initial joy.

She glanced down at that faded, blue frock, the battered, recycled canvas bag and the simple rubber thongs on her feet. The joy of reuniting with her sister, mixed with the immense pain of her grandmother's recent death, were intensified by a sudden and overwhelming sense of her own insignificance. She felt as if she were shrinking smaller and smaller with each step towards the kitchen. By the time she had walked through the swinging doors, past the huge pots of steaming food and into the small office near the back of the kitchen, Luz was sapped. When she slumped into a simple chair beside a cluttered desk, she was convinced further movement was beyond her. She clung to her canvas bag as if it were the only coconut tree keeping her from being swept away by a tsunami. She began to cry.

Lucinda closed the door and once more touched Luz's shoulder. "Dear child! There is no need to cry. Here, let me get you something to eat. You must be famished!" Lucinda opened the door just enough to call to someone in the kitchen to bring pork adobo, rice and papaya juice and then closed the door again.

"Now, child, how can I help you?" Lucinda sat in the desk chair and pushed it as far away from the desk as room allowed. She wore a tight smile, but her eyes were sharp and alert, scanning the whole of Luz's face. As the tears began to subside, she leaned forward and rested her hands in her lap, her fingers intertwined.

"I, I'm just looking to find my sister," Luz said. She wiped away tears with one hand and then used the back of her other hand to smear a clear string of snot across her upper lip. "Our grandmother died last night and, and... and I haven't seen Emmy in over a year, and I had no other place to go and I just want to, I just want my sister." Her breath hitched as she stifled another sob.

Interrupted Weekend

There was a quiet knock at the door and then it opened slowly. Had she looked around, Luz would have seen a gray-haired man, dressed in the stained, white uniform ubiquitous in kitchens the world over, backing into the room with a small tray. When he turned, Lucinda removed some catalogs and large envelopes from a corner of the desk to make room for Luz's meal.

The strong aroma of vinegar and soy sauce dried the remainder of Luz's tears as she turned to see the feast before her. The tray held an oblong plastic plate piled with food, a small glass of juice and simple metal spoon, wrapped in a paper napkin. The plate's red Chinese designs were hidden by a generous portion of boiled white rice flanked with pork adobo on one end and a vegetable dish on the other. Lucinda looked up at the old man who merely shrugged his shoulders and said, "there was a little *pinakbet* left over." He shot a quick grin at the puzzled young girl and then was gone.

Luz seemed stunned by the amount of food. She blinked at it and then looked into the gleaming eyes of this new woman in her life.

"Go ahead and eat as much as you want," Lucinda said. "That's right, turn your chair around." Lucinda reached across the desk and unwrapped the spoon for Luz. "Do you know how to use this?"

Luz nodded her head silently and began to scoot around in the chair. Lucinda went once more to the door and called out to the kind, old man again. "Arturo!" she said. "Find Ben de Guzman for me. I have something for him to do."

Chapter 21

Ben regretted the clumsy departure from Ace's Place but felt he needed to get out quickly. He didn't like the glitches which had developed in his plan. What he liked was control and he wasn't feeling much of that lately. What he needed most right now was to talk to Nestor and decided that he would go once more to the marketplace to talk to Esther. If he had to, he could wait until their scheduled rendezvous on Sunday, but he didn't want to.

Feelings of uneasiness had been building since seeing Boggs in Ace's Place last night. Throughout the day, those feelings got stronger, manifesting an almost physical presence in his brain and body. They seemed to be separating from his own identity, forming a different entity. Ben had questions, but those *other* feelings were starting to gain an independent voice and Ben feared that they too, would begin asking questions of him.

The actual events that transpired in the barrio were still unclear to Ben, but based on everything he had heard so far, the most likely outcome was that Nestor had killed Boggs' girlfriend instead of Boggs. His sources could not confirm anything, but his gentle prodding of several people throughout the day had produced a fair accounting of what might have occurred and, unknown to him, it was eerily accurate.

He was disappointed that the loud and popular enlisted leader might have escaped his plot, but he must carry on. He was also concerned that the death of a concubine might just be written off as some sort of lover's squabble gone wrong, but he couldn't worry about that now either. He assumed that Nestor left his note as planned and he felt that one dead American might be just as helpful as any other, as long as his narrative was not lost in the excitement. He decided to double down on the idea to encourage Luz to become close to the new American at the Naval Magazine.

In the short conversation they had that morning, Luz sounded a little reluctant to pursue Roy, but Ben suspected that she was more open to the idea than she wanted to let on. Since their first meeting, Luz had demonstrated a great capacity for survival and an independence of thought which made her slightly more difficult to manipulate than his typical source. But, as Ben understood, every human needed intimacy with others at some level. As a refugee from the slums of Manila, Luz had managed to find a small restaurant in a city over two hours away by bus from the only world she had ever known. Despite having never been in a vehicle, she was so hungry to reconnect with her sister that she navigated a complex transportation system while carrying everything she owned in a small canvas bag. She had also done all this on her own, with no previous experience, having just lost the only caring adult in her young life.

Back then, as a vulnerable twelve-year-old girl with little to count on but a promise made by an absent sister, Luz was guarded and distrustful. From that point on, she experienced many events which both supported and refuted that approach to dealing with others. Ben suspected that Luz had learned to meet those human intimacy needs much like he did himself, which was to form superficial and pragmatic relationships based on mutual interests and exchange of items of value. However, he had seen her mature over the years – even helped her in that capacity – and noted her development along the lines of social interdependency. He also understood that, while Luz may not need to have a meaningful and intimate relationship, she probably wanted one. Witnessing how she and Thompson got along the night before made Ben think that now might be the time for one to happen and he intended to help that along, as well.

Of course, he was not interested in Luz and Thompson living happily ever after. He wasn't interested in their lives at all except for how he might be able to use them to carry out his own plans. With others in the past, he had encouraged similar relationships, with varying degrees of success, always with an eye toward how they could be exploited. This budding relationship carried more urgency though, if only because of the current uncertainty.

Ben had heard the term "useful idiot" from time to time and had come to believe that most of those in his little network of contacts were just that; uncomprehending tools, laid out before him in a pattern most conducive to his manipulations. He could often get his bidding done by offering some advice here, telling a half-truth or lie there, discouraging a friendship, encouraging a minor infraction. He had learned some very useful tools about espionage and other types of "active measures" from his comrades and used them all effectively. Some people were very easily directed; others required the more direct route of a well-placed wad of cash. Nestor had turned into such an asset.

Nestor had been helping his sister Esther in her booth in the East Bajac-Bajac market when they first met. In the beginning, he had seemed very pious in his views towards the Catholic church, but as Ben became better acquainted with him, Nestor's eccentricities became more apparent. He loved the church, to be sure, but he also had a penchant for weaving some of his ancestor's more naturalistic, perhaps paganistic, ideas into the liturgies of the church. Ben recognized Nestor's intelligence early on, but eventually began to see a bit of madness, as well.

Ben helped Nestor get a job gardening on the base and it wasn't long after that when Ben began to ask minor favors of him. Nestor figured out fairly early in their relationship that he was being used by Ben, so it wasn't long before he started demanding money for the favors. Those insights made manipulating Nestor more difficult for Ben, but it also opened up all kinds of alternative uses for the cause. Regardless, Ben never warmed to the idea of having to depend on the discretion of another, especially one whose stability might be questionable.

Ben had a considerably higher opinion of Luz than any of his other assets, but still believed she could be guided into doing his bidding without suspicion. It was also possible that she wouldn't have minded doing some of those things for him even with full awareness. Ben had helped Luz pretty much from the time they first met, calling in very few favors over the years and he didn't think this last request would be much of a burden for her. He knew nearly all of her secrets; she knew hardly any of his.

Chapter 22

Frank slowed his car and flipped on the right blinker switch in an attempt to get the attention of someone among the clutch of tricycles clogging the driveway. A couple of drivers moved, but five others just sat on their bikes shooting the shit. He finally hit the horn with two short bursts and a place cleared for him to squeeze through. The short driveway dead-ended in front of a fenced compound which was flanked by a sari-sari store on the right and a small, windowless bar on the left. One car was already parked beneath a sign reading "Cutie's" and Frank parked on the far side of it. Two young boys ran up to the driver's side door and began yelling, "I watch! I watch!" before Frank could even turn off the ignition switch.

He opened his door and pointed at the tallest of the two. "One peso now, one when I come out."

"Okay, Joe!"

Roy looked over the six-foot tall cement block fence at a two-storied, stucco house, as well as the tops of some banana trees and towering palms. He could also see that broken glass had been cemented to the top of the wall to discourage anyone from trying to climb over. A wide, green, metal gate was located at the end of the wall closest to the sari-sari store and he noted that it was solid and high enough to obscure most of what might be hiding within.

"That looks like a nice place," Roy said. "Do you think the owners own these places too?"

"I doubt it. I know the owner of the bar and he has never mentioned living this close," Frank replied. "It would be a pretty short commute to work though, wouldn't it?"

The door opened for them as the two approached and a tall, light skinned, twenty-something woman flashed a bright smile as she beckoned them in. Her curly, brown hair was pulled back and gathered into a tangled ponytail. She had the most severe case of freckles Roy had ever seen and breasts so large that he immediately suspected the handiwork of a plastic surgeon. When she spoke to welcome them to Cutie's, her accent was as thick as that of any Filipina he had met so far.

Frank looked back at Roy, noting his scrutiny of their hostess and then said, "Yep. All that and she also has the whitest teeth I've ever come across." It was only later that Roy realized the comment was in reference to her talents in fellatio.

Instead of the dark, smoke-filled beer pit Roy imagined behind the stark front of the bar, he encountered a bright, sun-filled beer pit. The bar itself was not large. To the right of the front door was a single pool table and to the left was a single juke box, both of which were quiet. Four small tables with chairs were crowded into the remaining spaces. The short, Formica covered counter guarded the chest-styled refrigerator from the juke box and the rest of the bar and was very much like most other little establishments he would find.

What brightened this place so differently was the wall-to-wall sliding glass doors at the back of the bar. They highlighted an enclosed garden containing manicured plants and what looked like a small pond of some kind. The garden was the width of the bar – Roy estimated that at around 30 feet – and appeared to be about 40 feet deep. It was surrounded by the same kind of walls which protected the house on the adjacent property and had a solid metal door on the wall to the right.

The glass window ran from just left of the center of the room all the way to the far-right corner. On the inside of the glass, curtain rods supported two sets of drapes, both of which were currently pulled open. The outside of the glass was protected by sturdy iron bars with two hinged doors hung in appropriate places. One was wide open, allowing passage through a currently closed sliding door.

In addition to the hostess who had let them in, Roy spotted four other people in the courtyard. Three other females were engaged in what looked like a three-player version of mahjong and a white male sat at a table by himself, reading a paperback book and drinking a soda. The length of his hair and patchy beard identified him as being a civilian. He looked up as Roy and Frank entered and waved for them to join him. Frank waved back and by the time they reached the sliding door, the hostess had retrieved two beers and two frosted mugs.

Roy felt a breeze from a ceiling fan when Frank opened the door to the outside and only then noticed ten feet of poured cement porch and the roof which covered it.

"Hey, mate!" the man said. "Join me."

Pulling out a chair, Frank said, "Charles, this is Roy Thompson. Roy, this is Charles Pettit, Esquire."

"Fuck you very much, Frankie," he said, rising to shake Roy's hand. "And Roy, very nice to meet you." He spoke with an Australian accent which had been dulled slightly by many years away from the motherland. Charles seemed to Roy to be about average in every conceivable aspect. He had slightly greying brown hair to his shoulders and was about 5'10". He appeared to have been athletic at some time in his youth but was beginning to sport a little beer-belly and was somewhere between 40 and 60 years old. He was so unremarkable that Roy doubted he could pick him out of a line-up, even after having just met him.

"Roy here worked for me a while back and has just recently come to the P.I." The hostess had already poured his beer and Frank reached for it as he sat.

Roy shook Charles' extended hand and said, "Nice to meet you, as well, Charles."

"Charles is the proud owner of this fine establishment," Frank said. "He still won't tell me how he gets his beer so fucking cold without it freezing."

"I told you, mate. It's a state secret. I could tell you, but then I'd have to kill you, as you have heard before."

By that time, Roy's beer had also been poured so he picked up the mug and peered closely at the ice forming on his mug. "Yes, I can see that it is especially cold. I suspect refrigeration was involved."

Charles laughed and said, "I like this bloke! Must be a fucking detective!"

"Yeah, not much gets past him, for sure," Frank said. He sat down his half-empty mug and looked around the garden. "You got the place looking nice, Chucky. Get some decent hookers in here and you might scare up some business." One of the girls playing mahjong poked out her tongue and said, "*Bastos Kano!*" Frank raised his mug and smiled.

"I – and my girls – get all the business we need, fuck you very much, again," Charles said, smiling. "And what brings you to our sunny island, Roy?"

Roy gave him a short description of his duty station and an even shorter version of his connection to Frank.

"And," Frank interjected, "Roy was welcomed aboard with the murder of an American lieutenant last night. In Barretto." He looked over to the girls deeply engaged in their mahjong game and lowered his voice, "It sounds like NPA activity to me."

Roy remembered his earlier offhand remark, but they never discussed the possibility at length. The idea was broached at the early morning meeting at OPM, and he'd discussed it with Commander Pillotero, so he wasn't surprised that others had made the connection. He had done some research on his own about the organization shortly after getting ordered to the Philippines and was familiar with the NPA "problem."

Roy wasn't necessarily happy about Frank bringing up the topic, but since it was on the table, and both of these men might have some local insight, he couldn't help but to go into investigator mode.

Charles' interest had also been piqued. "And is this lieutenant someone I might have met?"

"No… at least, I doubt it very much. But you might know her boyfriend, Dennis Boggs. He is the CMC at the NAVSTA and might have ventured out here," Frank explained.

"Yes, I've met him, even if he isn't a frequent visitor to this part of the bay," Charles replied. "Friend of Turnbull's. Big gent, always happy, like he just got a knobber. Though, he never got one here, so far as I know."

Roy was still reticent to discuss any aspects of the murder, but he thought he might be able to ask relevant questions, just as soon as he could come up with some. For the time being, he was content to let them discuss what they knew and just listen for any insights they might reveal.

Charles said something in Tagalog to the mahjong players. The two youngest ladies immediately started packing the game tiles into a wooden box and the older one – the one who had called Frank a "vulgar American" – came over to whisper into Frank's ear. He smiled and said, "*Siguro mamaya.*" The lady then winked at Roy, picked up a few empty glasses from the table where they had been playing and followed the two others into the bar.

"It seems that Carmen wants to jump your bones, Royboy," Frank said. "I would recommend building up to that particular level of intensity. She is not a bronc you want to ride first time out of the chute."

While Roy was trying to think of a witty rejoinder, the door slid open and the woman who had met them at the front door came out with a tray holding three short glasses, a bowl of ice and a bottle of Glenfiddich scotch. She sat the tray on their table and left without saying a word.

"Let's drink to our new mate here," Charles said. He put a couple of ice cubes into each glass and then started pouring. "Like my mum used to say, 'Nothing says welcome to Paradise, like a little single malt on ice.' But she also used to say, 'If you don't like scotch, you're fucking wrong,' so there you go." They clinked glasses and after taking a sip and clearing his throat Roy said, "Far be it from me to argue with anyone's mom. Besides, she sounds like a sage."

"Now," Charles turned to Roy. "What makes you suspect the NPA?"

"I didn't say that I did," Roy replied. "Frank, why do you think that?"

"Just putting two together with the other two," he replied. "There's been some reported activity and there's a dead sailor who, I suspect, was in the wrong place at the wrong time." He finished the scotch in his glass and poured a bit more. "And considering that place was the residence of a highly visible American with sadly inadequate security, I think it too likely to disregard." He swirled his whiskey around in the quickly melting ice and glanced at Charles as he plopped in some more cubes.

"Am I right in assuming that nothing was stolen?" Charles asked.

Roy looked at Frank to answer and then looked back at Charles when he saw none was forthcoming. Charles raised his eyebrows as a way of repeating the question.

"I think that would be a safe assumption, yes," Roy finished his own scotch and then chased it with a sip of San Miquel.

Charles leaned forward in his chair and held his glass with both hands.

"I'll ask around," he said. "Nothing official, you know?"

"I'm not official either. Still checking in," Roy said.

"I like your thinking, mate. Cheers." Charles said, raising his glass.

Chapter 23

For hours after Scott left the bar, Luz felt disjointed. She continued to serve beer and make change and banter with patrons and all the other duties of her position, but she felt as if she were just slightly out of sync, as if she were witnessing her actions a fraction of a second after they happened; almost as if she were an echo of herself in real time. It started after Scott had mentioned the possibility that political assassins might be responsible for the death.

She was unexpectedly unsettled by the prospect of political violence hitting so close to home. And a large part of her anxiety resulted from her own definitions of "home" or "friends" or "family." None of those things, taken for granted by most children, were a source of stability for her as a child. Luz had reconstructed those aspects of her social life bit by bit since the loss of her sister and grandmother. But now, something – some insidiously ravenous beast nibbling at the perimeter of her conscious memory – was eating at the foundation of what she had made for herself.

Some facts of her childhood were never far from the surface of her memories and those had been playing on a near continuous loop since her absent sister's birthday. But for reasons she did not understand, those "facts" didn't seem quite as concrete as they had been. There was a nagging sense that there was more to them.

Luz's memories replayed throughout the evening and random additional scenes crept in, expanding here and filling in there. Eventually, flashing scenes and painful emotional scars started weaving themselves into a single narrative, focusing the story of her life with a new and terrifying clarity.

*   *   *

Shortly after arriving in Olongapo, Ben had been directed to take young Luz from the Mabuhay Restaurant to a house which sheltered about seven other young girls and women close to the restaurant. Some of them worked

147

in restaurants, some in bars, some in shops, but none worked at the Mabuhay and none of them knew anything about Luz's sister. Each girl paid for their rent and food from the meager wages they earned in their service jobs and, perhaps not surprisingly, there was usually little money left over at the end of the month.

As Luz was completing her first meal in Olongapo, Lucinda wrote a short note and sealed it in a professional envelope bearing the name of the Mabuhay Restaurant. When Ben arrived to deliver the young refugee to her new living quarters, he also delivered the note to the owner of the house. It was not the first time he had delivered such notes to that house, and it was not the first deal made between the two women, although both were blissfully unaware of just how long their relationship would last.

After Luz's stomach was full, Ben escorted her to the place she would call home for the next couple of years. The home was only a block or so away from the restaurant and once there, she was directed to a single bed in a small room with three others just like it. The beds were little more than metal tube structures, displaying remnants of white paint and strung with interlocking wire mesh, supporting a thin mattress. She carried her small cache of pesos on her body for three days before she felt comfortable enough to stash the treasure inside one leg of her bed. Until she left, she checked her nest egg at every available opportunity – adding to it when possible – and, as far as she could tell, it was never discovered. Who would suspect an itinerant waif of having anything of value?

From the beginning, Luz made little headway in her search for Emmy. Lucinda seemed always too busy to discuss the topic or would put her off by saying, "We'll have to discuss that at a different time. We need to focus on getting you taken care of right now!" No one else at the restaurant seemed to remember anything about her.

Ben had taken a shine to Luz and helped her to settle into the house quickly. She seldom saw the three other girls sharing the room except at night when they returned from whatever jobs they had. Once Luz learned that they knew nothing of Emmy, she saw no need to initiate any meaningful relationship with any of them. In the meantime, Luz was happy to do whatever she could to help pay her way. Within a week she was doing minor chores at the restaurant learning as much as she could about her new surroundings. Always learning.

Ben wasn't a constant presence at the house or the restaurant, but he was called upon quite often to run errands for Lucinda and others around that part of the neighborhood. Whenever he could, he let Luz tag along and help him with those errands, contributing to her ongoing informal education.

Ben loved to talk about the history of the city, the province and the country and at first didn't understand just how much Luz was observing. His realization of that intense curiosity happened by accident one day while he was talking to two men who Luz had never before seen.

Ben had been asked to deliver some food to an apartment a couple of blocks from the Mabuhay and Luz volunteered to help carry the bags. As they walked along, Ben explained that the apartment was close to one of the sari-sari stores that had once been owned by his parents. A few doors down from the store – little more than a wide booth fronting a small apartment – Ben greeted two men formerly and delivered the two bags he was holding and motioned for Luz to hand over the other bag she carried. It was clear to her that he already knew them. Handing her burden to the larger of the two men, she saw that he was staring at her empty and sunken eye socket. Ben received payment for the food and then gave her a couple of pesos and told her to get a snack at the store, which she was happy to do.

Luz usually didn't even think about her missing eye, but occasionally she would catch someone doing a double-take at her face and would be reminded once again of the injury. That happened quite a bit more since arriving in Olongapo and was beginning to make her feel a shame that she had never experienced in Manila.

Luz bought a few pieces of dried mango and as she waited for her change, she could hear the three men talking quietly, but intensely, about something she didn't quite understand. One of the men kept asking Ben questions about some particular Americans who had supposedly eaten recently at the Mabuhay. Luz at first assumed that it had something to do with the food at the restaurant and started to tune them out when a few of the questions began to pique her interest. They were asking about how often the Americans ate there, when they normally came in, when they normally left, who was likely to accompany them when they dined, and it dawned on her that the men were more interested in what those customers did after they left the establishment. It wasn't as if she was so interested in finding out what the questioning was all about, but just the fact that the conversation was so different from what she had expected to hear made her want to listen more closely.

Just as the girl behind the counter was counting out Luz's change, Ben stepped up to the counter and told her to bring him a few slices as well.

Returning to the restaurant, silently eating their sweet treat, Luz looked up at Ben and said, "Those men seem to think you know a lot about what people do when they leave the Mabuhay. Do you know where my sister Emmy might be, since she isn't there anymore?"

He hesitated for only a moment before saying, "No, I don't. But I might be able to find out something." Then glanced down and said, "What did you hear from my friends?"

"Not much," she said. "Just that they seemed really interested in what those *Kanos* do after they eat. Do you really think you can find out about Emmy?"

"I think I can," he said. "Just don't ask too many questions from anyone else… about anything." He took another bit of mango and chewed it before saying, "It is better if you don't ask questions from anyone but me. You might not want to believe what they have to tell you."

They walked a bit more in silence when Luz suddenly remembered the peso and change in her hand and tried to give it back to Ben.

"No. You keep that," he said. "A little payment for helping me deliver that lunch."

About half a block from the restaurant, Luz stopped abruptly and said, "Ben? I have a question." He was a step ahead of her and turned around to look into her earnest face. Wiping a tear leaked from her shriveled socket, she said, "Do you know someone who can fix this?"

"Maybe," he said. "Maybe we can work on it. You go back now and don't tell anyone about that money."

Having lived a more or less subsistence life before coming to Olongapo, Luz never paid much attention to the amount of time spent "working." She had learned to do whatever needed to be done, regardless of how much time it took and to do it as best she could. Had she ever bothered to think about it, she would not have been able to recall if that was some hard life-lesson hammered into her by her *Impó* or if it had come from some wisdom imparted during one of their long talks. She knew only that she had always approached living that way. It just was. Of course, she had learned the value of money early in life and had learned how to scrimp and save in order to accumulate as much of it as she could, but she never contemplated having a "job" where one performed services or labor, during a specified timeframe, in order to receive a fixed amount of money.

That mindset is what made her approach life more realistically than many of her peers might have, it also made her a good employee. However, her keen insight and independent nature could also be problematic. She did not suffer fools gladly and had to learn some early tough lessons about when to call people out on their bullshit.

A smart boss would put up with a lot from such an employee and Lucinda was a smart boss. She noticed quickly that Luz was bright, energetic and eager to help. It also didn't take her long to realize that a structured work environment would allow her to exploit those characteristics in an economically advantageous way for herself and her restaurant. For her part, Luz was ecstatic to be offered such an adult opportunity and was even more excited to be in a situation where she could actually accumulate some more money. She still had all of the money she had brought from Manila and even without Ben's warning, was careful to hide what she had earned since.

Luz had not forgotten about her sister, but she did realize that there was some aspect of Emmy's story that neither Lucinda nor anyone else was eager to discuss. But finally, after having been in Olongapo for nearly a month and having worked at the Mabuhay for a few days, Lucinda called her into the tiny office in the back of the restaurant. Lucinda maneuvered her chair from around the desk to sit across from Luz and took one of her hands into her own.

"I have been checking around because I wanted to be sure about Emmy before we talked about her," Lucinda began. "I suppose this is one of those 'good news, bad news' situations that you hear about."

Luz looked at her blankly, having never heard anything about good news or bad news or how that might have anything to do with her sister.

"The good news is that Emmy is happily married to an American marine," Lucinda said. She stopped at that, letting it sink in that her sister was safe and well cared for. The blank stare slowly turned into a smile, accompanied strangely by one eye still filled with questions.

"The bad news is that Emmy is already back in the States." The smile faded only slightly as Luz tried to process that she was not likely to see her sister again for a very long time, if ever. Luz had already begun to discern the dynamics between Filipinas and the American servicemen living there, but she never suspected that her sister would have been swept up into that, especially at such a young age. She still pictured her older sister as she had last seen her, not yet a woman but fully independent. It was a lot to take in.

Luz was told that Emmy had met the American while working in the restaurant and that she had been swept off her feet by the young, wealthy Marine. Evidently, Emmy had been living with the American and saving money in order to bring Luz and her grandmother from Manila, but the plan was derailed when he was ordered to transfer back stateside. They had to marry quickly in order for her to travel with him, which kept her from contacting them in Manila. Lucinda assured her that Emmy would contact her once she had settled in California. To wrap the whole story up, Lucinda said that she had just recently learned the last bit of information from Emmy's friend Mari, who herself was leaving Manila for the states within a day or two.

151

Luz was shaken by a mixture of emotions. Happy for Emmy's love, sad for her own distance from her sister and afraid of what her own future might now hold since her only living relative was halfway around the world, she sat stunned. Additionally, she could not know that the story she just heard was riddled with holes. Being unfamiliar with the machinations involved in international relations and travel, much less the requirements of American military personal marrying foreign nationals, she had no reason to believe otherwise.

This revelation about her sister came to Luz at about the same time as the onset of her menses. *Impo's* insistence that her grandchildren be inoculated against the warm embrace of ignorance insured that they understood the basic hurdles they would face. As cryptic as she may have been about the past, Luz's grandmother was completely open and honest about the future dangers of being a female in the patriarchal world in which they lived. As the changes in her body approached, she recognized them and prepared as best she could. To avoid disclosing that she had money hidden away, she asked Lucinda for advice and received an advance against her earnings at the restaurant in order to purchase any products she would need. Lucinda seemed pleased to be able to help usher Luz into her womanhood.

Lucinda surprised her even more by saying she would help with Luz's eye. She had contacted a local ophthalmologist, looking into the costs and risks of receiving an eye prosthesis, as well as the required recovery time. She estimated the time required to pay back such an expense by working at the restaurant. Then she contacted a colleague in Manila.

Within a few weeks, Luz had undergone the operation required to remove the damaged tissue in her eye socket and was fitted with a deep ocular implant. And after a few more weeks to heal, Luz received the first of three prosthetic eyes she would eventually own. The first one – made of glass and the very cheapest one available – made Luz feel as if she had won the lottery. It took weeks to get used to looking at her new face in the mirror and although she felt a bit of shame, she almost couldn't turn away. She was astounded by the pretty girl looking back at her and could barely believe she had been so lucky to have fallen into the good graces of Lucinda and the Mabuhay Restaurant.

That first experience with an eye prothesis took several adjustments, physically and emotionally. She had no recollection at all about the loss of her natural eye as an infant, but the loss of her first artificial eye was…

"Luz?" Gloria said.

Luz did not reply. She was leaning against the beer cooler with her head bowed, steadied by her right hand. With the other hand she rubbed absently at the brow above her left eye. Gloria's voice did not register.

Luz was back in the Mabuhay restaurant, feeling better than she could ever remember. She had adjusted to her new eye, she had adjusted to her new status as a young lady and she was wearing a brand-new set of clothing bought for her by Lucinda as a birthday gift commemorating her thirteenth birthday. Lucinda had personally taken her to a shop on Magsaysay to pick out the new outfit and had even taken her to a beauty shop to fix her hair and make-up. The dress she now wore resemble the Chinese inspired gown that Lucinda was wearing on the first day Luz wandered into the Mabuhay, though a brighter red and not quite as form fitting. Nonetheless, it highlighted the roundness beginning to appear at her hips and was cut to accent her young breast, such as they were. Her hair was piled into a similarly fashionable coiffure. Even her old, rubber flip-flops had been upgraded to dressier, faux leather, red sandals.

Luz had been performing the hostess duties off and on for several weeks and was expecting that she would be able to do that full time, now that she had clothing appropriate for such a position. Maria, the girl who had greeted Luz at the door that very first day in Olongapo, was still working there for the time being, but was expecting to move to a different place in the near future. Luz felt important, she felt empowered, she felt beautiful.

Maria smiled at them now, as Lucinda and Luz entered the restaurant and complimented Luz on her appearance. The two giggled like the young girls they were as Luz told her quickly of her experiences in the dress shop and beauty salon. Lucinda surveyed the few customers currently seated and waved to a middle-aged man sitting at a table near the kitchen. She sat next to him, and they began speaking in hushed tones as the two girls fussed over the new dress and Luz looked at her stylish hair in the mirror behind the cash register. They never noticed the man looking in their direction, his eyes shining with anticipation, as Lucinda continued to speak quietly.

Three young, professional looking men came to the door and Luz escorted them to an empty table near the window in the front, where they could see pedestrians passing by on the sidewalk. They each smiled at Luz in a manner she had never before experienced. She couldn't begin to describe what was different about the way they looked at her or the way they thanked her for the menus, but it was different nonetheless and she felt a tingling in her belly as she turned back toward the front counter. She saw Maria looking at her with a bemused smile and her eyebrows arched in a comical mask. She smiled back shyly and began to say something when Lucinda interrupted her train of thought.

"Luz, I have another surprise for you," she said.

Luz turned in her direction and saw the man to whom Lucinda had been speaking standing at her side.

"This is Mr. Smith," she said. Luz sized him up quickly but could not quite see the name Smith describing the man she saw there. He appeared to be in his late fifties and was wearing a very expensive Barong Tagalog which stretched snuggly across his ample stomach. His hair was thin and jet black, combed straight back over a peeking scalp. It seemed at odds with the wrinkled face and double chin over which it rested. He was slightly shorter than Lucinda and when he spoke his accent was clearly that of an educated Filipino.

"It is so nice to meet you, Luz," he said. "Miss Gordon has told me how very intelligent and ambitious you are, but she failed to mention just what a lovely young lady you are." He extended his hand and Luz pressed her forehead to it, in a show of respect she had remembered from some lost part of her past.

"Oh, please!" he said. "Surely, I am not so old, and you are certainly not so young!"

Luz's face blazed with embarrassment, and she said, "I am, uh, I am honored to meet you, sir."

"Luz, Mr. uh, Smith would like to discuss some possible employment opportunities with you," Lucinda said. "I have told him about your desire to reconnect with your sister and he believes he might be able to help you in doing that. He is very important in Manila and has many, many overseas connections. Wouldn't you like to hear what he can do for you?"

The mention of Emmy and the possibility that this person might be able to somehow help them reestablish contact blotted out any other consideration in her adolescent brain. Her normal, natural wariness had been short-circuited by the faintest possibility of finding her sister.

"Yes! Oh, yes! I would like that very much," she said. "What can I do?"

"First," Lucinda said, "Mr. Smith would like to talk to you and gather some more information about you and Emmy and then he can have a better idea of just what he might be able to do to help you find each other again."

Luz was beaming at Mr. Smith and trying to listen to what Lucinda was saying, but she couldn't quite get the picture of her and Emmy reuniting out of her head. It seemed to her that the perfect day just kept getting better and better.

"Of course," Luz said. "I have a very good memory. I can tell you just about everything since I was four or five."

"Well, I don't think we will have to explore anything quite that long ago," he said. "I am much more interested in how you have come along in the last few years." And then, after just the slightest of hesitation, "and how you and your sister came to be separated, of course."

Luz continued to smile up at this new hope and was unconsciously wringing her hands in excitement. She was blinded by the possibilities which had been presented to her and she could not wait to discover how this story would unfold.

"I would like to buy you dinner at my hotel so we can have a quiet conversation, uninterrupted by your normal work duties," he said. "The food is wonderful here at the Mabuhay, but I am sure you would like to eat something from a different menu, and it is a fine menu they have there, as well." He glanced in Lucinda's direction with a vague expression of query on his face.

"Yes. Yes, of course. Anything to help Luz's family," Lucinda said. "You two run along and take your time. Luz, I will see you tomorrow."

When they left the restaurant, Ben was walking towards them on the sidewalk. At first, he seemed not to notice them, but did a double take when he recognized Luz. He smiled and started to same something about the way she was dressed but the smile froze when he saw the man walking beside her. Luz smiled back but hesitated when she saw the look on Ben's face. Ben shook his head almost unperceptively and mouthed 'later,' hoping she would take the hint and not draw attention to him. He needn't have worried since Mr. Smith was looking at the keys in his hand and took no notice of Ben whatsoever. They walked only a short distance further when Mr. Smith stopped next to a late model Toyota sedan. As he unlocked the passenger door for her, Luz glanced back to the restaurant and saw Ben standing by the entrance, watching them.

Throughout dinner, Mr. Smith asked about her grandmother, her sister and about her friends and acquaintances in Manila. She wasn't necessarily proud to talk about her life in the garbage heaps, but she was as honest and forthcoming with him as she could be, wanting to contribute whatever she could to the possibility of reuniting with her sister. Again, looking back, he seemed to concentrate his questions around who she might still know or who might still be looking for her. Yollie may have been the only person still there who had any concern for Luz at all, but even that probably dissipated when she was able to move into the newly vacant shanty.

After the meal, Mr. Smith mentioned that he needed to go to his room there in the hotel in order to make some notes and fill in some paperwork. He assured her he would take her back to the restaurant just as soon as he had completed that simple errand. Luz's antenna started to pick up on something that wasn't quite right, but she was still giddy about how the day began and the possibility or finding Emmy, so she overruled it. And she believed that if this man was a friend of Lucinda, he must be honorable and trustworthy. After that day, she never ignored her sense of danger again...

"Luz!" Gloria repeated.

Again, she did not respond. She was leaning over the refrigerator now, both hands clutching her forehead.

At this point in her recollections, the newly emerging memories become sharp and distinct. Sometimes they rushed and sometimes they crawled, but they were crystal clear, as if she were living the scenes over again. She was there again, in that hotel. The smell of the grilled chicken, the melodies of the fancy, piped in music at the hotel restaurant, the texture of the cloth napkin and the shine of the silverware popped in her memory like projections on a wide movie screen. She was trying to think of the girl in the hotel as someone else, perhaps as some sort of actress in that movie pretending to be a Luz doppelganger. But it was her. She was there. "No!" an inner voice screamed at her. "You are there!"

The hotel is one of the best and most updated Olongapo has to offer. His room is on the second floor and at the very end of the hallway. He unlocks the door and walks in first, holding the door for her to follow. As she comes in, he motions toward the washroom and says she can use those facilities if needed. She declines and continues to walk toward the back of the room where a short sofa sits in front of a wide window. She hears the metallic click of the door latch as it closes. She pulls aside the curtain to reveal the side on another building within only a few feet. A small, brown bird starts to light on the windowsill but diverts at the last instant. The curtains are beige and have plastic rods located at the top, where they meet at the center of the window. She hears Mr. Smith placing his keys on a cabinet and shuffling what sounds like papers. She moves closer to the window and peers up at the adjacent building. She can see that it is at least one floor higher, and she can see that the sun is starting to go down. It has the effect of making the window more reflective and she sees a blurry image of Mr. Smith moving behind her. She thinks it funny that the dinner took so long to complete and turns to say something to that effect to Mr. Smith.

He is there. His Barong is gone, and his flabby belly is nearly visible beneath the thin undershirt. A few thin, graying hairs are protruding over its collar and his tan line makes a short "V" shape below his neck. His arms are also flabby, but they are strong, and he pushes her to the sofa. She is shocked and confused but sees the bump of his erection in the crotch of his pants and her sense of danger is now screaming at her to run. But she can't.

She starts to scream herself, but he puts his left hand over her mouth and grabs her budding left breast with his other hand, twisting her and pushing her onto her back. Through wide, terrified eyes, she sees his face strangely calm as he pins her head to the sofa and pulls open the top of her new dress, popping the buttons. It is buttoned to just past her knees and he continues to pull and rip until the gown is open all the way. A bit of spittle drips from one side of his tightly closed lips, inches from her face. She uses both of her hands first to try to remove the hand from her mouth and then to block his other hand, now pulling at her panties, but she is incapable of fighting him and begins to kick the sofa and buck. Over the shoulder of her attacker, Luz sees one shiny, red sandal sailing toward the corner of the room. Suddenly, the panties rip, he pulls his arm straight back and pounds his fist, still clutching her torn clothing, into her abdomen.

Every bit of her breath is expelled through his strong fingers, but she is unable to suck any air back in. Her eyes are now clenched tightly, her tears streaming and manages to get only a small bit of breath through her nose because of snot which seemed to appear from nowhere. Her hands go to her stomach, and she is sure she will die here, unable to breath, unable to speak, unable to resist.

He removes his hands from her for a moment and she gulps in air and turns her head to the side, spewing her still undigested dinner onto the floor. She feels the prosthetic eye become loose and then it is gone. She is still gagging and before she can spit out the last of the bitter morsels, his pants are off and his undershirt is wrapped around his left hand. She has just enough time to take in another deep breath, cough up more bile and see his pitiful erection protruding from his boxer shorts. Then he is on her again. Once more her mouth is covered, this time with the shirt, keeping his hand from slipping from her vomit slickened face. He has already worked his knees in between her legs and is rubbing her vulva with his thumb, pulling up and stretching her vaginal lips painfully. A few fine, wispy pubic hairs are visible, and he moans quietly as he falls on her, in her, plunging his angry penis inside her, ravaging her hymen and ripping her virginity to shreds.

The pain slashes through her like a jagged blade. She has now managed to scream, but it is muffled by his hand and shirt as he thrusts again and again. It seems an eternity for the man to spend himself, but he is actually done within just a few seconds.

He collapses on her, keeping his hand on her mouth but loosening his grip. He breaths heavily and her muffled screams subside to sobs as he pulls himself out of her, as he pushes up on his feet. He staggers to the washroom being careful to avoid the pool of puke, glancing back at the weeping girl.

"Smith," whose real name is Adolfo Aguilar, leaves the door open as he turns on the shower and pulls off his bloody shorts. He doesn't want to leave the girl alone for long but believes she will be sniveling on the sofa for long enough for him to clean up a bit. He has dealt with many girls like this one and he feels confident she will wilt away quickly, first into the corner of this room and eventually into the fetid underbelly of Olongapo, just like those before her. He was just soaping up his shriveled dick when he thought he heard the girl stirring outside the washroom. He quickly turned off the water and held a towel to his belly as he headed toward the door.

He saw Luz on her hands and knees at the foot of the unmolested bed. The torn dress draped across her back dragged on the floor as she appeared to be searching for something in the deep piles of the carpet.

"Get up onto the bed," he said. "I'm not done with you yet." The previous kind and helpful tones were totally absent from this voice. There was nothing but the cold commands of a rapist, convinced he had more to take.

Luz rocked back onto her heels, and using the bed to steady herself, she slowly staggered to her feet. But she did not get on the bed. The pain was still searing, but her blood was already starting to dry along the insides of her thighs and the rage in the pit of her stomach began to grow. Slowly she turned and looked at Aguilar defiantly through one good eye. Her prosthetic one was clenched in her hand. Her right foot slipped quietly from the thongs of the one sandal she still wore. He dropped the towel and exposed himself to Luz once again in an attempt to intimidate her and began to move toward the bed.

"I told you to…"

Her genitals were still throbbing, and she was a bit unsteady on her feet, but she took a deep breath and tried to focus all of her attention, all of her strength, into one potential move. As soon as he was close enough, Luz's right leg shot out from the front of the unfastened gown and the ball of her foot connected with the very tender and slippery balls of Adolfo Aguilar. He howled in agony and doubled over, instinctively covering his crotch and staggered to the side. Luz saw her opening and tried to run past him to the door. Her own pain resurged and caused her to falter for just a second, which was long enough for Aguilar to grab a handful of her hair. He tried to drag her down to the floor but, still weak in the knees from her well-placed kick, he stumbled and loosened his grip just a little. Luz extended her left arm as far out in front of her as she could and then swung in a roundhouse, backhanded undercut with all the strength she could muster. She didn't have much strength left but, as it turned out, it was enough. The back of her clenched fist connected squarely with the tip of his nose causing him to

158

completely release his hold on her hair. It was also forceful enough to dislodge the glass eye she had been holding in that fist. The eye flew through the air, landing in the vomit and the curses flew from Aguilar's mouth as he held both his face and his nuts. She wasted no more thought on the eye and concentrated on escape.

Adrenaline now coursing through her system, Luz was in the hallway in three seconds. She started to turn toward the lobby stairs but thought better of it and looked for an emergency exit which was just across the hall. In ten more seconds, she was at the bottom of the stairs looking at a chain which secured the door leading outside. She stood silently for just a moment, trying to think, but then heard sounds from the hall on the ground floor. She cracked the door leading to the hall and saw two hotel maids bustling around a cart filled with towels and sheets and tissue boxes, as they complained about their jobs. She could hear no noises of pursuit coming from the direction of her assailant but didn't feel as if going back up or staying in the stairwell were viable options. Slowly she opened the door wide and stepped into the hall. Both maids casually glanced in her direction and then did double takes as they saw the torn dress Luz was holding closed. They saw the mussed hair and the tear and mascara stained cheeks of the young girl. Again, she began to cry, refreshing those stains anew.

She continued to cry as the two tried to comfort her and ushered her into the laundry and supply room across from the stair well. She continued to cry as they wet towels and cleaned the blood from her legs and wiped the stains from her cheeks. Only when the two women began to discuss what to do next did Luz stop crying. She listened nervously as they talked about contacting the hotel manager or calling the police. Eventually they realized, as did Luz herself, that there would be no satisfaction in reporting to anyone the facts of the assault. The word of a poor woman carried little weight in this city and the word of an orphaned girl with no kin and few connections carried even less.

After calming Luz down as much as they could and assuring her that police would not be involved, they determined that she would probably not need medical treatment. Both ladies were grandmothers who had experienced hard lessons in their times and sexual assaults were not the worst of those. They decided eventually that the best – perhaps the only – thing to do was to get herself together, get herself out of the hotel and get herself back home.

They pinned her sad gown together and straightened her hair. And after checking the hallway, the stairwell and outside the back door, they bustled her into the alley. One on either side, they slowly walked her around to the street and hailed a tricycle.

Their hands, firmly clamped on both her arms, gave Luz a small sense of the security she was craving and for a fleeting moment she thought she might want to stay with them forever. Realizing the impossibility of that, she kept her eye peeled for any sign of the rapist or anyone else she might know. When the noisy tricycle pulled up, the maids helped her into the side car and gave the driver two pesos to take her wherever she wanted to go. Luz tried to smile at her two saviors as the trike pulled away, but she couldn't tell if that was what they saw. She clung to the front of her gown, staring down at her bare feet, as she softly recited the address of the house she shared with the other girls, thinking how sad it was that the house was her only home.

"Luz!" Gloria screamed. Grasping Luz's arm, she spun her away from the beer cooler. Luz gasped for air and slowly emerged from her past as the details of Gloria's face came together. Finally, the nightmare was over.

Chapter 24

"Come on, Royboy," the girl implored him. "I give you free sample. You like, you pay."

Roy smiled back into her dark eyes and thought of how the implied guarantee of satisfaction, based on a no-risk tryout of the proffered services, was a solid business tactic. And he was sure that it was a tactic which had proven in the past to be successful time and time again. However, it was a difficult thought for Roy to maintain in his mind, considering how the provider of those proffered services was at that very moment massaging his dick through his pants.

The girl, in full anticipation of Roy's acceptance of her terms, glanced down at his aroused crotch and started to unzip his fly. He slid his hand between the girl's eager fingers and his pants and said, "Thanks, but no thanks."

The girl looked back to him questioningly and with a bit of indignation. "You Benny Boy, Royboy?"

Having recently learned the term, Roy assured her he was not gay and made up the entirely unnecessary lie that he was married and didn't want to cheat on his wife. And, not for the first time that day, Roy silently cursed Frank for announcing his old nickname to everyone in the Philippines.

The girl raised her eyebrows, pooched out her lips in a petulant pout and then quietly returned to a table of her workmates next to a Rockola jukebox. Roy swiveled his stool around to the bar and picked up his empty beer bottle. Sensing he had reached a limit, he shook his head when the girl behind the bar offered a fresh one.

Roy had seen and met several beautiful, young and willing women since arriving in the Philippines and even though they were all desirable, the only face that seemed to matter was that of the cashier at Ace's Place. He recalled Frank's admonition to avoid falling for the first girl he met and would have laughed at the possibility if he weren't visualizing her at that very minute. He slowly shook his head and thought again about drinking a little more beer.

After leaving the little oasis behind Pettit's bar, they had traveled first to a place named "Stumpy's" and then to their present location, "Marilyn's." They were in Stumpy's for only one beer, during which time Roy was introduced to its owner named, appropriately enough, Stumpy. He had lost a leg to gangrene, or maybe to a war wound, or maybe to a shark. The version one was told depended on what day of the week one happened to stop by his establishment. Regardless, when Frank found out that his favorite girl had already been bought out of the bar for the evening, they moved on to Marilyn's.

They had been in Subic far longer than Roy thought they would be, and he was checking the time on his wrist watch when Frank came in the front door. He was trailing a prostitute who had obviously been in the game longer than any of the young girls currently chatting at their table by the jukebox. She disappeared to a room at the back of the bar as Frank sat next to Roy.

Even before Roy could broach the topic of returning to the base, Frank said, "It's starting to rain out there and I saw some message traffic this morning about a tropical storm heading our way. Probably ought to get back through the zigzags before it hits us."

"Sounds like a plan," Roy said.

The rain was not yet falling heavily, but the wind had started to pick up when the two climbed into Frank's car. However, by the time they were through Barrio Barretto, the rain had started to come in sheets and the windshield wipers were going full throttle. Frank turned down the music coming in on the AFRTS radio station and slowed the car's speed considerably.

"You still wanna go to Gordon Avenue?" Frank asked.

The image of Luz popped back into his head immediately. His body had demonstrated its ability to respond to sexual stimuli and he had successfully fought off the urge to satisfy his lust for the whole day. He might be able to do so for a while longer, but Roy didn't want to face the challenge that Luz might present. There was something about her that frightened him and in a frighteningly pleasant way.

"I don't think I would care to get stuck there, any more than I would want to get stuck in Subic City," Roy said.

"Well, I didn't think so, but I thought I'd ask."

"I appreciate your dedication to making me feel welcomed in the P.I." Roy said. "Which reminds me about some of the other welcoming I received today. I'm a little curious about Charles. He said something about nothing being 'official.' What do you suppose he meant by that?"

Frank cleared his throat a little and then said, "He used to... he says he is retired from a government job that required him to spend a lot of time in the Australian embassy in Manila. I first met him as you met him today, in his bar in Subic. Then I ran into him up on Roxas Boulevard in Manila. I was walking up to the Playboy Club for a drink and he was coming out of the U.S. embassy."

Frank shifted in his seat and adjusted the defroster switch to combat the fog forming on the windshield. "Over the last couple of months, I have talked to him about a few different things going on around this country and he always has what I would call interesting insights. He has never said anything concrete, but I've kind of gotten the idea that he knows a lot more about what is going on around here than the average bar owner, if you get my drift."

Roy looked sideways at Frank as he spoke and a faint memory from his days as a crypto tech formed in his mind. Almost from the first day upon receiving his security clearance, the Naval Security Group had reminded him that, while he was not a "spy," he would very likely become the target of spies. It was as if the Navy was trying to instill some sort of institutional paranoia surrounding any interactions with foreign nationals. That skepticism had stayed with Roy over the years, but he never really thought about it consciously. And he certainly never suspected that others might use that paranoia constructively.

"Notice I said that he was coming out of the U.S. embassy, not the Aussie embassy," Frank continued. "He told me he was involved with some kind of agricultural project between the U.S., Australia and the P.I., but it just never quite made sense to me."

They continued to ride in silence until they approached the back gate of the base.

"At any rate, that is kind of why I introduced you to him. He's a smart guy. He has insights. He knows people. He might be able to help with this Lieutenant Jackson shit show. Of course, as he said, it would all be unofficial."

There was no more talk of Charles or murder as they rode to the Cubi Point Chief's barracks. Instead, Frank recounted his encounter with the lady at Marilyn's and went on to recommend other women at other establishments. Roy looked out at the pouring rain and listened quietly as he tried to convince himself that Luz was only prominent in his mind because she was the first girl he met there. He wasn't successful.

*   *   *

The CD player had long since turned off automatically back when the mournful sounds of Miles Davis' "Witches Brew" came to an end. Now, the only sounds evident in the room were the drumming of heavy rain drops against the sliding glass windows and the competing sleeping noises of Dennis Boggs and Marvin Turnbull. Boggs lay on the bunk breathing heavily through his mouth, his shoeless feet moving rhythmically with each snore. Turnbull was curled up more quietly in a lounge chair in the corner. On the nightstand between them sat a near-empty Wild Turkey bottle. It had been full when Turnbull showed up just three hours before.

*   *   *

By the time Scott arrived at his apartment, the wind had come up slightly and a few drops of rain had begun wetting the sidewalk. There weren't many to start with, but they were big, heavy drops and they made such loud noises impacting the cement that Scott was reminded of the hail that fell much too often in his native Oklahoma. As he hurried to get through the gate protecting the empty driveway, he didn't notice that a light was on in his upstairs bedroom.

It was only upon opening the front door that he realized he wasn't alone. The smell of boiled rice, garlic, soy sauce and ginger filled the air and he stopped to inhale the rich aromas. He closed his eyes and smiled as a feeling of homecoming hit him. It was very much like the emotions he encountered when going home on leave for the holidays and it amused him that these typical Filipino kitchen smells were now competing with the likes of roasted turkey, honey-cured ham, and fresh pecan pie for such a coveted place in his heart. It was at that moment that he knew Judy would become the daughter-in-law his father most feared. The thought made his smile wider.

Scott closed the door and latched the deadbolt in one, semi-automatic move, calling, "Judy?"

From upstairs he heard her answer, "Yes! Are you alone?"

"I am! I was just coming home to…" Scott stopped midsentence as the slightly damp and nearly naked beauty came sailing down the stairway. Her sandals slapped the stairs and her firm breasts jiggled almost comically until she realized that she might need to be a little more cautious in her descent. The towel which had been wrapped around her head dropped to the floor as she stopped on the bottom step of the stairs and her shining black hair tumbled into long, damp curls around her shoulders.

Scott's growing erection was evident before Judy had covered the ten feet separating the base of the stairway from the front door. He held out his arms and said, "I was going to…" before she once again interrupted his speech and thoughts by embracing and kissing him hungrily. He held her tightly, running his left hand up her slender back and cupping one rounded buttock with the right one. The taste of eggplant and pork lingered on her tongue as it collided with his own and he couldn't suppress the chuckle that rose from his belly.

"What?" Judy said, pulling her head back, but still pressing her lithe body to the young sailor.

"I was just thinking," he said, successfully suppressing a bigger laugh, "that I was never before greeted like this at Thanksgiving."

"When Thanksgiving comes, I will do it again, okay?"

He could not suppress the bark of laughter which finally did reach the surface and he held her more tightly as he said, "I hope I don't have to wait that long!"

Judy changed subjects quickly and said, "I came back early because I heard a rain might come and I don't want to be stuck there *naman* and I'm so hungry I eat supper when I get home. Are you hungry?"

Instead of answering, he kissed her again, deeply and gently.

When their lips separated, she laid her head against his chest and said, "you were saying that you were going to do something? *Ano yan?*"

"I changed my mind," he said. "Let's go upstairs before Billy gets home."

*   *   *

The rain was slicing sideways in asynchronous sheets by the time Ben locked his door against the storm. He removed his soaked shirt and dropped it by the front door before completing his security routine and then retrieved a fresh towel from a shelf in the closet. He toweled off vigorously, trying to warm himself while drying and then stripped the rest of the way before completing the task. Only when he was satisfied that every drop had been soaked up, did he dress in his house clothes of flip-flops, gym shorts and tee shirt. He paced slowly between his bed and the propane burner on his kitchen counter, while dragging a comb through his thick hair, trying to think where Nestor might have holed up.

He stood at the foot of his bed and cursed the United States again. While they had well-trained people and highly technical equipment scattered across his country, his countrymen were still struggling with basic needs. Telephones were still expensive and difficult to acquire for the vast majority of Filipinos and he could not help but dwell on the fact that locating Nestor would have been much easier with them. His own government bore most of

165

the responsibility for managing an economy still incapable of providing that service, but the Americans were the ultimate cause of their poverty. He held that belief deeply within his heart. He knew it to be fact. He knew also that he would be the instrument to rectify that situation. He felt affirmation rumble in the back of his head.

"Yes," a voice said.

Ben spun around and crouched defensively, frantically scanning the open closet. There were no legs protruding from beneath his meager wardrobe. There was no intruder.

He glanced back into the lighted and still empty living room and then crept toward the small, dark toilet. He flung the door open and then swiped at the light switch on the wall. The light blazed to reveal the toilet bowl and small sink and nothing more.

Ben searched the rest of the tiny apartment and rechecked the front door just to reassure himself. Finally, he dismissed the voice as some random sound he had merely misinterpreted and then returned to sit on his bed.

Upon leaving Ace's Place earlier, Ben had gone to the marketplace and scoured the many faces once again. Esther had still not heard from Nestor but didn't seem much concerned with his absence. After that, Ben had gone to the apartment Nestor shared with Esther and her adult daughter, who worked in a restaurant on Rizal Avenue and was herself nearly as eccentric as Nestor and Esther. Ben had knocked on the door for a good while and looked through their dirty windows and, as far as he could tell, no one was home. Ben was just leaving Nestor's church when the first few heavy rain drops began falling.

This wasn't the first time that Nestor had been difficult to locate, but this last task had been more important than any other to Ben and he was quite anxious to find out what exactly happened in the barrio. He didn't like having to wait until their scheduled rendezvous, but he would have to.

Listening to the rain hammer against the windows of his apartment, Ben laid down and closed his eyes, mentally reviewing his plans for Subic Naval Station. He knew that his superiors would not be happy about the outcome of this last mission and would most likely not approve of his ambitious and aggressive plans for assaulting the Naval Station. Regardless, he felt confident they would like the results when he was able to detonate explosive devices at several places.

Much as he was certain the Americans were the cause of all of his country's problems, he was certain that his letter would make them focus their scrutiny on the Naval Magazine. The scheme had become more and more inevitable to him over the last few days, and he was now convinced it was simply a matter of time. Soon he would gather his other assets, assemble his munitions and blow the Americans back to their own side of the world. He was equally confident those results would propel him to a much higher level within the organization. To the level he deserved.

Those final few moments before slipping into slumber was about the only time Ben allowed himself to indulge in the fantasy of hero worship he craved. Consciously, he liked to portray himself as the most modest of patriots, humbly accepting the responsibility to save his country from evil Western imperialist forces. But in these last crumbling minutes of consciousness, he envisioned himself being hailed by his comrades throughout the Philippines and by those world leaders he admired. The voice he had heard earlier repeated its affirmation of his prediction, but it did not rouse him this time. The pounding rain soon became the roars of adoring countrymen standing before him.

*   *   *

From the warmth of her bed, Luz listened to the faint sounds of rain and wind assaulting the building. Lita's room was at the far end of hall and the intervening walls effectively blocked her soft snores. They were both snug in their own small rooms, insulated from the howling tropical storm and isolated from the rest of the drama unfolding on the streets of Olongapo. Her brain was buzzing.

After the jarring historic flashes of trauma she had endured earlier, Gloria and Lita insisted she go back to her room and rest. She resisted them at first, insisting that all was well. She just had a headache, she said. She was just tired, she said. She would be fine, she said.

The clientele had actually been slowly drifting out as the storm intensified, and the traffic on Gordon Avenue dwindled. Just as Luz was reassuring her workmates, Ernesto and Boy – Mama Nina's nephews – dropped by to check for any problems that might have occurred due to the storm. They hadn't witnessed Luz's episode and the girls did not relay it to them. Fortunately, the bar's occupants had been reduced by then to just Luz, Lita, Gloria and her customer. Luz told them they would close for the night after Gloria's bar fine was paid. There were no objections.

Luz's thoughts were now much more focused than they had been before the memory of her rape had played out. Those recovered memories must have shocked her mind into some type of hyper analysis mode. No matter how she tried to imagine different conclusions from the picture of connected dots in her mind, she always returned to the only one which made sense.

Interrupted Weekend

Very shortly after she had witnessed Ben talking to the two strangers about American's frequenting the Mabuhay restaurant so many years ago, an American Naval officer had been murdered on the highway between Olongapo and Angeles City, where Clark Air Force base was located.

The day after her sexual assault by Aguilar, Ben came to the restaurant early to check on her and was there when she arrived. He quickly drew her into a corner of the kitchen away from others and asked her what had happened. She was going to try to make up a lie but started crying softly instead and told him about the savage attack in hushed and embarrassed tones. He listened silently to her story and then handed her a clean dish towel to dry her tears.

Looking around, Ben insisted that she not trust anyone at the restaurant, especially Lucinda and then whispered to her that she needn't worry about "Mr. Smith" ever again. She must forget the whole incident. She started to ask why, but he stopped her with a raised finger and a quick shake of his head. He told her once again to forget what had happened, to never ask about it and to never, ever mention it to Lucinda. After another quick look around, he reached into a pocket and withdrew the glass eye she had lost the night before. He took her hand and placed it there, enclosing her fingers around it. She looked up with astonishment and started to ask how he had found it, but he held a finger to her lips. With one last look around the dining area, he told her one last thing, frowned and then left quickly.

Within the week, she heard news about a businessman from Manila, Adolfo Aguilar, being found dead at the same hotel where she was raped. He had been savagely stabbed to death with a large knife. She had never consciously connected Aguilar with the mysterious "Mr. Smith" until now.

Only two weeks after her assault, Ben found her a waitressing job at a different restaurant. She hadn't thought that Lucinda would allow her to leave the Mabuhay, considering that she had paid for her eye operations, the prosthetic eye and her rent for most of the time she had been in Olongapo. Nonetheless, Lucinda seemed very happy for her and wished her well. Additionally, Luz was allowed to live in the group home for several more months until she moved in with some girls from the new restaurant. By then Lucinda was gone and Ben told Luz she had quit her job and moved to Manila. Luz never heard from or about her again.

Luz really had tried to forget the whole thing, as instructed. And as she lay there listening to the rain, it was evident that she had been more successful than she thought possible. The recovered memories and the reemergence of those critical details about Ben's interventions in her young life crashed against her self-image and once more shook her concepts of

168

reality.

Had Ben shown some kind of unusual interest in Denny Boggs? Had he been watching him as closely as he had the customers of the Mabuhay restaurant so long ago? All of Ben's idiosyncrasies and peculiarities seemed to take on a sinister sheen. All of his "help" over the years seemed somehow less altruistic and much more manipulative. What she believed to be the final two pieces of the puzzle had fallen into place when Ben suggested the relationship with Roy Thompson and Scott proposed that the murder in Barretto might have been the work of a rebel group.

As she lay there trying to sleep, Luz was incredibly conflicted and unable to see a satisfactory resolution. Ben's connections to all those events seemed to be clear and unavoidable facts. Review of these memories had also reminded Luz again just how much help Ben had provided her over the years. While Ben may have done some terrible things, at least some of those things had been to Luz's benefit. Certainly not all of them could have been done with nefarious intent, she thought. Besides, could she trust these new memories? The previous ones had seemed solid and unequivocal. Now she was riddle with uncertainty.

Would it be such a bad thing to pursue a relationship with Roy Thompson? The idea was more than a little appealing to her and she couldn't see how a simple, sexual relationship with one American sailor could be problematic.

But two days ago, she also couldn't see how her oldest friend might be involved in multiple murders. Nor had she remembered then that her sister was also the victim of the same rapist who had taken her. Tears soaked into her pillow, and it was a long time before sleep finally came.

*   *   *

Nestor Dimasalang never had problems falling asleep. He slept soundly, comfortably. He had been ensconced in his own special haven for most of the day, praying in gratitude to his God. After all, he was God's natural angel, doing good works in the cause of eternal life. Tomorrow, he would begin a new role in that capacity. The world was balanced, and he was part of the equation. If he had dreams, they stayed in their own world, away from daylight.

Sunday

Chapter 25

The rain had slowed from last night, but it still beat steadily on his window. He wasn't yet familiar with the monsoonal cycles of the Philippines and wasn't sure if this was a part of that or not, so he made another mental note to find out. Roy had hoped to get in a short run this morning but when his alarm sounded at 7:00 AM, he heard the familiar drumming of rain drops, took one look out the window and promptly went back to sleep. Fortunately, the additional two and a half hours of sleep he grabbed seemed enough to soften the jet lag more than yesterday, so now his plan was to take another long, hot shower, piddle around the room for a while and then grab a leisurely Sunday brunch at the chow hall.

One thing Roy had learned after spending so many years living close to sea level, some of them in tropical climates, was the necessity to wage an ongoing battle against body fungus. So, after the shower, he made a mental note to purchase additional medicated foot powder while he was drying his feet. He dressed in a pair of comfortable slacks and a loose-fitting polo and then used his socks to get the last bit of moisture from between his toes. Deciding not to trust his mental note-taking abilities, he found a pad of post-it notes and jotted down Lysol spray and crotch talc along with the foot powder.

The piddling wasn't very productive and after rearranging just a few of his shirts in a drawer, he spotted the book he had begun on the flight over, laying on the desk beneath the alarm clock. He couldn't get through a single page without thinking of Luz and put it back down within minutes.

Fuck it, he thought. He was hungry anyway, so he went to the front desk and called for a taxi.

He sat in the same chair that he had on Friday afternoon but there was no sun glinting off rain puddles. This time the puddles were running quickly, and the sun was hidden behind thick, rolling clouds. Rain ran steadily from the slightly pitched roof, splashing noisily around a cement block which had been strategically placed below the gutter spout. It reminded him to make another mental note. In addition to the various medicated powders, he decided to get a large umbrella. He knew he was going to need a larger one for at least the rest of the day, regardless of whether or not monsoon season was upon them.

Brunch no longer sounded good by the time he got to the exchange, so he stopped at a canteen and gobbled down a double cheeseburger with spicy fries before going in to shop. Then he added Tums to his shopping list.

The quick shopping visit at the exchange did nothing to relieve his restlessness. His initial plan – after the idea of getting up early and running had died – was to do the shopping, hang around the barracks, maybe read a little. The prospects of that were as unappealing now as the idea of brunch had become earlier. The fact was that he wanted to see Luz again.

She wasn't the first thing he had thought of when he awoke, but her image appeared very quickly thereafter. The taxi waited for him as he put everything but the new umbrella into his room.

That turned out to be a smart move because the rain held at a steady drizzle as Roy walked out the main gate and back to Gordon Avenue. The traffic patterns were a bit different from what he had seen on Friday afternoon and what he saw today. There were a few less cars on the streets and considerably fewer trikes blocking the intersection. Also, some of them had more or less clear plastic sheeting hung in the entryway to the sidecar as a barrier against the rain.

Roy tried to assign some causative factor to his restlessness but couldn't pin it down to any one thing. He wanted to see Luz. He wanted to learn more about the murder. But he also wanted to be a part of something again. After the death of Lisa Bartow, he had burrowed into his work in Iceland, but now he hadn't yet started any work to embrace. He wasn't part of an official investigation, and he wasn't yet part of the security team at the NAVMAG. He felt disconnected and without purpose. Worse, he felt lonely.

The day spent with Frank Burkholdt had exacerbated those feelings by reminding him of the great camaraderie he had experienced at the beginning of his Naval career. The Naval Security Group had been a very exclusive, tight-knit and – by necessity – secretive cabal of unique individuals. He had certainly made other friends over the years and really enjoyed the work he had been doing as a Master at Arms, but he had never felt the same sense of professional family as he had since before leaving the SECGRU so many years earlier.

And then a strange idea occurred to him. Ace's Place suddenly assumed a status he would never have imagined before. It might have become the dubious nexus of Roy's salvation. He didn't know what he might learn there today, but Ace's Place was where he had met Dennis Boggs and it was certainly where Luz worked. He had also learned from Frank that several CTs frequented the bar regularly. That was enough of a connection for Roy at that moment.

Roy kept his umbrella open walking under the awnings on Gordon Avenue because they leaked so badly. He was amused by the vanity he felt about wanting to look good for Luz, but then felt an unfamiliar twinge of fear as he realized that she might not even be there.

As he got nearer, he berated himself silently for his scattered thinking around the situation. He was being silly. It had been what seemed like only a few months since the death of Lisa Bartow. There were beautiful girls all over the Philippines. He had known Luz only two days. Hell, he had been in the Philippines only two days and she was the first woman he had talked to. He wasn't a kid who fell in love with the first woman to talk nicely to him. At least, he didn't think he was. All those perfectly rational thoughts seemed to have won the battle for his internal narrative as he pushed open the door to Ace's Place.

Roy had only a few seconds to look into the bar before turning around and closing the umbrella outside the door. His eyes didn't need to adjust much to the indoors because of the gloom of the day and he saw there were only a couple of people there. He was tapping the pointed metal end of his new umbrella on the sidewalk when Roy heard the familiar, "Hello, come in, have a sit." He gave the umbrella a few more shakes and twirls before entering completely.

"You want beer?" Luz said. Her train of thought was interrupted as she recognized Roy. She really hadn't expected to see him for at least a few days, despite how much he had been in her conversations since having first met him. Her automatic smile instantly became more genuine after seeing him and her eyes reflected an enigmatic sort of questioning. For the first time in a long time, she felt the fluster that sometimes came with sexual attraction. It wasn't all together unpleasant.

Two young Filipino men sat at a corner table with Lita, sharing a meal of fried fish, boiled vegetables and steamed rice. Roy couldn't help but notice the faint, fishy aroma coming from the table. They all looked up casually but only Lita flashed a quick smile. He nodded at the group and continued toward the bar counter.

"Hi, Luz. I think I'll just have coke right now," Roy responded, pulling a stool out from the bar.

Luz sat two coasters on the counter quietly and then turned toward the cooler to retrieve the drink. For the moment her normal, friendly banter had abandoned her, and she stood over the open cooler, temporarily stuck for words or actions. Finally, she managed to say, "You want ice?"

"Nah. If they've been in the fridge, that'll be good."

She avoided eye contact as she poured cold soda into a squatty, clear glass and sat them both on the coasters before him. Roy tried to hang his umbrella on the counter by its curved handle, but it wouldn't stay.

"Can you stash this back there somewhere?" he said. "I have a feeling that it will come in handy over the next couple of years."

Luz obliged by leaning it against the wall, next the beer cooler and said, "*dito, nalang.*"

Roy either remember some of the Tagalog words he had learned since being there, or just intuited the phrase to mean that it would be "here." Either way, something about the way she said it made him realize that she wasn't quite the same as he remembered her being on Friday night. Something was bothering her, and he suspected he knew what.

"So," he said. "Did you hear what happened in Barrio Barretto?"

"I hear Denny's *novia* was, uh, maybe dead," she said, still avoiding looking into his eyes. "It is so sad."

"It surely is" he replied. Roy didn't let on that he might know any more about it than anyone else. He watched her as she busied herself behind the bar and saw that her eyes, those strange and beautiful eyes, were moistened with tears. The internal narrative which he had managed to silence before entering the bar, once again began the argument.

Lisa had actually been dead for nearly a year. She had killed herself because she could no longer bear the pain of her existence. The possibility of passing along HIV to Roy was just an excuse she had used to justify the ending of her steadily increasing emotional pain. It was a permanent solution to a problem for which she saw no end. It wasn't her fault that her mood disorder drove her to such a drastic decision; that it blinded her to the possibility of leading a more normal life. Just as it was not Roy's fault that he was now feeling much more than just sympathy for Luz.

And while it was true that Olongapo probably contained thousands of beautiful women – willing, able and ready to do whatever he wanted them to – it was also becoming clear that Luz was something else. What did it matter that she was the first Filipina he had met? What mattered was that she seemed intelligent and funny and emotionally connected to others' feelings. The rational voice he had heard earlier, was now considering additional evidence. As he was contemplating what to do with the new arguments presented by himself, Luz spoke.

"I know he had a girlfriend there, but I don't meet her," Luz said, wiping her eyes carefully with a tissue. "I don't think she is a secret *ngayon.*"

Roy wanted to tell her how he might understand what Boggs was feeling. He wanted to tell her how he too had lost a loved one. For some reason, he wanted to tell her everything he was feeling. However, as emotional as he was, his reason won out again and the investigator in him emerged.

"Did you ever see him anywhere other than here?" he asked.

"No. I only see... wait. I see him at the *ano*, the FILAM Festival one time. You know that?" The memory seemed to shake her out of her emotional funk for the time being. Roy shook his head.

"That is when the base has a, uh, *karnabal*? Like a fair they have by the main gate, and they have food and booths and games. A celebration of the Filipinos and Americans." She pronounced celebration slowly and with great caution, as if she had just acquired it and was taking it out of the box for the first time.

"That is the only time, I think," she said. "He is just talking to everyone like he is here, but I don't talk to him. I am with a... I was with a guy from the ship." Had Roy looked a little lower, he would have seen just the faintest of blushes creep up her neck. He was still looking at her eyes, even though she was still not returning his gaze.

"Have you ever heard anyone talk bad about him?"

"*Hindi*," she said. "I think he is friends to everyone." Roy was still watching her eyes and noticed that she closed her eyes for what seemed like just a fraction longer than she normally did. That didn't necessarily indicate that she was lying, but she might know more than she was willing to disclose just now. After she opened them again, he finally realized what had been "different" about her eyes. The pupil of the left eye never changed size. It seemed almost perfect in every other way but now that he noticed the pupil, he also realized that the brown and amber striations of her left iris were just a tiny bit darker than those of her right eye.

He smiled reflexively. He wasn't amused at the fact that she had a prosthetic eye, in fact, it increased his respect for her. And while part of him was happy he had figured it out, a deeper part was saddened by the idea of how difficult her life must have been.

"What?" Luz said. She was looking into his eyes now, with concern and curiosity at his grin.

"Nothing," he said. "I just noticed how beautiful your eyes are."

This time the blush was immediate and did not creep. It leapt up through her face in a flash as she realized he had discovered her secret.

"I, I," she stuttered. "*Hay nako! Bastos, naman!*" Her face was filled with anger and surprise.

"I'm sorry! What did I say? I'm just saying how pretty you are," Roy looked around as if for moral support. There was none to be had. The trio eating lunch were still at it and paid them no mind. It was only then that he realized that she may have been self-conscious about her condition. When he looked back to apologize again, Luz had turned her back and was standing with her hands resting on the beer cooler.

"Listen," he said. "I really am sorry! I was just..."

The front door opened, and an unusually cool and damp breeze interrupted him, mid-apology. Ben hastened to close the door behind him and started for the counter. He was carrying the familiar blue satchel but was also draped in a clear, plastic rain slicker that looked almost like a large trash bag. He glanced quickly around the bar as he plastered the professional grin on his face and approached Roy.

Luz had turned back when the door had opened and it appeared to Roy as if she had recomposed herself admirable, if she ever really was that upset in the first place. However, she wasn't smiling and said nothing to either Roy or Ben.

"You want peanuts?" Ben said. He flicked his eyes at Luz and realized immediately that something had happened between them. He couldn't tell what, but it didn't seem to be anything that would work in his favor.

"Sure," Roy said, reaching for his wallet. He then realized that he hadn't yet paid for his soda. He handed a ten peso note to Luz and said, "I'll go ahead and pay for my coke and get some change for peanuts, if that's okay." Luz took his money silently and put his change on the counter.

Ben reached underneath his clear poncho, pulled out a small rag that had been stuffed into the back of his trousers and wiped off the blue bag before setting it onto the barstool next to Roy's. He pulled out two small bags of nuts for Roy and then, in Tagalog, said to Luz, "Oh, I forgot to drop these off for you yesterday. These should come in handy for you around here."

He removed a thin plastic bag which had been opened at the top and placed it on the counter in front of her. In the bag were two yellow, rubber gloves; the kind meant to be worn for washing dishes.

"These come four in a bag, but I gave the other pair to another friend."

Roy spotted the gloves and then looked away quickly. Instead, he handed a peso coin to Ben and tore into one of the bags of peanuts.

"Salamat," Luz said and placed the gloves behind the counter.

In a move designed to keep his own eyes from being read by the peanut vendor, Roy took another peso from the counter and walked to the jukebox. He stood over the old Wurlitzer Zodiac looking up and down the list of songs; however, he wasn't thinking about anything listed there. He was thinking how the rubber gloves, now nestled behind the bar's counter, looked very much like the rubber glove he had seen in the crime scene photos that morning. He was thinking about how the bag which held them was already half empty. Then, for some reason, he was thinking about the picture in Pillotero's office and how an ARVN soldier could be fighting for his life alongside a group of American soldiers who couldn't be bothered to learn his actual name. He was thinking about the people talking in their native language behind him and wondering if his thoughts reflected some pathological paranoia or just the healthy suspicion of an all-too-obvious coincidence.

His eyes finally focused on the title "Girl You Know It's True," by Milli Vanilli and he barked an unconscious laugh.

"Roy, play D5," Lita called from her lunch table.

"Sure thing," he replied. "Luz, any requests?"

"I don't care," she said and then corrected herself. "How about B6."

He didn't bother to read the title of "D5" as he punched it in, but he couldn't help but notice the title of "B6" was "Da Ya Think I'm Sexy" by Rod Stewart. That gave him something else to think about as the rhythms of Lionel Richie's "All Night Long" started to fill the bar.

Ben had zippered his bag and was turning to leave when Roy got back to his stool.

"Thanks, hah?" Ben said in that strange idiom Roy had heard from several Filipinos. Roy waved and bobbed his head in recognition of his departure and climbed back onto the barstool to finish his soda. He decided to do what he could to mend fences with Luz and to try and get some information from her concerning Ben the vendor. Luz was busying herself with something in the sink until he scooted up and rested his elbows on the counter, when she turned and looked at him directly.

"You think I'm *pangit*?" she said. Although there was just a slight lilt at the end of her statement, he really couldn't tell if that were a question or an assertion of fact. Regardless, he didn't know what *pangit* meant.

"What?"

"Do you think I'm ugly?" she said again, much more plainly.

"Of course not. In fact, I believe I said just the opposite of that."

"You don't like my eyes."

"Nooo," he said in a voice that sounded patronizing even to him. "What I said was that I think they are beautiful." Looking into those eyes again, he was reminded of the spark he had detected just a couple of days earlier but felt she wasn't anywhere near as angry as she could get. And he also felt

179

lucky about that, so to keep from getting nearer that point, he decided to change the subject. He looked around once more to see Lita and the two young men engaged in an earnest conversation about something and then leaned in toward Luz again.

"Listen," he said in a voice too low to be overheard by the others. "How well do you know Ben?"

Luz didn't answer immediately. She was searching his face, but she didn't quite know what she was looking for. Honesty, maybe it was honesty.

"I know him well," she said, also quietly. "He was one of the first people I meet when I come here to Olongapo. I was very young and he, *ano*, he keep me from troubles. He help… helped me to work. He helped me to…" She began to tear up as she thought about the memories so recently unearthed, as well as the questions those memories begged. She reached for a tissue to wipe the fresh tears and then glanced over to ensure they were still not being watched. Convinced they could not be overheard, she searched his face again and found something – again, unsure about just what it was – that freed her to verbalize things she had not even considered divulging just a few days before.

"He helped me to get my eye," she said. There were no tears when she revealed that. The only thing now shining in her eyes was determination.

"He do… did a lot for me since before." She stopped and took a deep breath. "I know him for a long time, but I don't know now if he is always helping me for me. Sometimes I think he helps for his own." She felt a sense of relief but wasn't sure why.

"I know what you mean," Roy said. And he did understand, despite her broken English. "I have known many people who do that, and I might even do it myself sometimes. So, when I ask this, keep in mind I am asking for myself and for the sake of others. Do you think Ben might know something about what happened to Dennis Boggs' girlfriend?"

She hesitated just long enough to take another deep breath and was again surprised by the emotions that simmered so close to the surface.

"I don't think… I don't know."

"Can I see those gloves he just gave you?"

Luz silently retrieved the bag of gloves and put them on the counter in front of him. He looked it over and then took one out for a closer inspection. It was a common brand that he had seen in many stores and had even used himself.

"Can I have a piece of paper and something to write with?"

Luz reached for the pad of "night off" papers she had previously used to document when a girl was bought out of the bar and tore one off. Then

180

she turned it face down on the counter and placed a ballpoint pen on top of it. He noticed the pen was of the blotchy, U.S. Government type. After writing down the brand, size, place of manufacture and anything that even suggested that it might identify with the found glove, he folded the paper carefully into his wallet.

Luz didn't know what to make of Roy's interest in the gloves, but it was obvious that he had more than just a passing interest in Ben and the murder in Barrio Barretto.

She also didn't know what to make of all of the emotional turmoil currently swirling around her. Three days ago, she was fairly confident about her place in the world. She knew what her responsibilities were. She knew where her loyalties lay. She knew how to deal with customers. She knew who she was and the world in which she lived. Today, on this sad Sunday afternoon, she wasn't sure about any of that. Now she was in turmoil, questioning her friendships and her judgement. She was thinking and feeling things buried long ago. Things which were now fresh and raw. Now, she was disclosing things to near strangers just because... because of what? Again, she didn't know, and it was driving her crazy.

"You know," she said quietly. "I don't tell that before." She looked again into his eyes and then back to the occupied table.

"Almost no one knows about the... about my eye. But you see it. *Bakit*? Why you know about my eye?"

He started to explain his interest in details and his interest in her and his desire to get at the bottom of questions, but instead he said simply, "I like looking at you and I notice things... like beautiful eyes."

The blush was less pronounced this time, but still visible. She could not remember a time when she had been so flustered. Her normal flirtatious banter had disappeared. Her ability to deflect the flirtations of American sailors had diminished. And the impervious wall against emotional attachment, which she had been carefully constructing for so long, seemed to be crumbling at her feet.

Chapter 26

He wasn't necessarily surprised to see Roy in Ace's Place, but Ben was a bit concerned that he and Luz didn't seem to be hitting it off all that well. He decided to not worry about it for the time being, realizing that he had only seen them interact for a very short amount of time.

A voice said, "Yes." He had heard that voice a few times since the previous evening but ignored it. Just his overactive imagination, he thought. It will pass when things get back on track.

Right now, he would worry about finding Nestor and learning what happened in the barrio. He still had plans he needed to implement but didn't want to make final decisions until he had all the information. If the victim had been an American whore, other than the boisterous, glad-handing American he had planned for, it was just a small wrinkle he felt could be ironed out fairly easily. Nonetheless, it might require a little more imagination on his part.

He trudged through the rain, noting that it had abated slightly, and the sun was fighting a losing battle to break through the clouds, reflecting a thinning between the bands of the storm. The rain was a major reason Ben had not tried again this morning to track down Nestor. Anyway, he thought, there appointment time was near.

He tried to work out various scenarios in his head as he walked toward their rendezvous point but his thoughts kept circling back to the operation carried out on the previous Friday evening and the loop angered him. He didn't like having so many loose ends and it seemed that more were coming undone by the minute. He hoped to tie up at least one of those in the next few minutes. Yes, yes, the voice echoed silently.

St. Columban Parish church had a mass scheduled for 3:45 PM and Ben was to meet Nestor just inside its narthex at 3:00. As he stepped inside the outer gates, he could see that a couple of the parishioners were escaping the rain under the awning between it and the church. He joined them and took off his rain poncho, gently shaking off the rain. Looking into the nave, he could see Nestor lighting a votive candle, so he stepped inside and sat in the last pew, all the way to the right. Shortly, Nestor stepped back from the candles, crossed himself and moved toward the door. There was very little light coming through the windows, lending to the general dimness of the church so Ben wasn't sure Nestor could even see him where he sat. However, without ever looking in his direction, Nestor turned into the pew and sat down silently.

"I had hoped to hear from you earlier, since there seems to have been a… an adjustment required during your job," Ben said.

"Yes," Nestor replied. "Adjustments were made. That is a rule of life, isn't it? And sometimes, of death." Nestor didn't have nearly the number of wrinkles that his sister had, but the mischievous glint in his eyes was identical to hers.

"Your friend didn't arrive as scheduled but his friend did. And she was blessed in his place." Nestor had used that term for the two previous assassinations he had committed for Ben, as well. He didn't know if that was Nestor's way of avoiding an incriminating term, if it reflected some form of coping mechanism developed in order to deal with the services he provided, or, as Ben suspected, just the way Nestor had incorporated his interpretations of Catholicism into his personal, twisted idiosyncrasies. Ben had mixed feelings concerning the euphemism. His own thoughts about religion pretty much mirrored the Marxist view of it as a tool used by the powerful to maintain control over the ignorant masses. However, he hadn't totally escaped the guilt and fear he learned as a young child growing up in the mostly Catholic Philippines. Some lessons were very hard to unlearn.

"Were there any other problems to adjust for?" Ben asked.

"No problems. The key worked perfectly. The woman was blessed quickly, before I could tell it wasn't the man. She was peaceful. I cleaned up. I waited until 7:30 before leaving and there were no other visitors." He looked around toward the front doors as a few more parishioners began arriving for mass and then stood, looking expectantly at Ben. Ben also stood up and removed an envelope from his back pocket. Nestor received it, tucked it into a front pocket and smoothed his Polo Barong over it.

He started to leave and then stopped abruptly.

"It probably is nothing, but those gloves were quite hot and uncomfortable, so I removed them when I left the house," he said. The glint sparkled once more as he smiled at Ben. "Again, I'm sure it is nothing to be concerned with but when I arrived home, I realized I had only one in my pocket."

Ben was frozen. While his body was planted firmly at the far, right end of the last pew in the church, his mind was racing with questions. Had the glove been left at the house in Barrio Barretto? Had it been found? Could it be traced back to either of them?

"And now I must prepare for my first day as a lector," Nestor said proudly. "I have wanted to be a part of this service for many years, and I have now been given a chance." His smile grew even bigger as he nodded toward a stunned Ben and turned away.

Ben watched silently as Nestor cordially greeted a few people making his way through the church. He literally didn't know whether to bolt from the church or to kneel and pray. After a moment of total consternation, he took a few unsteady steps toward the exit, only to backtrack to retrieve his bag and the poncho draped over it. The first questions about the missing glove were now interlaced with questions about Nestor's new role in the church. Standing there with the slick poncho dripping residual rain drops onto his ankle, he contemplated the conflict between Nestor's roles of assassin and church lector. His thoughts even drifted into the neighborhood of his own deeply conflicted beliefs, but only for a very short visit. They quickly retreated back into the comfortable world view he had developed for himself, where his convictions still stood sturdy and virtuous, at least to him. He stood motionless for a moment, lost in thought, but eventually sank slowly back down onto the pew.

His hopes of tying up loose ends had been lost along with the yellow, rubber glove and he had more questions now than when he had entered the little Catholic church. He sat, staring vacantly at the podium at which Nestor would soon give his first public reading of God's words and decided he did not want to be a witness to that particular recitation. Nestor may have cleaned up his own mess after killing Boggs' girlfriend, but he had created a much bigger mess for Ben.

Finally, he realized that his only hope of salvaging any part of his plan for the Naval Magazine lay in learning as much as he could about what the authorities had found in the barrio. The fact that Boggs was still alive and that his officer girlfriend had been killed in his place, was now confirmed. That original plan, so carefully devised over months of observation and calculation, was souring quickly and would need to be set aside until he could gather more intelligence. Much of his original purpose for selecting Dennis Boggs for assassination in the first place, concerned the negative effect on morale that such a murder would have on other American enlisted men.

As he began to assess what to look for and who to contact, that now-familiar voice whispered just a tiny bit louder inside his head. What it was now murmuring, as yet unintelligible, were building at the back of his skull.

Other voices joined it. As the words began to take on meaning, a physical feeling spread around the cortex of his brain on an unrelenting march towards his prefrontal lobe. The voices began to assume familiarity, although he still couldn't fully identify them, and the words took shape. They know, the voices said. They know who you are and what you've done. They have the glove. They know where you got it. They know about the maid, the key, Nestor. He raised his hands to the side of his head and squeezed it. He ran his hands to the back of his skull, trying to force the words to retreat into oblivion. He hunched over planting his elbows on his thighs, aggressively massaged the back of his head until the voices abated. But they would not go completely silent. The murmurs remained, bubbling at the base of his skill. He stood slowly and pulled the rain poncho over his head still throbbing from the relentless voices, picked up the blue bag and ventured once more into the rain.

Chapter 27

Boy and Ernesto had disappeared into the back of the bar and were, judging by the sounds of it, moving beer cases around. At any rate, Roy heard the clinking of glass and heavy things being dragged along the floor. Luz and Lita had already moved the lunch dishes into the back as well and were, he assumed, washing them somewhere past the area where the restrooms were located. For the moment, he was alone in the front of the bar, so he swiveled his stool around to look out the curtained windows and listen to the muted sounds of the street. The rain was falling steadily and seemed a little less intense than when he first arrived. There appeared to be less traffic than when he was last on Gordon but attributed that more to it being Sunday than the heavy rain.

Just when he thought he might have the bar to himself for the remainder of the day, two figures stopped in front of the door and shook the rain from the umbrella they shared. Scott held the door as Judy walked through, looking around the empty room.

Emerging from the back, Luz exclaimed something in Tagalog and hurried to Judy for a hug. They stood in the center of the bar and chattered excitedly to each other as Scott moved to a table across from the jukebox where he dropped his collapsed umbrella. In the middle of their chat, Luz emitted a short squeal of glee, grabbed Judy's hand, and led her into the back.

Roy watched the reunion with some amusement and curiosity, smiling but silent. Alone now with a stranger, Scott raised his eyebrows and shrugged his shoulders in an open question as he approached the counter.

"I may be going out on a limb here," Roy said. "But I think they know each other."

"Little bit, little bit," Scott replied, sounding a little like Robert De Niro.

Scott climbed into the stool closest to the wall and called into the back, "*Gusto ko serbesa*, Luz."

"You wait," came from the back.

Scott shrugged again and said, "Nothing but the best customer service at Ace's." Scott had never seen the man sitting here now despite spending much of his free time at the bar. He wasn't ready to conclude that this stranger was the new Senior Chief he was expecting, but the thought crossed his mind as he slipped from the stool and walked back to the front door.

Luz came from the back and said, "Congratulations, Scott!"

"*Huwág sabihin sa*, uh, *ng*, uh…" Scott struggled for the Tagalog word for wedding. "*Ano, kasal*," he finally remembered as he came back to the counter. If Scott was in fact going to be working with the guy sitting at the bar, he didn't want to reveal his marriage plans to anyone in his chain-of-command just yet.

Luz glanced in Roy's direction and understood immediately what was happening. She retrieved a beer from the refrigerator and sat it on a coaster as Scott pulled a crumpled ten peso note from his jean pocket and tossed it on the bar, regaining his perch.

Wanting to avoid additional awkwardness, Luz quickly introduced the two.

"Scott, this is Roy and he is to be there where you work."

"Senior Chief Thompson?" Scott extended his hand. "Welcome aboard! I'm YN2 Chalmers, Captain's writer at the NAVMAG."

Roy shook his hand and said, "Nice to meet you, Petty Officer Chalmers. I take it you spend a little time in here?"

"Yeah… my girlfriend used to work here so I come in to complain about her every so often."

"Ah*, bastos*," Luz said jokingly.

"I see you have already met the resident virgin," Scott tilted his head in Luz's direction and grinned.

Luz let the joke lie unanswered.

Roy was oddly embarrassed by the reference to Luz. For some reason that remained unclear for the time being, he was uncomfortable joking about her sexuality. The idea that his feelings for her may have grown so serious, so quickly, resurrected his earlier self-questioning.

"Well, I am not sure about the status of her hymen, but I have enjoyed learning from Luz about other things around here."

"*Hay nako!*" Luz shook her head and turned to the refrigerator to hide yet another flush she felt rising through her neck. She wasn't exactly sure about the definition of the word "hymen," but she had a pretty good idea. And, not for the first time, she asked herself why she seemed to get so embarrassed around this new American.

Scott took a short swig of beer and started to continue the harassment of Luz but stopped himself. Instead, he leaned toward Roy and said quietly, "I was in the office when you were at that meeting at OPM yesterday. I'm sorry your check-in has been such a crappy one."

Roy cleared his throat and said, "Yeah. Well, I'm not sure it is the crappiest one I've ever had, but it certainly is one of the more interesting ones." He glanced at Luz, whose back was still to them, and continued, "Very interesting, so far."

Neither spoke for a minute or two but the silence was soon broken by Luz asking Roy if he wanted another soda.

"I think I can handle a beer now," he said. Then, turning to Scott, said, "You ready?"

He tilted his bottle slightly to ascertain the level of beer in the bottle and said, "I am senior, but let me get this one as a welcome aboard."

Again, they sat silently while Luz served their beer. As she was returning Scott's change, he said, "why don't you go ahead and play the jukebox."

"How long have you been here?" Roy asked. "You seem to speak the language pretty well."

"I've been here a little over a year. I got on the USS Nimitz just before her last Mediterranean cruise and rode her into the Pacific. I got orders to the NAVMAG after that. The NAVMAG is just my second tour of duty and might be my last." Female laughter arose from somewhere in the back of the bar. "But I haven't made up my mind yet."

Judy and Lita came from the back, smiling. Lita spoke rapidly to Luz standing over the jukebox, as Judy walked around and draped her left arm over Scott's shoulders.

"Judy, this is Senior Chief Thompson," he said. "He is the new guy I was telling you about. Senior, this is my girlfriend, Judy." She wasn't offended by not being referred to as his fiancé, since they had already talked about the need to keep that secret for a while. More precisely, they agreed to not tell his American friends. He knew that telling her Filipina friends was going to happen, regardless of his wishes. She said, "Nice to meet you."

"Nice to meet you, too," he replied. "Did you teach Scott to speak Filipino?"

"*Konti lang*," she said, smiling. "that means, 'a little bit'."

"Well, it seems like you're a good teacher."

"I'll go to church with Lita," Judy said to Scott. "Okay? And then we go to market, okay?"

"Sure," he replied. "Do you still want to go to the movie at six?"

"I'll be back before. I'll meet you to home, *nalang*."

"Okay. Have fun."

Judy, who still had her arm around Scott's neck, swung around on her tip toes and kissed him deeply, gently caressing his crotch. Roy averted his eyes and reached for his beer. When he looked back, Judy was smiling at Scott and said, "I have lots to confess!"

With that, she and Lita walked to the door and out into the rain.

Roseanne Cash was nearly halfway through "Runaway Train" by the time Luz backed away from the jukebox and went into the back to check on the beer resupply process. She didn't expect they would go through much product before the middle of the week, but she liked to know as much as she could about her domain, and she felt Scott and Roy might want to speak alone for a time. She wasn't wrong and Scott was turning towards Roy before the plywood door even banged shut.

"Senior, I know you can't say much – or maybe nothing – about the murder, but can you tell me if Master Chief Boggs is going to be okay?"

"Yes," Roy said. "To all of the above."

"I'm glad to hear that. I don't work for him, but I think he's a good man." Scott hesitated just a moment before continuing. "And I'd hate to think he was taken out by a fucking sparrow. It's bad enough if that's what happened to his girlfriend."

"Is that the scuttlebutt?"

"Well, partly, anyway. You know how bullshit goes around, especially when there isn't much being said officially. It's just the most rational rumor I've heard so far." Scott turned back to his beer but sat it back down without drinking.

"Have you ever heard anything out here on the streets that would make you think there were active sparrow operations around Olongapo?" Roy asked.

"Not really. I mean, I read things at work every once in a while, but I don't think I've ever heard anything out here. Most of the talk is about pussy and beer and the assholes we have to work with." Then, fearing he might not have properly gauged Roy's sense of humor, he hastened to add, "not that I am expecting that to happen to me any time soon."

Roy laughed. "Let's hope not!" he said. Adopting a more serious tone, he said, "What about the locals? Any reason to suspect anyone?"

"Naw…" he was scratching his chin in a near comical affectation of seriousness but before he could finish his thought, Roy said, "What about that Ben guy who is always selling something?"

"Ben? Oh, I can't imagine him being involved in anything like that. He's just a hustler, trying to make a peso off the *Kanos*. I mean, I see him around a lot of places, but he is always friendly. I can't see it."

"You might be right, but I can't be so certain of anything at this point. In fact, I need to get back to the base to check out something."

Roy picked up his beer bottle and decided to let the last half inch of beer remain there.

"Petty Officer Chalmers, it was nice meeting you and thanks for the beer," Roy said, as he stood. "I might be back out here later, depending on what I can find out on base. I look forward to working with you." They shook hands again before parting ways.

Roy walked out under to awning and saw that the rain was much lighter than it had been since starting the night before. In his urgency to get back to NISO, he totally forgot about his brand-new umbrella behind the bar at Ace's and began walking toward Magsaysay. As he reached the first corner, he heard a car horn beeping nearby, but had already learned to tune out such ubiquitous noises. It was only when he heard "Hey, Royboy!" that he turned toward the annoying sound.

The familiar yellow Impala belonging to Frank Burkholdt was slowly rolling through the intersection.

"Come around and climb in," Frank called. "We need to run out to the barrio for a little bit."

Roy started to refuse but realized the resulting argument would probably take longer than it would to just go along with him. Besides, there was no guarantee that anyone would be at the NIS office at this time on a Sunday afternoon and his suspicions about a possible link between Ben and the killing in Barretto were pretty tenuous so far. He looked both ways before abandoning the cover of the awning and dashing across the street.

"Okay, but we can't stay out late," Roy said as he rounded the front of Frank's car. "This is a school night, buster."

"Yeah? Well fuck you and jump in. And also, fuck you. You'll be thanking me soon enough."

They continued along Gordon Avenue and to Barrio Barretto beyond. Neither man saw Ben de Guzman trudging, zombie-like, through the rain toward Ace's Place.

Chapter 28

The rain was light, but it wouldn't have registered with Ben had it been a deluge. He was desperately trying to focus on the questions he needed to answer and was blocking everything else out. The concentration enabled him to squelch the voices in his head for now, but they seemed always on the verge of reemergence, like muffled conversations on the other side of a thick but unlocked door. He struggled to keep that door shut.

He was directly across the street from Ace's when Ben realized where he was. He stopped and turned, looking at the rain-speckled windows and the subtle, multi-colored lights emanating from the jukebox beyond the curtains. The image introduced him once again to the physical world for a moment and the voices at the back of his head grew ever so slightly louder. He continued to watch as a woman carrying an umbrella stopped in front of the door and shook the rain from it before entering the bar. He was aware that he knew her but couldn't be bothered with retrieving her name at the moment. Before he could command his legs to move, two young men emerged, laughing. They exchanged some friendly words before splitting up and going in opposite directions on the sidewalk. Again, he knew them but didn't care. They weren't yet important.

What was important now is that he find out what they knew. Perhaps more important, was finding out who *they* were. Of course, he knew that the authorities – the corrupt local politicians and police, the imperialist pigs who owned Boggs and his whore – were actively trying to uncover and understand details of his plot. The *they* he was fixating on at the moment were those around him.

He had learned early in their collaborations that Nestor's motives were money and "spiritual" connections. Being clever, he had played to those motives and was certain that his playing of that particular game was successful. Although staggered by Nestor's latest sloppy "adjustments" and loss of the glove, he knew full well that he could trust Nestor to do what was expected and to not be concerned with anything else about Ben's own long-term plans. But still.

Most of the various other assets he had employed over the years were also not a concern to Ben. They had blissfully gone about doing his bidding with no indication that they knew, cared, or were even capable of understanding what his true intentions were. But still.

There was one person he feared might have the background, insight and intelligence to see through his veneer as jovial vendor. There was one person who he knew to have the personal integrity, courage and a growing concern for others that might make them want to expose him. There was one person who had known Ben for several years and who had been witness to pivotal incidents. Incidents which might connect him to other violent acts.

As he stood there staring across the street, through the drizzling rain and dusty curtains and into the dim interior of Ace's Place, he saw the blurry shadow of that person moving behind the bar. He must discover what she knew. He needed to discover what she suspected. He needed to understand what she might do with that knowledge. Luz might be the key.

She *is* the key, the voices repeated. They were getting louder. She knows and you need to make her talk, they said. She needs to tell you what she knows. He began to step off the curb to cross the street when the voices spoke again. The thick door in his head creaked open ever so slightly. No. You might need help. You know where to find it. Go get it. She'll talk then. She will tell you what you must know.

He stopped and blinked again at the flickering shadows hidden by the curtains. The thick door in his mind slowly closed again as he thought about where it was that he needed. Yes, yes, he knew now. He would retrieve it and then he would talk to Luz. Yes, she would talk, didn't she always talk to him? Yes, but still.

Ben turned and walked toward his small apartment. What he needed was there, secure in a space in the wall between his closet and his toilet. It was resting there, waiting for him. It will be like my father is helping me, Ben thought. No, the voices said from beyond the door, it is your father's spirit helping you. He clenched his jaw while trying to ignore them and continued moving slowly home. He didn't notice the rain drops getting larger and falling harder.

Chapter 29

The two men began their trip to the barrio in relative silence as the rain started to increase in intensity once more and Frank cranked his windshield wipers to full throttle. As they approached the bend in National Highway, curving south around the cemetery, Roy finally had to ask, "So just why am I going to be thanking you?"

"I'm thinking we're going to meet someone at the BGU who might have some 'strictly unofficial' information that might help solve that murder," Frank said.

"Strictly unofficial?"

"Yes," Frank said. "You remember my friend, Charles?"

"Sure. Is that who we're meeting?"

"No, I don't think so."

"Then why did you ask if I remembered him?"

"Because of what he said about unofficial information."

"What the fuck are you talking about, Frank?"

"Remember when he said he would ask around, but that anything he might find out would be 'strictly unofficial'? Okay, so there's a phone call for me at the barracks about thirty minutes ago. The house boy comes looking for me, but I'm taking a shit and he can't find me, so he goes back to take a message but all that he is told is, 'there's something strictly unofficial at the Bad, Good and the Ugly Bar waiting for you.' Get it?"

"Jesus shit."

"My sentiments, exactly."

They didn't speak again for a few minutes as they made their way through the zigzags and were closing on the BGU.

"Listen. I am not shitting you here, Roy," Frank said. "If we hear anything that leads to something that helps in the investigation, you need to forget that Charles had anything to do with it. Strictly unofficial."

"Okay, so if we aren't meeting Charles, who are we supposed to meet? Did the phone message say anything about that?"

"No. But I have to think that he would have said something more if he

195

didn't think we would know who it was when we got there."

Just as they passed in front of the PC station, a gust of wind shook the car and sheets of rain threatened to rip off a wiper blade. And although there was at least another two hours of daylight left beyond the clouds, the storm had turned the day into an eerie dusk. All of the windows and doors at the BGU were closed against the onslaught, so Frank decided to back into a parking spot in front of the entrance, with the front of the car facing the wind. Maneuvering the Impala wasn't a problem because the parking lot was almost completely empty and the highway was nearly deserted; however, they could still see lights and shadowy figures moving inside the bar. Frank turned off the ignition and took a deep breath, blowing it out through flapping lips.

"At least they still have electricity," he said. "And if this works out, I expect free beer from you for the foreseeable future."

"You might get some of that even if this doesn't work out. Fuck."

"What?" Frank asked.

"I left my umbrella at Ace's Place."

"That's probably a good thing, because this wind would tear it to shit."

"Yeah? Well, fuck it anyway."

In unison, they shoved open the car doors against the wind and broke for the front entrance, which opened for them just as Frank reached for the handle.

"Mister Pronk!" Nathan stood behind the door and said, "You come in!"

Roy followed Frank through the door and very nearly fell on his ass because the concrete floor was slick with rain. As soon as he regained his balance and was through the door, Nathan pushed it closed again.

Frank took off his raincoat and shook it a few times before looking around to ensure there was no one to splatter. Roy simply tried to squeegee as much rain from his face and arms as he could with his hands. When they composed themselves and took a closer inventory of the bar, they saw two girls playing pool on one table and two young Americans playing on the other one. Roy believed they were all people he had seen the day before and the four played on as if the raucous entry of the two chiefs was commonplace.

"You want beer?" Nathan asked.

"Sure," Frank replied. "Has anyone been looking for us?"

"I don't think," he said, moving around the end of the bar.

Frank cast a quizzical look in Roy's direction and shrugged his shoulders. He then draped his wet coat over the back of a bar stool and sat on the one next to it.

"Are you fucking kidding me?" Roy said.

"I am not shitting you here," came the familiar refrain. "Take a seat and have a beer and whoever we're supposed to meet will show… or not. Nothing saying we can't have a beer while we're waiting."

Roy slowly shook his head and slicked back his hair with both hands before caving to the inevitable. But before he could sit, he heard a "tsst!" sound coming from the pool room area. A fortyish looking woman was standing timidly behind the corner of the wall which formed the backdrop of the counter.

Frank said, "Hey, Minda! Where is that ugly old man of yours?"

The woman didn't immediately reply, instead, looking around quickly to see if anyone else were watching. Satisfied that no one was interested in them, she flashed a "come here" gesture, whereby she cupped her hand at about chest level and pointed it at the two while making a downward scooping action. Not waiting for affirmation, she turned and disappeared around the corner. It was Roy's turn to look with a questioning face and he saw that Frank was already picking up his beer and coat. Roy followed his lead into the back of the bar.

The woman was already sitting down with her back to the wall. She was at a table near where Roy had seen the girls eating lunch yesterday and he could tell as he got closer that it was the most private table in the place. It was dimly lit and invisible from the entrance of the bar but in full view of the pool tables and the door leading to the rest rooms. If someone were looking for an "out of the way" table at the BGU, this was it.

The woman had a concerned look on her face and, even though Roy had never met her, it appeared to be one that she did not wear often. Frank must have noticed the same thing because as he sat, he said quietly, "Did you talk to Charles?"

Minda nodded her head and glanced nervously at the four pool players a last time and warily at Roy.

"Minda, this is Roy Thompson. He is an old friend of mine, and he is trying to figure out what happened at Denny's house a couple of days ago. Roy, this is Minda and she's married to Marvin Turnbull, who you met yesterday. Do you know something about what happened to Winnie?"

Roy sat down and then extended his hand across the table.

"Hello, Minda," he said.

She seemed to gain a bit of confidence and shook his hand tentatively.

"Nice to meet you," she said.

As his eyes adjusted to the light, Roy could see that Minda was probably a bit older than he had first thought. She was neatly dressed and judging by the dryness of her blouse, she must have come into the bar before the weather turned too nasty. It also appeared that her accent was not particularly heavy.

"Marvin tell, told, me yesterday about Winnie, but I haven't seen him since. I think he go to the base to see Denny."

"Probably still there," Frank said. Roy decided to say as little as possible. He was in "listener" mode again.

"I know Denny's maid," Minda said. That admission seemed to drain her even more. "She is Rosalita and I tell her to work for him when he said he wants a maid. I, uh, recommend her to him." She dropped her head and took a deep breath. Roy thought she might start crying, but she just shook her head and looked up again with pleading eyes. "I'm so sorry for her." It wasn't clear if she were sorry for Winnie or for the maid. After a hitched breath or two, she continued.

"I know her for a long time, and I think she is a good person, but she need money and I think, I think…" this time she did start crying.

"Minda," Roy said quietly. He waited for her to compose herself, which didn't take long. "Did she come back from Leyte early?"

"*Hinde*," she said with a tinge of anger. "That is why I try to find Marvin."

Roy and Frank remained silent, and Minda realized that she needed to be clearer about what she knew and why she thought it was important. She took another deep breath and spoke slowly and quietly.

"Rosalita has a sister in Leyte who is old and sick. She sends money there and goes to visit sometime. Denny pay her so much. Fifty dollars for two week!" Minda's voice had begun to grow louder, and she suddenly realized that she might be overheard. She looked around again and started talking again in lower tones.

"She always go there to Leyte on Friday, but last time she go Monday and said she come back on Saturday. So, I go to her house this morning to tell her about Denny's girlfriend and ask her to go to church with me. Her stuff is all gone! I look through the window and *wala*! I talk to her landlord, and she say, uh, said, Rosalita move out." Minda looked expectantly at Roy and Frank. Whatever she saw in their eyes must not have convinced her that this news was important enough to them, so she went on.

"She has a key to Denny's house. My friend there at church work at the market at East Bajac-Bajac. She say Rosalita have a key made there two weeks ago. Two weeks ago," she repeated for emphasis.

The two Americans looked at each and then nearly jumped from their seats as a burst of wind and rain rattled the windows. They had just started to laugh when the electricity blinked out and the jukebox went dark. The dimness in the bar deepened even more when the lighting above the pool tables died, and the pounding of the rain continued.

"Don't worry," Nathan called from behind the bar. "We got ice!"

Chapter 30

When Luz emerged from the back, her disappointment was evident.

"He said he might be back tonight," Scott said.

"*Sino?*" Luz responded coyly.

"You know who. Senior Chief Thompson."

"Oh. Okay," Luz said, as she busied herself rearranging beer in the refrigerator.

"So, what do you think?"

"*'Sus, namon!*" Luz retorted, spinning away from the fridge. "Why does everyone want me to fuck that guy?"

"*Teka minuto!*" Scott said, honestly surprised by her reaction. "I was just wondering what you thought about Judy and me getting married!"

Luz stared at Scott for a few seconds as she realized her mistake and again her face blazed with embarrassment. She lowered her head and placed both hands on her face as if to cry. Instead, she chuckled softly and when she removed her hands, she was smiling sadly and shook her head at Scott.

"I'm sorry, I'm not think straight today. I just…" her voice trailed off. "I'm just tired."

"Okay. So, what do you think about us getting married?"

"I'm so happy for you guys! I hope you have a big party."

Before he could answer, Ernesto and Boy came from the back of the bar, speaking in Tagalog. Luz seemed to answer a few of their questions and ask some of her own before their conversation was over and although they spoke too quickly for Scott to understand much of it, he understood the gist was mainly concerned with when they would return to the bar and what they needed to bring with them.

The front door opened, and Gloria walked in carrying an umbrella and small paper bag, half-full with banana chips.

"*Kumusta*, ya'll!" she said. She walked in offering the chips first to Scott and then to the others behind the bar. They all helped themselves to some chips while Luz asked her a few questions in Tagalog.

Scott said, "Why do you sound like a hick?"

"That guy last night, he's so funny," answering both of them, Gloria replied in English and then laughed. "I don't know what he say most of the time and I ask him if he really from the states. He's from 'Yarkinso,' he says. Scott, do you know Yarkinso?" By this time, she had moved behind the bar and placed the oil-stained bag of chips on the counter.

"I think he meant Arkansas," Scott replied and then popped another chip into his mouth. "That is the state just East of where I'm from."

"Why don't you talk like that?" Luz said. Her curiosity was genuinely tuned up.

"I come from a town that is kind of in the middle of Oklahoma, so it's quite a ways from Arkansas. And he might come from the country."

"Aren't you from the same country?" Gloria asked.

"Sure. But when I say country, I'm saying he might have lived out in the sticks, the boondocks, the boonies, the jungle."

"They have jungle in Yarkinso?" Gloria asked with just a hint of a smile.

"No, no, no," Scott said, burying his face in his hands. "What I'm saying is that he might have lived far from a large city."

Luz looked over at Gloria who had a mischievous grin. When Scott looked up, Gloria said, "Ha! Gotchu! What you think of me; *hungog*?"

Scott looked from Gloria to Luz and back, finally saying, "Fuck. I need another beer."

Luz and Gloria shared a laugh, but Ernesto and Boy had become inured to the banter between the girls and the *Kanos*. Boy raised his eyebrows at Luz and said, "*Sige mauna na ako.*" Ernesto, by far the shyest Filipino Scott had ever met, simply waved to the group as they turned to leave.

Gloria started toward the back but then stopped and pointed at the dwindling bag of banana chips. "You eat, hah?" She didn't wait for an answer and the plywood door slammed behind her.

Scott lifted his fresh beer and said, "Alone again, naturally."

Luz had heard that refrain somewhere and assumed it was from a song, so she did herself a favor by not following up with a question. She just picked a peso from Scott's change, said, "Okay," and walked to the jukebox. She didn't see that song title on the jukebox and wouldn't have seen Gilbert O'Sullivan's name there either, had she known he was the singer. She picked three of own favorites.

"So, Luz, can I ask you some things about Senior Chief Thompson, without you biting my head off?"

She walked back around the bar and picked up a banana chip. "Sure," was all she said.

"Who is trying to get you to, uh, two together?"

Luz's initial instinct was to deflect with the type of flippant conversations they were both used to. Instead, she took a deep breath, looked out the front window and then to the back of the bar. She put the deep-fried chip into her mouth, savoring the sweet and salty flavor before crunching it slowly.

"You are the one first," she said.

"You know I just joke around about that stuff," he said defensively.

"I know you joke but I get tired of jokes. And there is…" she still felt uncomfortable speaking aloud the suspicions and doubts she was having about Ben.

"Ben?"

It still surprised her that others might be having similar suspicions of him. She took a few moments to collect her thoughts before answering. She wanted to assure herself that her memories were accurate and not overthought. She hoped that the connections she made between the things she knew about his actions over the last several years were not tortured. Ultimately, she knew at her core that she was right about Ben, although she could not describe any one particular thing that would convince a judge. Regardless, she knew better than to disclose much to Scott.

"Yes," she said finally.

"Why do suppose he wants you to jump his bones?"

"I don't know," she said. "Why do you think?"

It was Scott's turn for reticence. He didn't want to share his conversations about murder with her, especially when those conversations were with a person within his chain of command and involved a possible suspect known to everyone on Gordon Avenue. Roy's question, 'what about that Ben guy,' had been repeating in his head since the Senior Chief had left Ace's. Maybe the question had merely stirred up some latent paranoia hiding in the back of his mind, but it did make him think back on his past interactions with Ben. That quick rumination turned up exactly zero things which might indicate that Ben was anything other than what he said he was.

"I don't know either. And I guess I don't think much either, except that the deal in Barretto is making me paranoid. And," he said raising his beer in Luz's direction, "maybe everyone else too."

"Maybe. But I know Ben for a long time and he…" again she hesitated. She just wasn't willing to spill any of her past to Scott yet. "I don't know… I guess he is concerned to me that I be a, uh, *matandang dalaga*."

"What is that?"

"That is like a…" she was still struggling to think of the English words.

"Virgin?" Scott said, only half-jokingly.

"No, but kind like that. Like a woman who never get married."

"Oh! You mean like an old maid?"

"Yes," she said, relieved that she recognized the idiom.

"Well, that is a reasonable desire for a friend, I guess. Nothing nefarious." Scott was absently twirling his beer bottle around. "But you could ask the question..."

"Why Roy Thompson?" Luz finished his thought.

Chapter 31

Ben stood inside the entrance to his apartment, staring at the butane burners sitting on his kitchen cabinet. He didn't know how long he had been standing there but the front door wasn't completely closed and rainwater was pooling at his feet. The voices which had wormed their way through the thick door in his mind began slithering back into the darkness. He blinked again at the burners and then leaned back against to front door, closing out the steadily increasing rainfall.

What passed for the rational part of his brain tried reasserting itself. He looked down at his soaked shoes and saw the growing puddle, still being dimpled by water dripping from his plastic poncho. He realized he was in his apartment and that he had returned for a reason, he just wasn't clear in his mind what that reason was.

Security check. Yes, that was the first thing. Make sure no one had invaded his sanctum. Make sure that no one had found him out. Make sure that no one had discovered his... 'father,' the voices said from behind the door. He dropped his blue bag onto the floor, splashing rainwater in a fan pattern around the puddle. Then he went about his survey of the apartment, finding nothing out of the ordinary.

He dropped to one knee on the floor of the closet, automatically looking for anything out of place around the false wall hiding his secrets. Finding none, he pulled the tab and the square piece of sheetrock separated from the wall easily. As he was reaching inside, a drop of rain dripped from the tip of his little finger and, in the dim light, it looked like a drop of blood. It stopped him in mid-motion. Although he was dimly aware that he was not bleeding, the image was enough to remind him to dry his face and hands before handling the little helper he had come for, so he retreated to the tiny washroom where he took off his poncho and grabbed a towel.

The act of wiping the rain from his exposed skin seemed to stimulate his rational thinking to the point where he realized his hair was also dripping wet. He vigorously dried his hair and then dropped the towel on the floor. He was about to strip in preparation for dry clothing when he spied the cubbyhole cover leaning against the wall. Immediately, the massive door which had until now kept his psychosis imprisoned, erupted into a million splinters. The hundreds of worms which had been squirming toward his reason, morphed into so many cobras striking at his sanity.

"Yesssss!" they hissed. "Embrace your father's spirit! Find the truth and act!"

He knelt reverently to retrieve the only item from his father he still owned. The knife rested snuggly in his hand and sent a jolt of energy up his arm making the voices in his head hiss in ecstasy. At that point, those voices became his voice. This **is** your father's spirit and the spirits of all your fathers before him who had fought against foreign powers. He somehow knew the spirit in that knife was the same that had slain Ferdinand Magellan in 1521. He knew that he – Ben de Guzman – would be the embodiment of Lapu-Lapu. That he and he alone, could rid his homeland of the Anglo intruders once and for all time. That Ka-Bar was his bolo knife, and he was Lapu-Lapu, José Rizal and Andrés Bonifacio all rolled into one and, more importantly, they were him. The peanut vendor turned NPA operative no longer existed. The newest liberator of the Philippines was now on his newest mission.

Chapter 32

Frank said, "Fuck."

Roy didn't respond since Frank had probably uttered that particular word ten times since leaving the BGU, and they weren't even through the zigzags yet. Additionally, the rain battering every inch of the car's body almost drowned out his monologue. He continued to look at the rain pounding on the window and the amorphous gray sky that obscured everything beyond his glass boundary. It was only after the car slowed noticeably that he looked forward to see blurry brake lights thirty yards ahead.

Before getting too close to the car ahead of them, Frank moved slowly into the oncoming lane to try and see around the obstacle. He turned back into his own lane and stopped about twenty feet behind the next vehicle, which to Roy looked as if it might be a white van.

"Fuck me to tears," Frank repeated. "There are three or four other cars in front of us and no one coming towards us. The last time I was stuck in traffic like that, on this part of National Highway, the road was closed for three days."

That got Roy's attention. "What happened?" he asked.

"There was a mudslide on the other side of the cemetery during the monsoons last year. It was raining like this then and kept it up for another ten hours or more. It took them two days after the rain stopped to clear all the shit off the roads and rebuild the parts that washed away."

"What did you do?"

"I sat in the car for about an hour and then went back to the BGU and got a beer and a blowjob. Not necessarily in that order."

"Let's not play twenty questions here, Chief." Roy sounded more like a Senior Chief than a friend and when Frank flashed him a sideways "bite me" look, Roy said, "You know what I mean."

"Yeah, well. I left my car at the BGU and paid a fisherman fifty pesos to ferry my ass around to Kalaklan gate in his bangka boat. That's a long-assed walk from there to the Chief's barracks, especially in the fucking rain."

"Shit. Could you see if that's what's holding us up now?"

"No. I couldn't see shit in this rain. But whatever it is, it must have just happened since there's only a few of us stuck here so far."

Roy looked out his side of the car again and realized that they were overlooking the bay, with a fairly severe drop off to some tattered buildings and the water. On their left was a high bank of dirt, rock and vegetation.

Frank looked in his rearview mirror and saw that there were already two sets of headlights waiting behind him. A third vehicle was veering over into the Southbound lane and edging toward them. "What's this ass wipe doing?"

As the car pulled around, they could see that it was a small pickup belonging to the Philippine Constabulary and neither spoke while the truck moved up to whatever was obstructing traffic. Frank leaned his head as far to the left as the window would allow to see what was happening. After a few moments he said, "That didn't take long. He's coming back."

There was a very narrow shoulder between the road and the bank, giving just enough space for the little truck to turn around. It was making its way back towards the barrio, stopping at each car on the way. When it pulled up to the Impala, Frank rolled his window down a few inches, trying to keep out as much rain as possible. The PC officer had no such concerns and had his window down all the way.

"There are some rocks, I'll get help," was all he said and then carried on down the line.

"We might have lucked out here, Royboy," Frank said with a smile. "Maybe we can get you back to some dry clothes and warm sheets before mommy checks on you."

"Cute. But I want to go back to Ace's and pick up my umbrella first, if you don't mind."

"No worries. I haven't been in there for a while anyway and it never hurts to check in on Luz."

Roy tried not to show his surprise at the mention of her name and quickly realized that it made perfect sense that Frank would know many of the people on Gordon Avenue. They had talked about bars on Gordon Avenue, but they hadn't discussed individuals.

Frank turned off the engine and said, "We can sit here for a little while and see what that PC considers 'help'."

They sat for a few minutes, lost in their own thoughts, listening to the drone of the rain on the car.

"So, what do you think of Luz," Roy said finally.

"She's a sweetheart, sharp as a tack and very easy on the eyes," Frank said, while still checking out things in the rearview mirror. "I paid her bar-fine a couple of months back, but she told me upfront that it was not for an over-night. I wanted to take her to dinner and try to get in her skivvies. She said dinner was okay but that she didn't do old guys like me." He said it matter-of-factly and with no apparent animus.

"And you paid her bar-fine anyway?"

"Sure, why not? I can get laid anywhere, any time. It's harder to find someone who's smart and honest, that you can have a conversation with."

"I am not shitting you here, Royboy," Frank continued. "I don't know how many squids I've known over the years who married some sweet, young thing only to figure out later that they were going to have to eventually talk to them. I've made that mistake myself, a time or two." Then he grinned at Roy and said, "And I may not even be the only person in this car to do that."

"Good point," Roy said. "So, what did you talk about? You and Luz."

"What makes you think I can remember shit like that? We talked, we laughed, she ate enough chicken for three people, and I drank enough beer for the both of us. I just remember enjoying the dinner and wishing I was younger."

Frank sat silently for a few seconds and then started chuckling softly. "I was too late yesterday, wasn't I?"

Roy said nothing, but he thought he knew where Frank was going with his question.

"You are already sweet on her, aren't you?" Frank's chuckle graduated to a single, barked laugh. "I knew it! I knew you would... look!" Frank sat up in his seat and looked in the side mirror. "It looks like the cavalry is on the way."

Roy twisted in his seat to see the blurry image of a green, military-styled truck slowly backing up to the obstruction in the road. As it got closer, they could hear the irritating beeping of a reverse warning alarm in the truck and see several men in rain slickers sitting in its bed. As the truck passed them, Frank started to pull his raincoat from the back seat of the car.

"I'm gonna mosey up and see what we're looking at," Frank said, trying to wriggle into the coat while still behind the steering wheel. "Be back," he said before looking in the mirror a last time and swinging the door open. The wind had abated some, but the rain was still heavy, and Roy could see muddy water rushing downhill between the hillside and the shoulder of the highway.

Mentioning Luz had sparked some struggling ember of awareness at the base of Roy's consciousness. But the awareness for now was only at the emotional level. He had been grappling with various emotions since climbing out bed, but this new idea was different. Roy could not yet attach it to any specific thought or memory, and he struggled to give structure to the growing, uncomfortable feeling in his gut.

After a few minutes, the rain-distorted image of Frank emerged through the windshield, watching his steps carefully and holding his raincoat closed. He paused outside the car for just a moment and then opened the door, pulled off his coat, tossed it into the back seat and got in as quickly as he could. Once behind the wheel, he reached behind Roy's seat and pulled out a towel to dry off. It was the same well-rehearsed set of actions he had taken when leaving the BGU.

"Good news," he said. "There was just some smallish boulders and some mud washed across the road. Those guys in the truck are making short work of things and we should be moving in just a little while."

While Frank continued to dry off, Roy thought more about Frank's knowledge of Luz and Gordon Avenue. He had the impression that Frank was about to probe into his own thoughts concerning Luz and he didn't want to chew on that bone just yet, so he decided to move him off that topic and ask about Ben first.

Just as Frank wiped his glasses and settled them on his face, Roy asked, "What do you know about that peanut vendor on Gordon Avenue named Ben?"

"Don't trust him," was his short reply. "Don't know why. There's just something about him that's always seemed a little creepy to me. You'll be drinking and shooting the shit with someone and the next thing you know, you look up and he'll be hanging around like a perv at a grade school playground. And he's always fucking smiling! He reminds me of a fucking dolphin at Sea World. Nope. Don't trust him. I won't even buy peanuts from him."

"Why don't you tell me what you really think, Frank. Quit beating around the bush."

Frank reached forward and started the car. "Naw, I prefer to keep my opinions to myself."

"That's what I've always liked about you."

"Wish we would've brought a couple of beers with us," Frank craned over to his left again to see any progress that might have been made. "Maybe there's a sari-sari store close by."

Chapter 33

Luz and Scott spent a few minutes talking about why Ben might be interested in her love life. Their discussions broke in two basic directions; that Ben was an old friend who wanted happiness for a woman he had known since she first came to Olongapo as a girl, or that Ben was part of a terrorist organization that wanted to foster relationships with the person who would be primarily responsible for the security at a weapons magazine for the U. S. Navy. They were both leaning in the same direction but were unwilling to share with each other the level to which they believed it. Eventually, as is the case with so many human interactions, that reluctance to dig deeper into the topic resulted in a gradual return to their more comfortable repartee about the trivialities of life in Olongapo.

Whether or not they cared to debate the serious nature of the implications they both recognized, they nonetheless shared the same nagging questions floating in their minds. Questions – about the motives of those close to them, of their own motivations, concerning the level of responsibility they bore about the things that happened to them – were pondered in different languages and images. They were asked within different contexts, and they would be answered in different ways. They were the types of questions that often troubled deeper thinkers but seldom visited the psyches of most of Olongapo's bar workers.

*   *   *

At that moment, Gloria she was thinking about taking a nap. She had taken a quick bath in the small washroom in the common area at the back of Ace's Place and was laying on her back looking at the ceiling of her room. The quiet drumming of the rain against the roof and walls was soothing and the heavy towel draped over her bare skin imparted a sense of security, like a warm hug. She absently rubbed her pubic mound under the towel and thought of the clumsy sex she'd had with the even clumsier American sailor from Arkansas the night before and that morning. Yes, she thought, it was clumsy, but it was still fun and she made some money in addition to what the bar fine brought in. She smiled remembering how crooked his penis had been and then fell into a peaceful slumber.

*   *   *

"I think I'm going to head home and wait for Judy," Scott announced.

"What movie do you see tonight?" Luz asked.

"I'm not sure, but it is something with Kevin Costner. I think it's another baseball movie, but it has something about "dreams" in the title. Man, she has the hots for that dude."

"He is dreamy!" Luz rolled her eyes and batted her lashes comically. "I think I let him have my cherry!"

"You still got that thing?"

"Sure! I put on ice cream all the time." She tried to look serious while answering but was unable to keep a straight face.

Scott merely shook his head in a show of mockery, but also couldn't keep a smile from creeping to his lips.

He took a last swig from his beer and slid off the barstool, headed for the umbrella he left under the table. Judy had shared Lita's when they left for mass earlier.

"If the electricity stays on but the weather stays crappy, we'll go straight home after the movie. If it goes off, we might drop back by," Scott said. "So, see you tomorrow, maybe."

After Scott left, Luz's mind snapped back to the more mundane aspects of running a bar. She looked around the empty room and realized that it would probably remain that way well into the evening. It wasn't an unreasonable expectation for a rainy, Sunday evening. It was not uncommon at all.

The capiz shell lamp hanging nearby emitted the same glow it always did. The jukebox, with its silent blinking lights, still punctuated the atmosphere with alternating shades of color. The dusty curtains still guarded the same windows they had since before Luz's journey to Olongapo had even begun. But now, everything she could see seemed diminished by the dreariness of the weather and she was suddenly seized by a feeling of despair. She was not a pessimist nor prone to bouts of depression, but the feeling was real and jolted her savagely, perhaps even more so because of her normal optimism. She just wasn't familiar with the idea of abandoning hope.

She had clawed her way through some of the nastiest barriers that life in the Philippines could build against an orphaned and destitute female, but she always saw a gap through which some small ray of light would beckon. The power of her rational mind seemed to overcome emotional impulses which might cripple shallower thinkers. And although she could not express those mental processes in any of the languages or dialects that she spoke, she still understood instinctively that this was what she needed to do now. That beacon of rationality, dimmed but not extinguished, still glowed inside her and she began to stoke it as she always had. She looked at what was before her. She assessed what would help and what would hinder. She carried on.

She had never taken a psychology course, nor heard the definition of melancholia, pragmatic realism, or grit. Nevertheless, she understood that her normal attitude was being assaulted by history she could not change, as well as dreams which may never come true.

Luz stood behind the bar, looking out through the curtains at the steady rain and absently wiping a spot on the counter which was as clean as it would ever be. She was already starting to feel a better about the day when her grandmother's voice echoed from some protective shelter in her memory. "Don't think about how you are going to enjoy the papaya," it said, "while a cobra still protects the tree." The memory of her grandmother's voice brought a spontaneous smile to her face. She was still smiling as a blurry figure approached the front door and it froze on her lips as Ben entered the bar.

Chapter 34

While Frank was seriously considering getting out in the rain to track down some San Miguel, the headlights on the PC truck came on and the brake lights on the car in front of them blinked off.

"Never mind, Royboy. It looks like we are about to weigh anchor," Frank said, looking sideways at Roy. "Maybe we can get you into Luz's warm sheets tonight!"

"Me? Or you?" Roy said.

"Oh, I think you're the only one in this car with a shot at that," Frank said, turning on the ignition. "Besides, I'm thinking I may not want a bunkmate with that much on the ball. Next thing you know, she'll be questioning my description of eight inches."

Roy let the penis reference pass.

As their car slowly approached the road blockage, they could see a young Filipino male in a brown poncho waving them around debris still covering the opposite lane. A traffic barrier had been set up there, on the other side of the mud.

"I guess they had to empty the truck before cleaning up the rest of this crap. Just happy we were going the right direction," Frank said.

Roy hadn't told Frank about the rubber glove but thought he might get some insight without letting too much out of the bag.

"Do you know much about how they clean houses here?"

"What?"

"You know, what kind of cleaner they use in the kitchen, what kind of accessories they employ, that kind of stuff."

Frank glanced quickly at Roy before getting his eyes back onto the slick road. "Why? You thinking about what Denny's maid might've been using?"

"Yeah, kinda."

"I haven't paid much attention, but I'm sure it's pretty basic. Probably just elbow grease and maybe a little Ajax if they have an extra peso. Have you seen those short, wispy looking brooms everyone has? Pretty sure those are mandated by the government. Of course, if someone made enough money, they would want to get the best they could. You probably haven't been here long enough yet to notice, but Filipinos tend to love their status symbols.

"Denny may have been pushing the limits of fraternization, but I gotta believe he would be very sensitive to possible black-market violations. He probably just gave her enough money to buy what she needed to get on the local economy."

"Yeah. That's what I was thinking, too."

The rain was steady, and Frank slowed the Impala as they passed Kalaklan gate. The traffic would be getting thicker from there to Gordon, so Frank concentrated more on his driving and Roy dug silently into his thoughts. He was no longer surprised that those thoughts were more about Luz than they were the murder of Winnie Jackson.

Chapter 35

Scott left Ace's, heading toward the small group of trikes occupying space on the corner of Sixth Street and Gordon Avenue. Rain was being blown sideways by the storm and he tilted his umbrella down just enough to protect his head and face from the stinging and surprisingly cool, drops. His thoughts were buzzing around all the recent events in his life. He had decided to stay in the Navy after Judy accepted his proposal the night before and he was really happy with that decision. In fact, it seemed to relieve some of the stress he had been feeling over the last couple of weeks.

The only thing that seemed burdensome now was the issue of the murder of an American officer. He believed that Boggs had been the original target and that the assassination was committed by some rebel group. If that were the case, he knew that any American could be the next potential victim. With that idea bouncing around his skull, he saw Ben coming from the direction of Perimeter Road on the sidewalk across the street.

Ben was covered in a plastic rain slicker and carrying his blue bag, but there was something else that didn't quite seem right about the way he carried himself. He was walking stiffly and seemed preoccupied with his own thoughts. Ben was normally very aware of his surroundings, always looking for the next customer for his merchandise, but to Scott he appeared now to be focused on something specific. It was an odd enough feeling that Scott dipped his umbrella back down to block his face from Ben's view.

Scott backed away from the tricycles and lifted his umbrella's edge just enough to see Ben cross the street towards Ace's Place. Was he being paranoid? Did his earlier discussion with Luz warp his thinking about Ben? He didn't know, but he still felt compelled to keep an eye on him. He felt he needed to do something.

Ben strode to Ace's front door and stood there for just a moment before pushing through the door.

Ben stepped silently into Ace's Place and then let the door close behind him, his blue bag hanging just below the edge of the clear poncho. Luz immediately recognized the changed demeanor from only an hour or so

217

before, seeing a much more subdued character than the exuberant salesman she had come to expect.

"Hello, Luz," he said. "I forgot to ask you about something when I was here earlier." That voice in Ben's head alternated between being his personal guiding spirit to the combined voices of his Filipino forebearers but the message was at least now consistent; be calm and find out what she knows. He walked casually up to the counter and sat his bag on a bar stool, not bothering to first wipe rain from the bag. Insanity can wear the mask of reason quite comfortably, but it doesn't really fit. The voice Luz heard coming from Ben also didn't seem to fit.

Luz didn't know what to make of Ben's altered affect, but she hoped her stiff smile didn't betray the emotional frailty of which she herself had only recently become aware. She marshalled the strength which had sustained her for the past thirteen years and willed herself to stay in the moments. She pulled a roll of paper towels from beneath the counter.

"Here," she said. "Why not dry off?"

Ben unrolled a couple of sheets and silently wiped the rain from his face and arms, his eyes never leaving Luz's face. His gaze was unnerving. She intensified her efforts to present a façade of calm.

"Luz," he said, placing the damp paper towels on the top of his bag. "Where did Thompson go? I was hoping to ask him some more questions also."

"He went to the base, I think."

"Is he coming back here tonight?"

"I don't think so. He has to go to work for the first time tomorrow."

"So, you aren't going to fuck him tonight?"

The vulgarity of his questions surprised her, and it evidently showed.

"I, I don't think so," she said, again, feeling the blood rush to her face. "He has only just arrived to the Philippines, so I think I have plenty of time to determine whether or not to sleep with him."

"Yes, you do," Ben said. "But perhaps I don't."

"I don't see how that matters to you," she replied. However, she was convinced more now than ever that it mattered to him a great deal. Still, she tried to convey a sense of naiveté and innocence.

"It matters to me because it matters to you, Luz," he said. There was just a hint of a grin on his face as he said that, and his eyes were still glued to her face. Then he said, "What does Thompson know about the American who died in the barrio?"

The abrupt question caught her off guard, and she was hopeful that the look of innocence was still effectively hiding her concerns.

"I don't know," she said. "He doesn't talk to me about those things." She had the capacity to lie, but it wasn't a skill she employed often. And when she did, it was usually about some trivial interaction with a customer.

Ben's grin broadened appreciably, but there was no humor in it. It reminded Luz of a scary comic she had seen somewhere.

"I have known you for a long time and I have always appreciated your honesty," he said. He absently wiped the top of his bag with the wad of moist paper towels, slowly moving up one side of the zipper and back down the other side. "I suppose that is why you have never gotten particularly good at lying."

The realization that Luz and Roy had discussed the death of Boggs' girlfriend, however casually, placed a narrow pry bar under the lid that Ben had clamped over the voices in his head. The murmurs were getting louder with every passing second that Ben imagined what the two might have discussed. The time for stealthy questioning was quickly sliding away. Ben's sense of urgency grew exponentially along with the volume of the spectral voices haunting his mind. He wanted to stay calm. He wanted to continue to lead Luz down a path of full disclosure without her knowing she was even walking. In his current state, that was an unattainable goal.

"What did he say to you, Luz? Does he have any clues about who killed the American whore?" His grin had disappeared, but a slender strand of saliva dripped slowly from one corner of his mouth.

At the same time, Luz was starting to lose confidence in her ability to stay calm. She sensed sanity abandoning Ben but could feel her own self-control beginning to faulter as well. She looked at the spittle seeping from Ben's lip and wanted to scream for him to wipe it off.

"I, I don't know what you mean," she stammered. "How am I supposed to know that?"

Ben's gaze did not weaken. "I know you have talked to him. I know he has talked to you. I know everything about you. I know how you can lie to yourself very effectively when you need to, but you are an open book to anyone else. That is why Mama Nina trusts you to run this pathetic bar. She knows you can't lie to her." Ben caressed the zipper on his bag and quietly started to pull on its tab.

"And yet, you continue to lie to yourself about your sister. Whenever I hear you tell that story about her living the dream in the States, I see how your brain has swallowed the lie like a magic elixir. You have heard everything about her death, except her voice describing it. You have seen all the evidence, except her rotting corpse. You know she was raped and killed by the same monster that raped you and yet you still cling to the fantasy that she is somehow living a perfect life where she doesn't contact her only sister. You probably still believe that the bitch who sold you both to that businessman from Manila just conveniently decided to leave Olongapo after you escaped him. Do you think that she would just leave a lucrative position like that? After spending so much money on you? Do you think that the rapist would just go back to Manila and decide to quit raping and murdering young girls? Are you that stupid? I don't think so." He finally did wipe the spit from his chin with the back of one hand and, without taking his eyes from Luz, continued to pull open the zipper of his bag.

"No. You aren't that stupid. And I can see now that you might have even stopped lying to yourself," he said, easing his hand into the bag. "You know their bones lie rotting together in the jungle. You know I'm the one who put them there. And you know that I did it for you!" His voice had been rising as he recounted this part of their shared history and the thread of spit had formed again at the corner of his mouth. But as his hand rested on the leather handle of the Ka-bar, calm returned.

"I did it for you," he repeated softly. "And now… and now you must do something for…"

The front door suddenly burst open, and a raft of wind and rain blew Scott through it. He turned to push the door closed after collapsing his umbrella, not bothering to try shaking it outside.

Luz gasped at the entrance but was otherwise frozen. Ben turned quickly toward the commotion and took his empty fist from the bag.

"Holy shit! It's getting hairy out there," Scott said, turning toward the bar. "Sorry to break up your pow-wow, but I need to take a dump and I didn't think I'd make it home!" Scott hurried toward the back, brushing past the two quickly. "Sorry! My system did not like those banana chips! Hold on, Luz, your turn is coming!" he said as the flimsy door slammed behind him.

Ben looked back to Luz and shook his head slowly. It was a warning. Her startled expression had returned to one reflecting more the anguish which had been building in her over the last several minutes. The drumming of the rain and the two walls separating them, fortunately muted the sounds of Scott's diarrhea and Ben took the time to quietly warn Luz against alerting him to their conversation. She averted her eyes as Ben wiped his chin once more.

"When he leaves, you will tell me everything you know about Thompson and what you have already talked about with him. You will do whatever it takes to get him in your confidence. If that means fucking him, you will do it. Whatever it takes. Do you understand?"

Luz nodded almost imperceptibly until the sound of a flushing toilet startled her again.

"Don't try to keep him here," Ben said, gesturing toward the restrooms. "If he doesn't leave right away, tell him you will close early because of the storm. Just get him out of here."

Scott exited the restroom noisily and opened the door leading to the bar. Ben moved closer to his bag to give Scott plenty of room to get by him and out the door, but Scott just stood in the doorway. Neither he nor Luz noticed Ben's hand in the blue plastic bag.

"That was not pretty," he said. And then, "Oh! Almost forgot my brolly." He grabbed it and was back in the doorway within a few seconds. This time he was stopped by the strange look on Luz's face.

"Are you okay?" he said. He glanced quickly in Ben's direction and then back at Luz. "Is everything alright?"

He looked back to Ben and then his eyes flew open as Ben thrust the Ka-Bar into his solar plexus. Ben tried to twist the blade, but his left hand was too weak to complete the action. He quickly moved closer to Scott and continued to twist with his right hand, pushing Scott back across the floor and against the men's room door. He leaned into Scott's face and looked directly into his surprised and shocked eyes.

Scott's life did not flash before his eyes. He saw only the dull, sinister face of his killer. However, as his blood gushed around Ben's hand and onto the floor, his mind did flash back to the previous night's passionate love making with Judy and his earlier conversation with Roy Thompson. With those images fading dimly from his mind, only two weak words managed to escape his trembling lips. "What? Why?"

Ben did not answer. Instead, he pulled the knife from Scott's body and plunged it once more in an upward motion, aimed at his heart. Scott's legs buckled and his lifeless body slumped to the floor, pulling the knife from Ben's blood-slickened hand.

Chapter 36

Frank flipped on his left blinker by force of habit. There were no cars coming from the base and the closest one coming from behind was at least two blocks back. There were a few brave souls crossing Gordon Avenue, trying to find shelter from the increasing wind and rain, but they too would not have noticed his feeble attempt at driving courtesy. Those pedestrians were being pushed along Magsaysay by the rain coming sideways from the South and Frank doubted they would lift their heads again until they found a dry place to hunker down.

"I'll go up and make a U-turn," Frank said. "There might be a parking spot close to Ace's, but if not, at least you'll be able to open the door without drowning me."

"Thanks," Roy said. He would have delivered a snappier comeback, had he been listening more closely, but he was really being bothered by the jumble of thoughts and emotions vying for attention in his head. He knew intellectually that the stress of the murder, before having any chance to settle into a new duty station, were amplifying the already existing and still unresolved stressors related to Lisa.

He used his new umbrella as an excuse to have Frank drop by Ace's but in reality, Roy had resolved to let Luz know he was interested in seeing more of her. He had left Ace's earlier that day without saying goodbye to Luz and he actually felt more guilt about that than he did about wanting her. Whatever level of guilt he still felt about moving on from Lisa, he knew that positive, intentional behavior was what he needed. He would simply retrieve his umbrella and tell Luz that he would see her the next day. Simple groundwork, he thought. I'm just letting her know I'm interested, he repeated to himself. Positive, intentional behavior.

As they crossed Sixth Street, Frank said, "Hey, there's a spot near the corner. I'll go up to 10th and turn around, let you out in front of Ace's and then park. If you're not out in five minutes, I'll assume you found safe harbor in 'port Luz'."

"Funny. Okay. I should be out in less than that, so keep the engine

223

running."

The only thing visible inside of Ace's as they drove by were the pulsing blue and red lights, filtering through the curtains.

* * *

The sudden attack on Scott so surprised Luz that she jumped backwards, toward the little bar sink next the wall. She was aware that some noise had escaped her lips, but didn't know if it was a scream, a moan, or a whisper. She now stood with her butt pressed against the sink and her hand pressed against her mouth, watching Ben push Scott against the men's room door. Within a second, the door between them slammed shut, pulled by its spring.

She seemed welded to the sink. She stared at the fading paint on the plywood door and started to become aware of faint scuffling sounds coming from beyond. Additionally, a small voice rose slowly from the back of her mind. It was the voice of a one-eyed, twelve-year-old, orphan girl who had just lost her grandmother. It was a weak voice, at first. The words it formed were distant and unintelligible, but they were getting louder and clearer. Finally, "Run, RUN, **RUN!**" screamed the scared, little girl from the past.

Luz took only one step forward before the sad, plywood door squeaked open.

* * *

A noise woke her. She didn't know what it was or from where it came, but it didn't fit with the comforting sound made by the rain pounding on the secure structure around her. Gloria threw off the warm towel and stretched while still laying naked on the bed. After a minute or so, she pulled on her panties and stopped to listen for any additional foreign sounds coming from the front. All she could hear now was the still heavy drumming of rain drops.

After putting on some shorts and a tank top, she quickly checked her appearance in a small hand mirror she kept bedside before daring to go out front. She ran a comb through her hair, looked down at the thin cloth covering her otherwise naked breasts and smiled as her nipples hardened underneath. She owned a few bras but had never felt comfortable wearing them and believed after leaving the confines of her home village she would never again have to. However, she had since gained a level of sophistication and viewed them now as a sometimes-necessary evil. Now though, she felt as if she had to be ready for whatever adventure, or customer, awaited her.

224

Interrupted Weekend

As she turned the key on her door's deadbolt, Gloria heard muffled voices coming from the front. And although she couldn't really make out what was being said, they didn't sound like the conversational tones she was used to hearing. She decided to take a cautionary look through the peephole rather than crashing onto the scene, as she was usually happy to do.

*   *   *

Ben stood silently in the doorway with his foot holding it open. The front of his rain slicker was now covered with Scott's blood and behind him, a pool of it crept slowly across the bare cement floor. He had retrieved the knife from Scott's torso and blood dripped slowly from its tip.

Scott's body lay in a heap against the men's room door, his eyes half-closed against the indignity of death. To Luz they seemed somehow accusatory – as if she should have warned him about this possibility – and the scene threatened to push her to the edge of her own madness.

Ben's eyes were eerily unexpressive. If anything, they reflected a total disconnect from reality and rejection of self-agency.

"See what I must do?" Ben asked. "See what must be done for you and for our homeland? The occupiers must be expelled at all costs. All costs." He stepped from the doorway, allowing the door to close quietly and then moved to the right, leaving just enough room for passage. He motioned toward the front door with the knife.

"Go lock the door," he said. "I'll watch."

Luz tried to move but leaned against the counter when she thought her knees might buckle. She bowed her head and saw her legs trembling. She then glanced at the door and back at Ben's stony face.

"Go," he said quietly.

She took a deep breath and slowly began putting one foot in front of the other. Moving around the corner of the counter, she could hear Ben following closely behind and experienced a flash of terror. The feeling did not diminish when she realized he was just making sure she didn't escape. But while trudging toward the door, Luz's fear began to change. She was still terrified, but her anger was also being rekindled.

*   *   *

Frank rolled to a stop in front of Ace's and as Roy was about to open the door he said, "Fucking asshole."

"What?"

225

"That jerk just took my spot."

"That's okay. I won't be a minute. I'm just gonna run in and grab that damn umbrella. I trust Luz, but a fifteen-dollar umbrella is likely to grow legs before the night ends around here, so just sit tight. Back in a jiff." Roy jumped from the car and slammed the door behind him, dashing between two cars just in front of Ace's front door. Remembering how he almost fell on his ass at the BGU, he slowed before opening the door and was stopped dead in his tracks after entering.

Luz stood only five feet from the door and Ben was just a step behind. Her normal smile was nowhere to be seen but her face projected a jumble of mixed emotions which set off an array of alarms in Roy's head. His eyes dilated and the crimson smear of blood on Ben's poncho jumped to the front of his attention. His mind flashed to the idea of somehow signaling Frank, but the door was already closing behind him and Ben was reaching for Luz's neck. Before he could think of any plan of action, Roy saw the bloody knife swinging around to Luz's cheek. But he knew, somewhere below the conscious assessments now flying around his brain, that Ben would not kill her just yet. Roy opened his hands completely and spread his arms wide in a display of open submission.

"What do you want, Ben?" Roy tried to keep his voice as steady and reasonable sounding as he could.

Ben didn't respond immediately. Whatever was going through his head was not evident on his face, but it seemed to Roy that perhaps he was still asking himself that exact same question.

Ben had his left arm around the front of Luz's chest, grasping her right shoulder and restricting her arms. In his right hand, the bloody blade hovered above her jugular. He stared at Roy and slowly started pulling Luz backwards. It was only then that Roy had questions about the first victim. Who was it? Were there more than one and where were they? Were they alive or dead? Instead, he gave voice only to the question now in front of him.

"What can I do for you? What do I need to do for you to let Luz go?" Roy asked. He did not step towards them but opened his arms even wider.

Ben said nothing. He just continued to pull Luz backwards, shaking his head slowly, stiffly. Roy assumed that the bar had a back door, and he was moving towards it. He tried to keep his eyes locked with Ben's and take in the details behind them at the same time. He discovered nothing that would help him, but when he focused back on Luz, he saw less fear and more anger. He saw a determination to overcome and then he saw Luz moving her eyes to her left and then back to him repeatedly, as if trying to signal something.

*   *   *

Through the peephole, Gloria saw what at first appeared to be a pile of wet clothing stacked against the men's room door and then gasped when she saw one bloody arm sticking out from beneath. Only then did she notice the pool of blood, looking like so much spilled ink in the dim light.

Her first instinct was to run out the back door and, as far as she knew, there was no other instinct. However, she froze, her eye glued to the peephole, one hand over her mouth and the other on the deadbolt. With a thousand questions blaring in her head, her right hand quietly unlatched the deadbolt, seemingly of its own volition. One instinct she had forgotten was the one to help others in need.

*   *   *

Roy remained motionless as Ben slowly dragged Luz behind the counter. As they approached the door, Ben said something to Luz in Tagalog. He spoke it in tones so low that Roy would not have understood, even had he spoken English. Ben quickly moved the hand holding the knife behind him and pulled the door open, propping it open with his right foot. Then the knife was back at her throat. He began backing through the door, pulling Luz with him.

Gloria could see a plastic rain slicker moving slowly through the door and reflexively stepped away from the peephole, although curiosity forced her to return. She could see a man backing through the door who seemed to be pulling someone else along with him.

Just as Luz was passing through the doorway, Ben stepped into the still warm puddle of blood. He shifted his position to keep Roy within his field of vision, altering his center of gravity ever-so-slightly. It was enough. His foot slipped wildly, and Ben tumbled backwards, pulling Luz with him. His right elbow cracked against the cement floor and sent the sharp blade slicing cleanly across Luz's cheek. There wasn't much blood at first, but then it came in a gush, mixing with Scott's.

Roy rushed forward, knowing he would have no better opportunity, but the door slammed shut before he could reach it. The smack of Ben's elbow hitting the floor, was followed closely by a muffled grunt and the scream of a woman. And with no weapon equal to the Ka-Bar, he grabbed his umbrella leaning against the wall before reaching for the door handle.

Roy jerked open the door to see three bloody bodies on the floor. His heart leapt to see that Luz was alive and crawling away from the mess but was less happy that Ben was nearly on his feet and had moved the knife to his left hand. His right arm dangled loosely at his side, at least temporarily stunned into uselessness. Roy hoped it would stay that way for a little while longer. He held his umbrella like a pugil stick and faced Ben, careful of the blood-slickened floor.

Roy didn't feel like trying to reason with Ben now. What he wanted to do, was to stick his umbrella as far up Ben's ass as it could possibly go, but instead he struggled to keep his voice moderated and said, "Ben, there is no need for anyone else to get hurt. Put down the knife and we can talk about this." He had no real expectation that Ben would do anything close to that, but he hoped to keep him distracted long enough for Luz to get farther away. He was focused on Ben's chest, but he could see peripherally that Luz had made it to the locked door of their living quarters and was on her knees, reaching for the doorknob. Unfortunately, there were two other things he saw peripherally which were much more concerning. He could see blood seeping from Luz's cheek and Ben's eyes flicking towards her.

Ben lunged toward Luz with the knife in his left hand. Roy instinctively swung the handle of his umbrella and was able to hook Ben's wrist just before it plunged into her side, but it couldn't stop the momentum completely. As it jerked down, it cut through her blouse, drawing more blood. She screamed again and squeezed as close to the wall as she could.

Roy pulled back on the umbrella, hoping to dislodge the knife, but instead he tripped over Scott's dead hand, pitched forward, and landed at Ben's feet. He had twisted while falling and landed on his left shoulder, managing to keep a firm hold on the umbrella.

Ben looked down at Roy's head between his feet and released a primal scream of anger, fear and frustration. He raised the knife above his head and brought it down in a wide arc, aimed at the middle of Roy's chest. Roy gripped the umbrella with both hands and swung the umbrella straight over his own head, plunging its metal tip into the pit of Ben's stomach. Ben's wrist cracked against the umbrella before he could stab Roy, but he held fast to the blade as he doubled over in pain. Roy pulled the umbrella back down and felt a flashing sense of satisfaction at the sight of blood on its tip.

The rage engulfing Ben's awareness did not allow for many other feelings to register, but he was still aware that his stomach was injured. He didn't care. His only goal now was to destroy the intruder lying before him and he tuned out every other consideration as he started to lift the knife above his head one more time.

Gloria had been watching the melee from behind her sturdy door and inconspicuous peephole. However, she was aware that Luz had been injured and was trying to get through the door, so when Roy hooked Ben's wrist, she opened the door and quickly pulled Luz to safety. The first thing Luz did was to rise to her feet and fling open the door once more. She didn't know what she could do, but knew she had to do something. She looked desperately to her right and saw a cooling pot of rice on the stove. With no further thought, she grabbed the pot by both handles, stepped through the door and swung it with all her might at the head of her former friend. It bounced off his left shoulder before connecting with the left side of Ben's skull with a metallic thump.

Roy jabbed once more at the center of Ben's stomach and heard the pot meeting Ben's head at the exact same time. The dual assault caused Ben to finally drop the knife and it clattered to the floor, inches from Roy's face.

Ben's head recoiled slightly, but the force of Luz's blow ensured he would fall to the right as all the other muscles in his body went limp. He was still conscious as he fell, but unable to command his body to fight the pull of gravity. Ben crumpled to the floor and the right side of his head whiplashed into the bare, cement floor. He was conscious no more.

Roy kept the knife within his sight from the moment it left Ben's hand and twisted around to his side to scoop it up as quickly as possible. He banged his back on the woman's room door scrambling to his feet and automatically went into a defensive crouch. The blood-soaked Ka-Bar was clenched in his left hand and the now-bent umbrella was in his right.

He saw Ben lying mostly on his right side, with his shoulders at a thirty-degree angle from the floor. His right arm was pinned underneath and across his body and some of the fingers on his right hand twitched spasmodically under the clear plastic of his rain poncho. Luz was standing just outside the door frame still holding the rice pot with both hands. She was staring at Ben and breathing heavily, as if in preparation to hit him again, should he rise up. Gloria stood behind her, although Roy couldn't currently remember her name.

"Are you alright?" he asked.

Luz's eyes never left Ben as she said, "*Oo.*"

Roy dropped the umbrella and reached down to check Ben's neck for a pulse. There was one, but it was weak. It was then that he noticed blood tickling slowly from Ben's ear and his head was eerily flat against the floor. Roy turned to the other body on the floor and was shocked to see the pale face of the young sailor he had met just hours before. He held no hope that Scott was still living, but he felt for a pulse anyway. There was none.

Roy turned just in time to see Luz slump against the door frame and hear Gloria exclaim something in Filipino. He reached for her as the pot fell from her fingers, spilling what was left of the rice. Both he and Gloria then walked her to one of the kitchen chairs and began tending her wounds. Very little blood was coming from the cut on her side and Roy reasoned that, judging from the way she had wielded the rice pot, it had resulted in no major damage. The slice on her face had bled fairly heavily in the beginning but had slowed to a leak, seeping from a quickly forming clot. Gloria went to the sink, soaked a wad of paper towels, and returned to wipe away as much blood as she could.

"I'll be okay," Luz said. She looked directly into Roy's face and said, "I am good, but I need to, *ano*, lock the bar."

Gloria pressed a few squares of paper towel against Luz's cheek and said in Tagalog, "Hold this here and I'll go lock the door."

"Not yet," Roy said. "Let me go send my friend to get the police and an ambulance. I'll be right back and then you can secure things until help gets here."

He stood to leave and only then realized that he still held the knife tightly. He laid the bloody weapon on the table and said, "I don't think we'll need that again for a while. I believe our friend out there is about done for."

A familiar voice came from the front of the bar.

"Holy fuck me to tears! What the fuck?"

Roy stuck his head around to see Frank standing at the edge of the carnage.

"Chief, I need you to go to the main gate and notify the OPM and the Shore Patrol that there has been another murder out here," Roy said. He slipped so easily into the role of crime scene supervisor, he surprised himself.

"Roy! Are you okay?"

"I'm fine. Luz is hurt but going to be okay, I think. That kid from the NAVMAG is dead and," gesturing toward Ben, "the peanut vendor here is almost there. I guess you ought to let them know we need a medic too."

"Shit," Frank said, leaving the bar. "I'll be back ASAP."

Gloria peeked around Roy's back tentatively, looking for a clean path through the puddles of blood. She gripped Roy's arm, but it had none of the flirtatious elements of Friday night. Finally, she chose to pick her way along the restroom walls until she got to Scott and then crossed over. She did not avoid all of the puddles and left bloody tracks from her flip-flops as she went to the front of the bar.

Luz was resting one elbow on the kitchen table while pressing the makeshift bandage to her face. With her other hand she rubbed her eyes as if the pain was starting to register. She started to lean against the table and then winced when its edge came into contact with the cut on her side.

"Let me look at that," Roy said. His voice still carried the authority of a crime scene supervisor, but Luz's face effectively conveyed the fact that she didn't give a shit about his presumed authority. Still, she turned in her seat to present the wounded side for his inspection. Lifting her blouse, he could see where the blade had sliced through part of her bra and then shallowly into her flesh. The cut was less than two inches long and had already begun to scab over.

"This one doesn't look bad," he said. "Hold on." He wet another wad of paper towel and dabbed at the dried blood, being careful not to disturb the fresh wound.

The flimsy door dividing the bar opened and they heard Gloria call to them. "I'll stay in front. I don't want to see that *na naman*." The door slammed shut, cutting off any discussion of the matter.

Roy retrieved more wet towels and pulled a chair up next to Luz.

"Let me see this one again."

Roy put his hand gently over hers and pulled the compress away from her cheek slowly. She looked sideways at him, trying to detect any alarm her condition might have raised, but saw none.

"It's a good thing this knife was very sharp," he said. "I don't think it will leave much of a scar, but I'll feel better when Frank gets back with some medical help." He wiped gingerly at the edges of the cut, then looked into her eyes again. "Here. Hold this for a sec."

He took her hand once again and raised it to the damp towels at her cheek. He might have held it for just a little too long, but Luz didn't mind. She didn't want him to let go at all.

They sat quietly, listening to the rain pound against the roof until the sounds of approaching sirens finally cut through.

Chapter 37

It was nearly two hours before Roy got back to the Naval Station. Frank's Impala sat beneath the streetlamp outside the OPM building, reflecting a flickering yellow blob through the rain-soaked windows of the Shore Patrol's van. It was well after 1:00 before Frank delivered him to the Chief's barracks in Cubi and almost 1:30 when he finally laid in his rack.

At 3:15 he was still lying there, looking at the dark ceiling. An hour before, he had rolled up a towel and stuffed it under his room's door to keep light from the hallway bleeding in. He now blamed his inability to sleep on the three swigs of spiced rum that Frank had insisted he drink while heading up to the barracks. However, as soon as that thought of blame popped into his head, he dismissed it. He realized that his current sleeping problems were the result of all of the fucked-up things that had happened since his arrival in the Philippines, poured on top of a significant jetlag and blended together with a dash of loneliness and a good helping of self-pity. One good thing about my brain, he thought, is that I can't lie to myself for very long. Of course, he had also been replaying the day's events over and over in his head, which was also not conducive to sleep.

After the initial mission to retrieve his umbrella had turned into a certified shit-show, the fun continued for a couple more hours. Investigative and medical teams from the base were the first to show up at Ace's. Both contained Americans and Filipinos who drilled regularly to respond to such emergencies and were very well coordinated in their efforts. Philippine Constabularies and Olongapo Police came later.

The medics were very professional and worked on Ben and Luz at the same time. Ben was stabilized at the bar and then transported to a hospital in Olongapo with two fractures of the skull and two shallow puncture wounds to the abdomen. Luz's cuts were irrigated, treated with anti-biotics and covered with butterfly stitches. Scott's body was taken back to the base per the Status of Forces Agreement with the Philippines.

Roy, Frank, Luz and Gloria were all interviewed individually. At one point, an Olongapo policeman started to get aggressive with Roy and Frank but was hauled out of the bar by two PC officers who had been briefed by the OPM.

After the preliminary investigation into the incident at Ace's, the authorities determined that Luz had acted in self-defense and that there would be no arrests made. Gloria was then allowed to notify Mama Nina, who insisted the bar stay closed for at least a few days and arranged rooms in a nice hotel on Rizal Avenue for any of the girls who might come back to the bar before midnight. She left Boy and Ernesto there to take care of them, should they come in.

Roy told the investigators about his earlier suspicions concerning the rubber gloves, so they were bagged and taken into custody. Frank was allowed to drive his car back to the base, but Roy was driven back by the OPM and Base Security team. He was debriefed for a couple of more hours and basically recounted, with a few omissions, his entire experience after arriving in the P.I.

However, one other specific lie crumbled beneath the scrutiny of his self-reflection, one more fact he could not dismiss as unnecessary. The vivid scene replaying in his head that mostly kept him from the sweet arms of slumber was that memory of those other arms that had held him earlier that night. Roy had been preparing to go back to the base with investigators when he heard that Luz would not be charged. He turned to her instinctively and without speaking, they embraced. Her slender body melded into his as she lay her face against his chest and they held tightly to each other for several moments, blocking out the others around them. Reluctantly, he pulled away just far enough to kiss her forehead.

"*Magandang gabi*," he said.

Luz looked up at him, tears glistening in her eyes. "Bye, bye," she said and then with a mischievous smile said, "See you never."

He could still feel the warmth of her body, the firmness of her breasts pressing against him. He wanted to feel that again. He needed it. He knew that 'never' was not an option.

While lying there, he had listened to the rain's intensity surge and recede several times and now it was nearly silent against his windows. Finally, he slept.

Monday

Chapter 38

Roy waited. Past is prologue, he thought. It will come, he thought. He sat waiting for someone to interrupt his morning. Perhaps a call, delivered by the front desk, would give him some new direction. Maybe Bill Eikleberger would show up in his overstuffed uniform to cart him back to yet another meeting about the sad death of Winnie Jackson. But this morning was different. Nothing happened.

He watched the dim numbers on his alarm clock and as 7:00 AM approached, he decided that the expected would not happen. He picked up his briefcase and walked to the front desk. His khaki uniform was freshly ironed, and the vinyl covered combination cap sat squarely on his head, ready for any additional rain that might fall during the day.

At their lunch on Saturday, Roy and Bill had agreed to meet outside the barracks this Monday morning at 7:00. That seemed like an eternity ago now. As he stepped from the barracks, he was happy to see that the sun had returned after so much rainfall and not just because his brand-new umbrella had been ruined the night before. There were still a few clouds blotting out the mostly blue sky, but sunshine cut underneath them on the horizon and made him wish for sunglasses.

Squatting in practically the same spot as he had on Friday afternoon, Daddy puffed on a crooked cigarette. He peered up through a cloud of smoke and flapped a hand at Roy.

"Good morning, Senior Chief," he said. "Do you have laundry?"

"Good morning. Yeah, I've got some, but not much," Roy replied.

"How was the weekend?"

"It was, uh, busy."

"Did you hear about that murder?"

"Yes," was all he said in return.

Bill's little white truck turned into the barracks parking lot and stopped with squeaking brakes and Roy waved to acknowledge his arrival.

"Take care, hah?" Daddy said.

"Sure. Hey, what is your real name?" Roy said.

"Ernesto Benigno Dela Cruz," he said.

"It's good to know it, Daddy, thanks," Roy said as he started toward the truck.

After he climbed into the truck, Roy exchanged morning pleasantries and then sat silently looking at the jungle foliage through the side window as Bill took him to finish checking in at work.

"Did you like the barrio?" Bill said.

"It was okay," Roy responded. "But I met a girl on Gordon Avenue." He fell silent once again and Bill, completely out of character, thought it best not to pry. Roy hoped that he could now begin a normal tour of duty at his new command and spend the next two years writing up AWOL sailors, monitoring security procedures and battling jungle rot. And maybe, he thought, he could find time for a girl.

*   *   *

There was light rapping on the door and Luz awoke with a start, jerking up from the bed. A sharp pain grabbed her just below her left armpit and then slowly released its hold. The cut on her cheek brought the pain of a throbbing, dull kind and she involuntarily reached up to feel the butterfly stiches binding her wound. Gloria had given her some kind of "sleeping" pill after they arrived at the hotel and Luz had been in no mood to question its pharmacological properties. Whatever they were, she had slept soundly through the night and could recall no dreams whatsoever. For that, she was grateful.

Sunlight was streaming through the narrow gap between the curtain and the window's edge, reflecting off the wall and making her squint. The sunshine seemed just a little out of place to her, but she was too groggy to realize why that might be the case.

There were additional taps on the door and then Mama Nina's voice came from the other side.

"Luz, are you up?" Nina asked again.

"Oo," she said, throwing the thin sheet off her legs. She pivoted to plant her feet on the floor but was too dizzy to stand up immediately. Whatever the pill had contained, it was still making itself known in her system. Yawning, she finally stood and pulled her oversized tee shirt down towards her knees before going to the door. She cracked the door enough to see Mama Nina alone in the hall, so she removed the security chain and stepped back, allowing Nina to enter.

"How are you, little girl?" Nina asked.

"I think I'm going to be okay," she said. "I'm sorry for all of the problems."

"Nonsense! I never trusted that crazy bastard anyway! I am just sorry that you got hurt and I want you to know that Boy or Ernesto will be there every night until you close, from now on." She put her arm around Luz and walked her back to the bed.

"I appreciate that. I don't know if it's needed, but I appreciate it."

"Listen," Nina said, sitting on the bed and pulling Luz with her. "Don't worry about it. I don't know when we can get back in the bar to clean up, but don't worry about that either. I want you to rest and try to forget about all that mess for the time being." Nina opened her handbag and pulled out several fifty-peso notes which she offered to Luz.

"Here. You can go to the movies. You can go to dinner. You can go to the beach. You can just stay here in the room if you want," she said. "I just want you to feel good about coming back to work when you feel better."

Luz looked blankly at the handful of cash and then back at Nina. "I don't..."

"No," Nina said. "I want you to take this and not worry about anything for a while." She took Luz's hands and forced the bills into them. "Just relax."

With those words, she leaned over and kissed Luz on the forehead. As she walked to the door, she said, "I will check on you tomorrow, but if you aren't here, don't worry about that either." She then smiled and left the room.

Luz sat quietly for a moment, looking at the 450 pesos in her hand. The truth is that she had been thinking about taking some time off for a while. She had never been to Pangasinan and the recently refreshed memories of her *Impó* had sparked an interest to investigate the place that her grandmother had talked about so longingly. Perhaps now, she thought, might be the perfect time for that.

Luz stood and walked to the side of the bed closest to the wall. She looked around, purely by habit, before lifting the side of the mattress and reaching underneath. She withdrew the tattered canvas bag which had served her so well over the years and emptied its contents onto the bed. Small bundles of American dollars and Philippine pesos tumbled onto the sheets. A few bank notes from other countries were thrown into the mix and together they amounted to nearly every cent she had been able to save since leaving the trash heaps of Manila. She removed the rubber band from a roll of fifty-peso notes and slid the new ones on top before rolling them back together and tossing them onto the bed. Then she located a little, spiral notebook under the bills and took it to the desk near the window where she carefully recorded the addition of money to her savings.

Looking at the pile of money laying on the bed, she wondered if it might be time to start trusting a bank and deposit the money into an account. She thought it might be. She wondered also if it might be time to start looking for different work, perhaps in a restaurant. She thought that might be a good idea too. Finally, she wondered if Roy Thompson might be interested in having a relationship with a Filipina who didn't work in a bar. She wasn't sure about that, but she really wanted to find out.

Stifling a yawn, Luz reached over and pulled the curtain closer to the edge of the window, trying to shut out even more sunlight. Then she returned to the bed and replaced all the money into the bag before stowing it safely under the mattress once more. She thought for a fleeting second about showering but instead fell back into bed and covered up with the sheet. Curling into a fetal position, Luz remember how comfortable and safe she had felt in Roy's arms last night, even if only for a moment and realized she wanted to have that feeling again.

Ben de Guzman was nowhere on her mind as she fell back to sleep.

*   *   *

Roy sat at his desk, doodling on a legal pad. He had just finished writing down everything he could remember having done since arriving in the Philippine Islands until he reported for duty that morning. Again, he did not believe that the inclusion of Charles Pettit's name would be of interest to anyone reading his account. Also, at the back of his mind stood the isolated possibility that that particular, unsubstantiated connection might possibly come in handy over the next couple of years.

LCDR Pillsbury had already read the relevant reports concerning Roy's altercation over the weekend but felt he needed to have first-hand knowledge of every pertinent fact. He was an officer who normally trusted his senior enlisted people but didn't yet know Roy and he felt the exercise would be beneficial to them both. He insisted on being in the loop directly, certainly at this stage of the threat and Roy had absolutely no problem with that decision.

Roy continued to reflect on the things that had happened and the people he had encountered during this first, long, bizarre weekend of his tour of duty. He knew from experience the pain that friends and family of Winnie Jackson and Scott Chalmers would suffer, and he ached again for his own loss. They would move on eventually, as he had, and restart the stories of their lives, begin new narratives with new characters and altered story lines.

The missing characters would not be replaced or forgotten like those on some network sitcom, but they might help the survivors appreciate those still living just a little bit more. They might encourage them to say just one more kind word or stifle just one more cruel comment. He wished that outcome for them and he wished it for himself as well. He also wished to see Luz again. He felt confident that wish would come true quite soon.

*   *   *

Nestor came onto the ward with a small bible and a smile. He exchanged a few quiet words with a nurse and then walked to the third bed on the left. Ben lay motionless, an oxygen mask and gauze encircling his head. Plastic tubes and monitor leads snaked out from under the thin sheet, connecting him to the world outside his senses.

A craniectomy had been completed to relieve the pressure created in Ben's skull by swelling of the brain, but the hospital had done the minimum procedures necessary to keep him alive while trying to determine the level of his health care coverage. Ben, living in a near vegetative state, was oblivious to such bureaucratic concerns and hadn't been very concerned with them even before Luz had laid him low with a pot of rice. His tenuous hold on awareness had no energy to expend on them now.

At the very depths of Ben's mind was a dark pit, like the unlighted stage of an amphitheater. Occasional pulses of light would illuminate the stage in fleeting flashes, allowing Ben to see himself beside his heroes. Lapu-Lapu, Bonifacio, Rizal and others surrounding him, enthusiastically applauding Ben de Guzman at center stage and chanting his name.

These brief displays of imaginary honor were invisible to those charged with caring for his physical body, but they might have detected the slightest flicker of an eye movement had they been watching closely. What they witnessed instead was Nestor pulling a chair close the head of Ben's bed, opening his bible and silently reciting some passage of hope. Of course, they could not see Nestor's eyes scanning the bible nor hear the prayers coming from his lips. If they could, they might have been surprised.

In the eternal passages of darkness between Ben's fantasy appearances on the stage, random pulses, muffled murmurs, and alien echoes filtered down from all around the highest seats of his personal amphitheater. Rhythmic beeps and actual words would sometime break through the darkness, like the threatening calls of wild beasts, urging him to step out from the protective umbra of the stage. But he could never leave that stage.

Nestor looked at his former employer lying motionless on the bed and a short, reflexive smile danced across his lips. We all finally reach our place in this world, he thought. Leaning forward in his chair, Nestor opened the bible to a random page, but did not read from it. Rather, an old verse rose in him, and his lips moved ever so slightly upon its recital.

> *"Monkey, oxen, pig and hen,*
> *All become the food of men…*
> *…If he fails to heed the call,*
> *Man becomes the food of all."*

The End

Acknowledgements

I would like to thank all of the people who have aided and abetted me since beginning this endeavor so many years ago. First, I want to thank my wife, Joanie Cole Scifres, who offered encouragement, advice and substantial editing skills to get this into a publishable form. With that said, if there remain any typos, word misuses or grammatical errors, they are my errors and mine alone. I also want to thank all the shipmates and civilians I have met and worked with over my twenty years of active duty and several years since. Specifically, I want to thank Joe and Jovy Pipes and especially Dave and Trudy Oster, all of whom provided invaluable friendship, guidance and insight into both the culture and worldview of the marvelous Filipino people and the beauty possible in intercultural relationships. I could otherwise never have effectively imagined the joy and sorrow that can result from such families. Next, I would like to acknowledge my fellow faculty members at Eastern New Mexico University – Roswell who endured my incessant chatter about "my book," with the good humor and tolerance that good friends display every day. Thank you, Bob Bender, Bill Kuehl, Bob Phillips, Daniel Wolkow, Jennie Bower and Annemarie Oldfield. Finally, I want to thank those who have paid good money for this book and took the time to provide helpful feedback and encouragement for future writing projects. I hope that you enjoyed this interrupted weekend in Subic Bay and that you feel you got your money's worth.

About the author

R. L. Scifres was born in West Texas, raised in Roswell, New Mexico and joined the Navy two weeks after graduating high school. He spent twenty years in the Naval Security Group and spent about four years total in the Philippines between 1974 and 1981.

Upon retiring from the Navy, he completed a Master of Science degree in Clinical Mental Health Counseling from Troy State University and worked as a counselor and educator at various institutions before retiring from Eastern New Mexico University – Roswell as an instructor of Psychology and Sociology in 2017.

Today he lives in Arizona with his lovely, young bride, Joanie.